I0525324

THE ONE WITH ALL THE KIDNAPPING

POPPY WATSON

CHAPTER 1

CHLOE

*A*s the Greyhound bus barrels down the freeway, I close my eyes and try to picture what comes next: the new life waiting for me in a town I've never seen, with a grandmother I'm not even sure is real.

But every time I shut my eyes, my anxiety wakes up.

The fact is, I'm not safe on this bus.

I don't know if I'll ever feel safe again.

The guys my dad owes money to—gangsters, loan sharks, mafiosos, call them what you will—chased me out of New York.

My dad and I were staying at the Ritz-Carlton. If you haven't stayed there, it's nice. I recommend the room service lobster mac and cheese. But like most high-end hotels, no matter how many $100 bills you pass to the doormen, management gets suspicious when your bill tops $50,000 and the credit card you have on file won't go through. Normally, my dad handles things at that point. But this time, he wasn't around.

Dad disappeared two weeks ago.

Now those mobsters are after me, trying to track him down. Make him pay up. I know they're not above kidnapping me, holding me for ransom. Or worse.

So far today, I've:

Yeah, it's been a day. A week. A life.

As THE BUS TRAVELS NORTH, the city fades away, and the smell of tuna fills the air.

Who would eat a tuna fish sandwich on a bus?

That's Greyhound life.

I fix my tear-streaked makeup, using my phone camera to see my face. The phone's just a mirror now, since my dad didn't pay the bill and the service got cut off.

I look more like my mom than my tall, pale blonde dad. My mom had heaps of long black hair wore heavy bronzer. She loved Ylang 49 perfume, sticky-sweet, and heavy gold jewelry.

I haven't seen my mom since I was nine. But when I look in a mirror, I can almost see her face.

I rub glitter off my nose. Must have picked it up at Hustlin' Hunks. I swear, they pipe glitter into strip clubs the way they pipe oxygen into casinos—anything to keep you awake, alert, and spending that cash.

I'm only sixteen, but growing up with my dad, I've been everywhere: clubs, casinos, racetracks, you name it.

I wonder about my grandmother. What is she like? Would she eat tuna sandwiches on a bus? Does she snore, like the old man in the row behind me?

I don't know her. I've never met her. I don't even know if she really wants me to visit her. But I'm pretty sure she knows I exist.

My dad always called Granny my PLR. Person of Last Resort. He used to say, "If things get bad, go to your Granny's. She lives in a little town called Sweet Harbor."

And sometimes, with Dad, things got bad. There were a lot of lows. But a lot of highs too.

Life with my dad was never boring. That's the con artist lifestyle: thrills and chills—mostly chills.

But things were never this bad. Never, my-dad's-missing-and-I-don't-know-if-he's-alive bad. Never, I'm-all-alone-now bad.

A lump rises in my throat. What if I never see him again? I bite my lip to stop the tears from flowing. Never show weakness in public. It makes you an easy mark.

Sweet Harbor. I try to think positive. The name sounds adorable. Just hearing it makes me think of innocent, grandmotherly things: apple pie and hugs. Maybe Granny has a dog, like a lovable little collie.

I've never been able to have a pet. My dad and I have moved around too much. Mostly running away from people he'd scammed, or people he owed money.

I bet Granny lives in a cute little cottage, with dormer windows and geranium-filled boxes. And somewhere in that house is the key my dad swears he left me.

It's a key to a bank safe deposit box. He said there's emergency money in it. Money I could use to pay my dad's debts.

Then, maybe, he could come stay with me at Granny's. Clean up his act. Running away from the mob is not exactly fun. Maybe he's ready to make a change.

I close my eyes, picture him. Hope he's safe. I swipe at my eyes. This is no place to cry, but the tears come anyway.

Dad knew this would happen. That one day, his debts would catch up with him. That's why he kept reminding me about that safe deposit box.

"When all else fails," Dad always told me, "you can go back to your Granny Riding's. I've hidden a key for you there. It goes to safe deposit box number 311 at Sweet Harbor Bank. Inside that box, you'll find everything you need for financial security. It's all there, in case of an emergency." He even made me repeat back to him the box number, 311, just in case.

I asked him why we didn't just go to Granny's. Get the box. Get the money he'd saved.

"It's complicated. Plus, I'm not welcome in your grandmother's home," Dad said.

I understand why my grandmother might be angry with my dad. I love him. But he's not always reliable.

Somehow—maybe it's the setting sun, or the motion of the bus, or just comforting thoughts of an actual grandmother—I fall asleep, leaning against the window of the bus.

I WAKE up with a start when the bus jerks to a sudden stop. We're not at a bus stop. We're in the middle of nowhere.

Maybe I'm being paranoid. But something feels off.

Outside, the fog is thick and dark trees crowd the road. My throat goes dry.

Usually, I have a plan. An exit strategy. That's what makes me comfortable.

But here, what will I do? I want to call for help, but my phone doesn't work. Besides, there's no one to call. Not really. Not anymore.

I *think* I threw those mobsters off my tail.

But am I sure?

A feeling like one of those lobsters in a tank comes over me— you know, the ones with the rubber-banded claws? It feels like someone's rubber-banded my heart. I can't breathe.

I would feel safer if my dad were here.

Behind us, headlights pierce the fog. They're set high. Like the mobsters' Suburban headlights.

"Let me off this bus!" I yell, standing up.

The snoring old man wakes up with a start. A girl with the

4

vivid blue hair gawks at me. I note the remains of a tuna sandwich in her lap, and wonder why she's staring.

I start to exit the bus, and the driver scolds me. "Now just hold on, miss. We're calling our Roadside Assistance now, it's just a flat tire—"

"Let me out!" I punch the bus door and the driver, startled, opens it. I hop out into the smothering fog.

Those mafia guys have connections. They could engineer a spike on the road to give the bus a flat. Then they could ambush the bus. Staying here would make me a sitting duck.

But I am not a sitting duck. I am Chloe Riding, and if those guys want to catch me, they're going to work for it.

I set off on foot toward Sweet Harbor. It's late summer, but I can't shake the shivers. I reach into my Birkin bag. It's soft gold leather with gold hardware, one of the few things I have left from my mom. Fortunately, it's roomy enough to carry a black windbreaker and stocking cap. This will keep me warm and make me less visible.

My breath hitches when I hear an engine. I duck into the trees as headlights sweep across the road, heart pounding, ready to hide.

CHAPTER 2

CHLOE

I hold my breath, hiding behind a tree, and peek between pine branches. I can't see much.

A car door slams. In the beams of a truck's headlights, a rangy shadow moves toward me. My throat catches.

I can't see him, but I can hear his sure, steady footsteps.

I yell out: "Get the hell away from me! I swear, I've got a gun. Back up!"

Silence falls. A branch snaps. "Easy," the guy says, in a low, comforting tone. "Easy now." He's talking to me the way you'd talk to a skittish horse.

"I said, get away," I repeat.

"I've got my hands up, and I'm not coming any closer," he says. His voice is firm but gentle. "I can't even see you in this fog. I stopped because I saw something moving out here, kind of limping along—thought someone had hit a deer. But you sound scared. Are you okay? Did someone hurt you?"

"Who do you work for?" I ask. My heart is pounding so hard I can barely hear myself speak.

"Huh?"

"Who do you work for?" I don't trust his voice, because I can feel it working on me. There's something calming about it. Something that makes me want to drop my guard. And that's exactly what's so dangerous about it.

He laughs a low, lazy laugh. "I wouldn't call it work, exactly, what I do. But sometimes I run delivery for Shady."

"Shady?" I repeat. "Shady Who?" My dad owes money to people with a lot of unusual nicknames. But I don't recall some gangster named Shady.

"Shady WHO?" I demand.

And suddenly, infuriatingly, the guy starts singing. "When the moon hits your eye like a big pizza pie, that's a-Shady," he bellows, in a wolfish tenor, "When you're hungry, just call, we deliver it all, that's a-Shady."

An owl hoots on that last note. Some part of me wants to laugh. The gullible part of me.

"I deliver pizzas, is what I'm trying to say. For Shady Cove Pizza?" The owl hoots again. "You're not from around here, are you?" he asks.

He really does have a great voice; even in the darkness, I can sense his personality—his confidence, his sense of humor.

But charming people can still kill you. They're fatal, because they make you *want* to you to drop your defenses.

"What makes you say that?" I snap.

"Shady Cove Pizza? Everyone around here knows that ad. My buddies always say that on our deathbeds, the song from that ad is going to run through our heads, chasing us for all eternity. But I guess... an eternal pizza earworm is a fair trade for the world's best pizza. And Shady Pizza really is the best. If you're a tourist, you should definitely try it. It's more of a French bread type of crust, with a cornmeal dusting, just the right amount of grit."

His easy voice calms me. It's like my heart wants to trust him before my head's caught up. And somehow, even in the darkness, without seeing my face, he can tell I've let my guard down, because his tone shifts, grows low, and he says,

"Are you okay? Do you need help? Can I call someone for you?"

"There's no one to call," I say. My voice comes out in a tearful squeak. I hate how it sounds, how it gives away just how alone I am. Sometimes it feels like once I start letting go, I won't be able to stop. I babble on, spilling my guts to this stranger in the dark. "I fell. And my ankle—now it really hurts."

As soon as I admit the pain, it flares up, searing in a way that takes my breath away. I stumble into the trees, but he's there in a flash, catching me, enveloping me in a warm, rich scent of green lava soap and cedar.

"Put me down," I say.

"Just let me carry you out of the woods," he says. "There are a lot of tree roots, you'll fall again—"

I kick and squirm, trying to show some resistance, but it's such a relief to be off my ankle. My arms wrap around his neck before I even mean to. There's something about being carried by him, being cared for, that feels relaxing, safe.

If I have to, I can always knee him in the nuts later.

When we reach the road, I see his truck. It's a battered old Toyota pickup. I relax even more at the sight of it. It's not the vehicle anyone mobbed-up would be driving.

My heart calms just a notch. Maybe he truly is an innocent civilian, just trying to help me out. If such a thing even exists.

With one hand, he opens the truck door and sets me on the seat. At first, I think from the way he's reaching out that he's trying to grab my butt, but he says, "Sorry—there's a broken spring in the seat. Just trying to set you down clear of it."

It's so dark I can't get a good look at the guy as he crouches down to inspect my ankle. He slips off my shoes and hands them to me with a gruff, "Here, Cinderella," and shines his phone flashlight directly over my feet.

In the flashlight's glare, I get a view of my fresh pedicure and my swollen ankle, but all I see of the guy is a flash of sandy hair and a bit of bristly jaw.

"Hold on," he says. He clunks around in the bed of the truck and returns with something in his hands. Something that makes a familiar ripping sound.

Tape. Duct tape. AKA, kidnapper's best friend.

I quickly kick him in the gut before he can tape my mouth and wrists and drag me back to whoever he's working for. He gasps and doubles over in pain.

"Hey! What did you do that for?"

"I have a gun!" I insist. "In my bag."

"Oh yeah? Go ahead, shoot me, put me out of my misery. That really hurt."

"What are you doing, getting out duct tape? Freaking serial killer move," I say.

"It's first aid tape," he says. "I was going to wrap up your ankle."

Oh. Oops. I don't know what to say.

The owl hoots again. I press my palms to my face, my cheeks hot with embarrassment.

From somewhere in the foggy dark, he sighs. "All right. Give me your ankle. I'll tape it up."

"I won't kick you this time," I say.

"You better not." His voice is firm, but his fingers are gentle as he winds the tape around my aching ankle.

"Can I give you a ride somewhere?"

My chest tightens. I shouldn't tell him. But what choice do I have? "I'm trying to get to 1022 Harborview Drive, Sweet Harbor."

He whistles. "What you got going on over there?"

"My grandmother's house," I say.

He whistles again, another low whistle.

"What's that whistle about?" I ask. "Is that a bad part of town?"

He laughs. His laugh is fantastic. It rumbles through the night, sending a little shiver through me. I want to make him laugh again.

But I still don't trust him.

He says, "You'll see, Cinderella. You'll see."

Then he climbs into the truck and starts the engine, its low growl cutting through the fog and dark.

CHAPTER 3

TYLER

I've got a Sweet Harbor girl in the truck, and I'm driving her home. Damn. That's a first.

The girl doesn't seem like a Sweetie. She doesn't have *the* accent. (They all speak in this pretentious rasp, like a fly crawled down their throats.) And right away, that pricks at my curiosity, because if she's not one of them, what's she doing here?

But she's going to Harborview Drive. Her grandma lives there. So the girl belongs to them—the Sweeties.

Everyone I know in Shady Cove works hard all day. Meanwhile, the Sweeties a few miles up the coast in Sweet Harbor spend their time racing their yachts, crashing their Lamborghinis, and plotting layoffs at the factories they own.

Still, this girl doesn't seem like a Sweetie. Sure, she's got Sweetie shoes—heels so spiky a balloon would take one look at them and pop.

But she doesn't sound like a Sweetie or smell like a Sweetie.

(Sweetie perfume is so stinking sweet it'd make cotton candy blush.)

In fact, this girl smells incredible: fresh and sharp, like lemony heaven. And her hair, when I carried her, brushed my cheek and felt like silk. And her body, in my arms. It felt just right.

So right, I'd call her Goldilocks—except I have no idea what color her hair is, and besides, thinking too much about how she felt in my arms is dangerous. No good ever came from getting mixed up with a Sweetie.

I'm lucky the interior light in my truck is busted, so I can't get a good look at her.

Still. It's funny how you can feel someone's presence without seeing them—just hear a shift of breath, the way they settle down into silence, and you can know all about them.

I didn't even see what she looked like when I was binding up her ankle. I wanted to shine the flashlight over her. Get a glimpse of the girl who felt so good in my arms. But that would've been rude. And truth be told, it might've only gotten me in trouble.

"What's your name?" I ask, now, as I pull out onto the highway.

The fog is so thick it's like driving into a blanket. I go slow. Which I don't mind. It's giving me more time with her. Whoever she is.

"Chloe," she says, after a beat.

I wonder. Is that her real name? Don't know why she'd lie to me.

But then again. Don't know why a Sweetie would limp around in the woods by Shady Cove, pretending to have a gun, either.

I try not to ask too many questions. The girl's scared of something, I can tell. Even in the dark, her posture tells me things—how she shifts, how she's gone still, how her voice tightens. There's a weight in her silence I can feel through the dark.

If there's one thing I know, it's that you have to calm people down before you can get anywhere with them. So I start talking. "I'm Tyler," I say. "I live over by Shady Cove. You know where that is?"

She's silent. What? Is she judging me for my address? Or is she really so clueless she doesn't know that no self-respecting Sweetie girl would be seen in a Cove-man's truck?

Finally, she says, "Is that where the famous Shady Pizza comes from?" She even sings the jingle a little. "That's a-Shady," she trills.

"Very good," I say. "You should sing in the ad."

Good. She's relaxing. Joking around. That means she feels safer. She shifts back a little in her seat. I tell myself to keep it light, keep her laughing. She's halfway between running and trusting.

"Your grandma *really* lives on Harborview Drive?" I say, half-hoping that she's actually going there to rob the place.

"Yeah," she says. "I don't know her too well, actually. I've never been to Sweet Harbor before. Once, when I was a baby. But my dad grew up in Sweet Harbor."

"Where is he now?" I

It's the wrong question, and I know it as soon as the words are out of my mouth. Chloe freezes up. **I can't see her face, but the silence sharpens, and I can feel her shut down.**

I keep my hands on the wheel and my mouth shut, giving her space. She doesn't say anything. Not when we drive past the neon spectacle that is the Shady Sweet Drive-In. Not when we climb the ridge and get the first view of the harbor way down below, sparkling with all the lights from America's richest small town. Not when we wind our way down Mountainview Drive.

At last she says, "Is someone following us?"

"Huh?"

"Look in the mirror. Is there someone—"

I glance back. The road is dark and empty. Just fog.

But like I said. You've got to calm people down before you can get anywhere with them. "Well, if they *are* following us, they won't any more," I say.

I whip the truck into the parking lot of a steakhouse and hide, parking behind a giant Land Rover. "We can watch the road from here without getting spotted."

"Mm-hmm," she says, and I can hear nervousness. I can't make out her expression, but from the way she fidgets in her seat, I can feel her fear. I don't know what's scaring her, but I wish she could understand she's safe with me.

I breathe in her fresh clean scent of citrus and cotton, lemonade and honey, and remember the feel of her body in my arms—oh, my friends would *kill* me if I took up with a Sweetie.

My buddies would call her a Sweetie Snack. The kind of girl that'll give you diabetes, then jack up the price of insulin. The kind of girl that'll drive her spike heels through your heart and her Range Rover over your entire family. The kind of snack you better skip, if you know what's good for you.

But hiding in a dark truck with this Chloe girl, I forget all that. There's a softness in her voice, a shakiness, that hits me in the chest. I want to be the one looking out for her, making sure she's okay.

"There!" she says. A black Escalade zooms past on Mountainview.

"That's who's following me."

"Some soccer mom on her way home from hot yoga?" I say.

"What?"

"That's who drives those things," I say. "Sweetie mommies. Let me show you."

"Don't!" she says, but I pull onto the road and floor it, catching up to the shining black Escalade.

Even though we're in a hilly no-passing zone, I know I can make it. I pull into the other lane and floor it, passing the Escalade. I want to show this girl she's got nothing to be scared of.

"Take a good look!" I tell Chloe, who's all scrunched down in her seat. She peeks her head up and sure enough, we pass a teensy blond woman at the wheel of the enormous vehicle.

"Oh," Chloe says, relaxing. She laughs, and something inside me unclenches too. "I guess I was a little paranoid."

"What are you worried about?" I say.

She waves her hand, still laughing. "Nothing," she says. "This is Sweet Harbor, right? My dad said I'd always be safe in Sweet Harbor. Maybe he was right. There's nothing to worry about here."

"Not if you're a Sweetie," I say.

"What do you mean?"

"Not if you belong here," I say. "There's nothing to worry about if you belong here."

I turn onto Harborview Drive. The older mansions are out here, spaced far apart and hidden down long, tree-lined driveways.

Chloe perks up, begins looking around. "I thought my grandmother lived in town," she says. "But maybe it's more like a farm?"

Yeah, I think. A diamond farm. A Cadillac farm.

I smile to myself. If Chloe doesn't know it yet, she's about to find out: Grandma is one rich old lady.

CHAPTER 4

CHLOE

*I*t's so dark in the truck I can't see my rescuer's face. He seems young, though. Maybe my age, maybe a little older.

He said his name was Tyler. And he's been nothing but nice.

So far.

I was a little nervous when we skirted downtown and drove more into the countryside, but when he turned down my Grandmother Riding's street, Harborview Drive, I felt reassured, if a little confused.

Did dad grow up on a farm? Has he been a farm kid all along? It's easy to picture him at the gaming tables in Monte Carlo, but it's much harder to imagine him squatting down to milk a cow.

Tyler turns down a driveway next to a mailbox with Granny's name on it. Immense pine trees shade the long, twisting lane. The trees are so dense, it feels like driving through a narrow tunnel, which opens into a wide clearing—and a stunning Georgian mansion.

My jaw drops. Granny's house is a palace. It's brick, three stories, with huge white columns out front and wide white balconies strung all across the top.

"1022 Harborview Drive," Tyler says, in that lazy, rangy voice that makes me feel so warm and squirmy. How can I be attracted to someone I can't even see? How can I feel safe with a stranger who just basically picked up a hitchhiker?

Maybe it's that voice that's making me melt. Or maybe it's just the overall damsel-in-distress situation. Either way, it's annoying. It's not safe to feel this way. It's dangerous to feel safe.

And yet here I am, practically swooning. God, get a grip, Chloe.

"Home, sweet home," Tyler says.

"I had no idea her house was like this," I say as we drive closer. "It's weird. My dad always said growing up here felt like growing up in a prison."

"A prison of prosperity," Tyler says, in a voice that smirks, and as we approach the house, its security lights snap on, illuminating truck's cab—meaning I can see Tyler.

He's looking at me.

And he's got a pair of blue eyes that would make your heart stop.

I swallow. I don't know which is more impressive—Tyler, or Granny's mega-mansion.

The security lights blink out, maybe because we haven't moved in a while, or maybe they're on a timer. I wish they'd come back on so I could get a better look at Tyler. I have a feeling I could stare at this truck-driving, ankle-taping guy all night.

But we're in the dark again.

"Should I leave you here?" he asks. His voice is ragged with concern. Again I feel it. That scary feeling. Safety. I pull my Birkin bag closer to my chest, clutching it like a $10,000 security blanket.

Because I barely know Tyler, yet there's a part of me that doesn't want him to go.

Which means I have *got* to get *out* of this *truck.*

No matter how good he smells.

"Granny goes to bed early," I lie. "She said I should use the back door."

The truth is, my grandmother has no idea I'm coming. But I don't want Tyler to know that. I may trust him enough not to murder me on a five-mile drive, but I don't trust him with everything.

I hop out of the truck, careful to land on my good ankle, and lean against the truck's open doorframe.

"Can you make it okay on that ankle? Need help getting to the door?" Tyler asks.

Yes, I think. *Please pick me up and carry me again. Pretty please.* But I say, "No, I'm fine."

Because the last thing I need in my new life is a liability.

"You sure?" he says.

My ankle is throbbing. I can barely stand, even leaning against the truck. "It's feeling a lot better, since you taped it. I'll be fine," I lie.

I'm used to lying. It's easy for me. But for some reason, I don't, especially, like lying to Tyler.

Because he's been kind, when most people aren't.

"It's probably good if you go on your own. Because if your grandma owns this place, she's liable to have me arrested for kidnapping if she sees me with you."

"What do you mean?" I ask, surprised by the edge in his voice. Like he's joking, but he means it, too.

"Oh, you'll find out, I'm sure." There's that edge in his voice again, rough and raw.

"I'm sorry I kicked you in the stomach," I say, gently.

"I'm sorry my first aid tape sounded like creepy duct tape." His voice is softer now, velvety.

"And thank you for the ride."

"Sure."

I fumble in my Birkin for the tiny wad of cash I have. "Do you want some money? For gas, I mean?"

"From you?" That rough edge returns to his voice.

"I mean, gas costs money—"

"Not everything is about money. Have a good time at your grandmother's. Sweetie."

Sweetie? The way he says the word, it comes out twisted, part-tender, part-teasing, part-something else.

That edge in his voice—there's history there, something sharp under the charm. I shouldn't care. And yet... I want to know why he sounds like he's choking back emotion when he's just dropping me off.

I stand there and watch as the old beater of a pickup chugs back toward the main road. The word TOYOTA, painted in white on the tailgate, has all but worn away.

Only the letters Y and O are left. YO. I watch until the YO disappears.

Well. That was it. That was Tyler.

Now... this is something else.

The night is silent again, except for the sound of the ocean. I can hear it surging somewhere beyond the house. When the wind blows, the tall pines creak. An owl hoots. I smile, thinking again of Tyler singing to me about pizza while I pretended to have a gun.

My ankle throbs. I'd give anything for an ice pack. But there's no chance in hell Granny Riding is going to swoop to my rescue with ice and Advil.

She isn't expecting me. We've never even met—thanks to the fight between her and Dad—and for all I know, she thinks I'm still twelve

And what if I knock on her door and she calls the cops, freaks out about some strange teenager ringing her bell in the middle of the night? An old rich widow, all alone in this big house, might be jumpy.

It makes more sense for me to find some place on the property to sleep, at least until morning, and then show up around breakfast.

But my ankle hurts so bad. And I'm thirsty. And an ice pack and a soft bed would be so good. And she *is* my grandmother. She'd *want* me to be safe and comfortable.

Wouldn't she?

Because there's a third option, something between pounding on the door and sleeping in the yard.

I could break in. Sneak upstairs.

Why not? I could tiptoe around. Maybe find an unused guest room? The place is big enough.

I limp around to the side of the house, leaning against the brick walls to rest when my ankle hurts too much. Around back, I discover that someone's left the kitchen window slightly open.

It takes me a couple of tries to launch myself (everything's harder on one leg). But I pull myself in through the window.

Soon I'm sliding face-first into a polished marble sink. My elbow knocks the faucet on. I hold back a shriek as icy water soaks my shirt. I've barely gotten the faucet off when I hear a sound that's even more chilling.

It's the sound of someone racking a shotgun, loading the chamber. My blood turns to ice. My breath stops.

Because my grandmother is about to murder me.

CHAPTER 5

CHLOE

"Get out of my kitchen." The woman's voice is shaky, but I doubt her aim is.

The trick with people who need you to know they're powerful? Let them think you're weak. Sometimes, they'll feel sorry for you and protect you.

Even though I'm terrified, I summon my most babyish, most innocent voice. "Grandma? Is that you? I'm scared," I say.

Silence falls in the dark room.

I don't dare move.

The light snaps on. I blink against the sudden glare, eyes adjusting to the gray-on-gray kitchen.

There are no kitschy oven mitts or bright magnet collections or cozy, punny mugs in *this* kitchen.

Everything's sleek and gray—rich-people gray—the walls, the cupboards, my grandma's hair and manicure. Even her skin has a wintry undertone, like pencil lines erased too many times.

I want to take in her face, study it, see if I can detect traces of my dad, but she hasn't put the gun down yet.

"Stay where you are," she hisses. "Explain yourself."

"It's me. Chloe. Chloe Riding. My dad is Harry Riding, and I think you're my grandmother, Elinor Riding."

"Drop your purse on the floor," she says.

I do, and pointing my toe, I kick it toward her.

Still training the gun on me, she picks up the Birkin bag and rifles through it. She fishes out my wallet. Looks through my ID cards. "Cassie Everly. Caitlyn Montmorency. Cordelia Cordray."

"Those are fake," I squeak. My dad and I have a ton of fake IDs. They're useful for all sorts of things—like, say, renting cars you don't plan to return.

"And I suppose this Chloe Riding ID is fake too, then?" Granny Riding asks. "And these other IDs must be for all the other heiresses you're impersonating? All the other grand-mothers to whom you're giving heart attacks?"

Heiress? I know my dad grew up well-off, but it's never occurred to me that I could be considered an actual heiress.

I mean, I've eaten my fair share of lobster and filet mignon (mostly dine-and-dash). But I've also eaten out of garbage cans and food pantries.

Money was never a steady thing for me and my dad. Not like the word "heiress" would imply. But now that I see this house…

Maybe I *am* an heiress.

"The Chloe ID is the only real one," I insist. "I don't know how to prove it. Except I can tell you things about my dad. Things only he would know."

My heart is gunning like a getaway car. Dad definitely told me a lot of stories—enough stories to fill a podcast season.

But my dad also tells a lot of lies.

I don't know which of his stories will turn out to be true, and right now, a game of "true or false" feels a lot like Russian roulette. But I can't think of a better option.

"Very well. What was your father's dog's name growing up?" Granny quizzes.

I know this one. Dad was always telling stories about Penelope, the perfect poodle.

"Penelope," I say.

Granny scoffs. "No. It was Chloe. I hate to admit it. But he named you after that little shih tzu. Now, hold still. Don't move. I'm calling the police."

"Wait!" I say. "Maybe my dad just didn't want me to know he'd named me after a dog."

The truth is, being named after a dog does kind of hurt my feelings. Even with a shotgun pointed at my head, my ego still manages to whimper.

"All right," Granny says. "One more chance. I haven't seen my granddaughter Chloe since she was a baby. Back then, she had a certain distinguishing birthmark. Do you?"

Finally, something I can prove. I have a birthmark in the shape of a strawberry on my left shoulder. "Yeah. Can I can take off my windbreaker?"

Granny moves to inspect me, still carrying the gun. She licks a finger, rubs it against my exposed shoulder. Then she claws at my birthmark with her nails.

"Ow," I say as her gray talon scratches me.

"Well, it's not coming off. Either it is a tattoo, or you are indeed Baby Chloe. Lightning round. What was the name of your daddy's sailboat? The one that sank in harbor?"

This one's easy. Dad told me all about the parties he used to have in high school on the Sweet Suite. According to what he told me, he was ragingly popular—despite having no aptitude for football. Instead, his quick wit and keen sense of human weakness propelled him into the spotlight.

"The Sweet Suite," I tell Granny Riding. "The first sweet like a candy, the second suite like—"

"Where did your parents go on their honeymoon?"

This one's almost tragic. "Vegas—where they eloped. And yes, an actual Elvis impersonator married them."

"Where is your mother now?"

"The United Arab Emirates, I think. I haven't seen her since I was nine."

"And your dad?" Granny's steely voice cracks a little at those words. There. That's it. I've spotted it—her weakness.

My dad broke her heart.

"He told me to come here," I say. "He's on the lam. Some loan sharks are after him—"

"He won't get any money from me. No matter how many charming granddaughters he sends to break into my kitchen."

"So you think I'm charming?" I say, tilting my head and gazing into her eyes. I know from looking at pictures that at this angle, I look more like my dad. The more I remind Granny Riding of him, the softer her heart will be toward me.

"Don't get cute," Granny says. "I raised your father. I know all his tricks. Cuteness, cleverness. I want none of that."

"Okay," I say.

"Just honesty. Why are you here?" she demands.

"I've got no place else to go," I say. "And not a dollar to my name. Honest."

At last, Granny Riding puts the gun down. "You can stay here with me, Chloe. But as long as you do, you'll live by my rules."

"Okay," I say.

"The first rule is, do not wake up your grandmother in the middle of the night. A lady's beauty sleep is sacred."

"Got it," I say. "Sorry."

"Follow me," Granny Riding says. She leaves the gun lying across the kitchen counter.

"Um, are you going to put the gun away?"

"Oh, Helga will get it in the morning, when she cooks break-fast. Now come along. I'll show you to your room."

"Could I get some ice? For my ankle?"

"Of course. But there is no need to use those puppy dog eyes on me. I am a human being. Not a monster."

Granny Riding pulls a frozen gel eye pack out of her enormous freezer. "Try this," she says, tossing it to me.

Upstairs, in my luxurious but sterile gray guest suite, I think about where my dad might have hidden this safe deposit box key.

But I'm so tired—too tired to look for it—and the king-sized bed looks so inviting—that I give in and go to sleep.

CHAPTER 6

TYLER

*D*riving home, a Lexus almost T-bones me on Harborview Drive.

Okay, maybe I'm not paying complete attention.

I'm still breathing in the lemony, summer-morning scent Chloe left in my truck. Still wondering who she is—and what she's afraid of.

Then some rich, drunk Sweet Harbor High Sweetie pulls out onto the main road without looking.

I slam on my brakes. The Sweetie driving the Lexus doesn't even seem to notice. Entitled moron just drives off down the center line like he trusts everyone to get out of his way.

But that gives me an idea.

I've been trying to think positive lately. Look for silver linings. See opportunity—not just Sweetie jackassery.

So now, I turn around and check out the driveway the Lexus came from. The house is set way back, so all I can see is the glow of distant lights. But I can hear the low throb of bass.

Someone's having a Sweetie party.

I text Benny and Cyrus. I know my boys are close by. The three of us were racing down at the dunes earlier tonight, and the two of them were going to hit up some girl's party at the Dock & Drink beach.

Cy texts they'll meet me right away. The party's busted. Deana didn't even come. (That's Cy's ex. She's all he ever talks about lately.)

Benny texts that the party sucks because his ex, Rach, showed up and made a scene.

Which, knowing Benny, could mean she just *talked* to him. Once Benny's done with a relationship, he's done.

It's not cool. But I understand where it comes from. His home has been a wreck since we were kids, and breaking up is easier for him than letting anyone in. He's really messed up about girls. It's not his best quality. But he's a good friend.

Cy, on the other hand… he wears his heart on his sleeve. So it's easy to tell when that heart is broken. Which, right now, it is.

That's the main reason I'm looking for opportunities to mess with Sweeties.

A little prank will be just the thing to cheer Cy up.

Where I come from, people don't have a lot. But we have each other. That's Shady Cove.

Even if your friend is being an idiot—and even if they are an idiot most of the time—you stick by them. It's who we are.

I pull off the road and wait for Benny and Cy. My thoughts turn again to Chloe. Her voice, clear and sharp, like a new pair of scissors.

She didn't talk like a Sweetie. But she didn't sound like anyone else I'd ever heard, either. She almost had an accent like she'd lived in a million places, absorbing a little bit from every place.

She's a puzzle I can't stop trying to figure out. And maybe

part of why I'm so intrigued is, I can tell she's carrying something heavy, too.

I tried to calm her down, get her to trust me, open up—and the little I'd been able to glimpse had only made me want to know more.

It's so dark out, I jump when Benny knocks on my window. Or, okay, maybe I jumped because I was remembering wrapping Chloe's ankle.

The way she held her breath, like she didn't want me to hear how much it hurt. What kind of girl grows up afraid to show weakness?

I noticed while taping her ankle she's got very soft toes, like silk or butter—not that I care about toes, especially, it's just—my mind keeps running over the details of her. Trying to figure her out.

She's still a Sweetie—right? Obviously. Look where her grandmother lives.

But she doesn't *know* she's a Sweetie. Does it still count?

Benny knocks on my window again, and Cy hops in the truck's bed. The truck sinks under his weight.

Cy is huge, six and a half feet tall, and made of solid muscle. He doesn't look like a guy who'd break easy, but when Deana left, it was like watching a bear curl up for winter.

"Cy hardly talked to anyone at the beach," Benny tells me, leaning into the window. "All he did was stare out at the waves. You know Julia? The hot one, with the tattoos? She went over to talk to him. But she came back and told me all he talked about was Deana."

"He's not right in the head," I say. "We gotta fix him up."

"He says he'd be down for a game of Gas Station," Benny says. "Unless you had something better in mind?"

"I'm cool with Gas Station," I say.

"Anything to get Deana off Cy's brain," Benny says.

"Yup," I say, and Benny slaps the roof of my truck twice, then climbs in the truck bed with Cy.

I KEEP the headlights off and drive slowly down the curving driveway to the house. It's one of those modern houses that looks like a giant glass shoebox. It's lit up so I can see all the Sweeties inside it, like some dollhouse, or a shoebox diorama you'd take to school.

Inside the house, all the girls are taking selfies, making faces with those fake plump lips that if you kissed them would probably pop like balloons.

All the guys are doing keg stands, high-fiving, and chest-bumping.

Normally, I wouldn't pay much attention to Sweetie parties.

But now I wonder. Next time I see a swarm of Sweeties—will I see Chloe, too?

And if I showed up at her grandmother's house, what would happen? Would Chloe pretend not to know me? Would her grandmother call the cops? And what if they caught me?

I think about what happened to Benny with that Sweetie girl, Virginia, last summer. The Sweet Harbor Police pulled him over and beat the crap out of him. Told him to stay out of Sweet Harbor.

Next day, the news reported that Virginia's family had just made a $100,000 donation to the Sweet Harbor police officer's union. Later, I learned Virginia's parents sent her away to boarding school, too.

All that history is what's cycling through my brain.

But my brain doesn't feel very in charge of me just now.

Because the truth is, no matter what the stakes are, I'm sure, 100% sure, I'm going to find Chloe again. I just don't know when.

In the meantime, we play Gas Station. Here's how the game is played.

First, Benny goes around and finds the valets. They're usually somewhere vaping, getting high. And they're usually guys we know, regular type guys earning a few bucks parking Maseratis and Lambos at a Sweetie party. It beats handing out snacks on toothpicks inside.

Usually, Benny distracts the valets, tells them jokes. Meanwhile, Cy and I go around siphoning gas. Filling up gas cans for free from all the Sweetie vehicles.

It's an easy, fun, low-stakes prank. Technically, it's a crime—but it's a petty one. A hobbyist crime. Just for fun.

Tonight, for the first time in days, Cy looks alive. He's grinning from ear to ear, running around with this tiny little gas cap key he ordered special on Amazon. It's supposed to open any and all gas caps—and it actually works.

We skip over the Teslas, for obvious reasons.

But for the rest of the vehicles, it's fair game. We open the gas caps, stick rubber hoses in the tanks, get them going with a little suction, and fill our own gas cans.

"Hoo, boy, time for some mouth-to-mouth action," Cy says when he gets his hose down a Lambo's tank.

He's having so much fun he actually sucks too hard and gets a mouthful of gasoline.

Then he spits the gasoline out and flicks his lighter, so an arc of dragon flame bursts to life—way too close to his face.

I tackle him, cursing under my breath. Second time today I've needed the first aid kit. But Cy's laughing when I hand him a pack of Band-Aids for his burned-off eyebrows.

When we've filled all my gas cans, we load them in the back of my truck. I whistle for Benny, and we head out.

But the night's not over.

We drive toward downtown Sweet Harbor and park the car on a side street, hiding behind a Dumpster out front of a building that's getting renovated.

Cy and Benny climb up in the cab with me, and we wait to watch the fun.

Soon we'll see a parade of luxury vehicles running out of gas —one by one.

First it's a gray Audi, coming to a stop. The driver gets out and pops the hood. A girl climbs out, texting.

Out of his pocket—Benny always has things in his pocket— Benny pulls some firecrackers, lights them, and tosses them in the Sweeties' direction. Not close enough to hit them—just enough to scare them.

As the firecrackers explode, the Sweeties run away screaming, the she-Sweetie tottering on her high heels, the he-Sweetie pushing her down in his rush to get away. Imagine shoving your date out of your way so you could get to safety first. That's love— Sweetie style.

It feels good to see Cy smiling. And it's even better that tomorrow we'll get to play Santa Claus down at Shady Cove trailer park, filling everyone's gas tanks for free.

CHAPTER 7

CHLOE

*S*leeping in the gray guest room at Granny's, I have an amazing dream.

I'm back in that old Toyota truck with Tyler, the guy from last night. In the dream, we pull up outside Granny's mansion and Tyler says, "You don't have to go in there if you don't want to. Let me take you someplace safe."

Then he drives me to the beach and spreads a pink blanket on the sand. I lie down next to him, and our legs tangle together. I inhale his rough, soapy, woodsy scent and relax as waves rush onto the shore.

I wake up to a stern rap on my door. "Miss Riding? Get dressed and come downstairs," a woman barks.

Helga, I think. This must be the housekeeper Granny was referring to last night—the one who was supposed to put the gun away.

As I get dressed, it hits me what's crazy about this house.

I barely got a look at it last night. I fell asleep the second my head hit the pillow. But now, in the morning light, I can see it.

Everything in this house is gray.

The walls in my room are dark green-gray, like the sky before a storm. They're decorated with black-and-white photos. The fine wool carpet is pearl gray, and my comforter, sheets, and pillows are shades of ash. Everything in the en-suite bathroom is charcoal gray, from towels to tub to tiles.

It's like living inside a charcoal drawing.

As I rummage around, looking for the key my dad supposedly left somewhere in the house, I notice the extremeness of the palette. Drawers lined with gray shelf paper. Pictures backed with gray matting. The silver picture frames shine like little warning bells. It's like someone burned down this house and resurrected it in expensive cinders.

My ankle's feeling better, but I'm still limping as I walk downstairs and find my way to the kitchen. A hulking woman in a gray-and-white housekeeper's uniform introduces herself as Helga. She lays out a dark gray place setting for me on the light gray marble counter.

When she serves my egg, I note the bluish-gray shell—the sign of a fancy breed of chicken. But in this setting, it makes me feel like I'm living in a black-and-white movie.

I check my reflection in the back of the spoon to be sure my lips are still pink. "What is this place? Is my grandma a big fan of *Fifty Shades of Grey*, or what?"

Normally, joking with staff works. You always want to get in good with them. Workers are helpful allies.

But Helga gives me a glare that could freeze lava. "I don't appreciate off-color jokes."

"My apologies," I say.

Inside, my stomach's tight. It's been hours since I checked for messages, but my phone's been dead since yesterday. Dad's last words echo in my head: *"If you get stuck, I'll find you."* Sure, Dad. Any day now.

"Be advised, I will count the silver," Helga warns.

I roll my eyes. But she has a point. Scrap silver's selling for $26.15 an ounce; the spoon in my hand is probably worth something.

But I wouldn't want to get caught stealing from Granny. Even I have limits. Right?

Sure, Granny's welcome was a bit... frosty last night, gun and all. But I did wake her up in the middle of the night.

I'm sure today she'll be more grandmotherly. Tea, stories, maybe she'll even let me stay awhile. It's been years since I've felt settled anywhere.

All I've ever wanted was a place to land. Somewhere to hang my backpack without checking for the nearest exit.

I dip a corner of toast into the warm, runny yolk. "Delicious," I say, even though I can hardly swallow with Helga staring me down.

"Mrs. Riding seems to think you're her long-lost granddaughter. I am not so sure."

I pull down the neck of my T-shirt. "Want to check out the birthmark?"

Helga peers at it. "That is the strawberry," she admits. "But it's too convenient. You showing up the day before Mrs. Riding was about to make her bequest."

"What bequest?"

Something sharp enters Helga's gaze. "Oh, don't act so innocent with me. You know very well your grandmother was planning to leave her entire fortune to the Historical Society. Now, naturally, she's revising her will. Leaving everything to you. Of course, you'll need to clean up your act."

Helga shakes her finger at me. "She can cut you out of the will, the same way she cut your father out. Mrs. Riding has the highest of standards. She expects you to act like the Riding Heiress if you're going to be the Riding Heiress. And so far, I'm rather doubtful you can succeed."

She whisks the plate out from under me, even though I've only taken two bites of toast.

"Now get dressed for school."

"What?" I say, still dazzled by all this information.

"School," Helga says. "Or does the Riding Heiress think she's too good for that?"

Heiress.

If Granny really is revising her will, do I stand to inherit this gray mansion? I take another look around. The marble counter. The Viking range. The French doors to the patio overlooking the harbor. The silver spoon, heavy in my hand. Why would I even think of stealing it? It practically belongs to me.

I'm still blinking when Helga says, "Hurry up. I have to get you to school and then get down to the fish market before the good crab's taken."

"Where's Granny?"

"Occupied," Helga snaps. "Haven't you anything more suitable to wear?"

"Just this," I say, gesturing to my T-shirt and jeans.

"No luggage?" Helga says.

"It got lost," I lie. Because the truth is, it's still at the Ritz. I couldn't take much when I ran off.

"Your grandmother won't like you wearing those rags," Helga says.

"Maybe we should wait for her to get home," I say, stalling for time. My chest tightens. Because I've got no phone, no money, no way to disappear if this all blows up—and I don't know about the "school" business.

The truth is, I've never been to school. Not really. My dad and I were always running.

For a while, before my mom left, we were living in London. I went to school for almost a whole year. I think I was in—what was it called? Fourth form? But that was a long time ago.

"No," Helga says. "We'll go now. You have a suitable handbag, at the very least." She holds up my Birkin bag.

"Hey! You took that from my room."

"There is no such thing as your room. Every room in this house belongs to your grandmother. And so does everything in it. Don't you forget," Helga hisses.

"Be nice to me," I say. "I'm the Riding Heiress."

"I don't work for you," Helga says. "I work for Mrs. Riding. I have been her housekeeper for twenty-five years. She trusts me. If she's going to believe one of us, it's going to be me. Not some teenager who claims to be the daughter of her son, who happens to be a well-known pathological liar. So you be nice to me, Miss Riding."

She snaps open my bag and paws through it.

"That's mine—"

"What did I just say?" Helga tuts. "Nothing is yours anymore. Get used to it."

Helga opens my wallet. She clucks, pulling out my fake IDs. "I knew your father as a young man," Helga says. "I had his number from Day One. So it's no surprise he's got his daughter wrapped up in his scheming. But the buck stops here."

She reaches into the pocket of her apron and pulls out a shining steel scissors.

"Those IDs aren't yours," I say.

But as Helga snips my fakes in two, it hits me like a punch: there's no plan B. No escape hatch. Just me, the mansion, and a whole lot of gray.

Helga hands me my purse. "Now, Miss Riding." She says it like it's an insult. "Time for school."

CHAPTER 8

CHLOE

*S*weet Harbor High is a low, modern building perched on a cliff on the far side of the bay. From a distance, I can spot the glass elevators that scale the cliff wall, leading to the private marina where the school keeps a fleet of boats. Their bright sails, in the school colors—yellow and blue—look tiny.

When we get close, Helga joins a parade of luxury vehicles in the drop-off line. It winds through huge, carefully manicured rose bushes.

Being in line makes me nervous. I don't like feeling trapped. What if the mob guys are after me? I've got no phone. No way to call for help.

The only escape route? Jump off the cliff.

As we crawl up the congested drop-off lane, I keep one eye on the rearview mirror. Behind me, a gorgeous girl steps out of a Mercedes SUV. Her honey-brown hair cascades down her shoulders expensively—a clear indicator of a fresh blowout.

"That's Sophie," Helga says. "Your grandmother will expect you to befriend her, no doubt."

"How would you know?"

"Sophie Cortez is one of the most well-connected girls in Sweet Harbor. You can understand the importance of befriending her, right?" Helga's gruff voice drips with condescension.

I can understand the importance of getting to know her to run a scam. Other than that, I don't see it.

"Your grandmother expects you to live up to your family's reputation," Helga says. "The Ridings are the best of the best. We socialize with the crème de la crème. We—"

We. Helga says it like she's a member of the family, not a servant.

"We are the most successful. We get the best grades. Win the athletic competitions. Win prom queen, homecoming queen. You're the Riding heiress. Those are the expectations. And if you can't live up to them, your grandmother can always leave her money to the Historical Society after all. She wanted me to make that quite clear to you. Is it?"

"So, your job is to make it clear to me that my grandmother's love is conditional?" I say. "That she'll love me as long as I'm totally perfect?"

"Not perfect," Helga says. "No one is perfect. But someone is always the best. And that someone should be you."

I slink down in my seat as we inch along in Granny's Land Rover. It's a lot of pressure for your first day at school—your first day ever at an American high school—just twenty-four hours after you ran from the mob, sprained your ankle in the woods, and got rescued by the hottest pizza delivery boy you've ever met.

Then, a few cars back, I see it. A black Chevy Suburban.

Calm down, I tell myself. It's probably not the mafia.

More likely, it's a parent who drives a Suburban because they need room for lacrosse gear.

Still, my heart pounds.

I'd be lying if I said I wasn't nervous about starting school. I haven't been to school in years. I don't know how to act. I don't even know what grade I'm supposed to be in.

But if anything can make me less nervous about being the new girl, it's worrying about the mafia. Dad's old advice flickers up—always fight problems by creating bigger problems.

Helga pulls up at the main door. "Go in and find the principal's office. Your grandmother has called. They're expecting you."

Inside, Sweet Harbor High looks more or less like what I'm expecting. Granted, my expectations are based on movies.

There are, in fact, lockers. Hallways. Tons of students. So many I can slink through them unspotted.

I sit down to wait on a leather bench in front of a glass-walled office labeled PRINCIPAL.

Sophie, the swishy-haired girl from the drop-off line, sashays past. She's accompanied by three other girls. At first, from a distance, I think they're identical quadruplets.

They all have the same gold-brown blowouts, bodycon dresses, and boots. They move in sync, whipping off their square Bulgari sunglasses at about the same moment, revealing long, thick fake lashes.

But when they get closer, I start to tell the four girls apart. For example, the one I saw in the drop-off line, Sophie, has a small, dark mole above her upper lip. Sophie stops walking when she sees me.

"So, you're the Riding girl?" she says. "My grandmother texted me today. She heard about you." She looks me up and down.

Her nearly-identical friend snaps a pic of me, bracelets jangling on her wrist.

"Hey," I say, holding up my hand in front of my face. I'm careful about being photographed. Facial recognition technology

39

is improving every day. Selfies are a great way for cops or loan sharks to find you.

"Get a shot of her bag," Sophie tells her braceleted friend. "It will be perfect for the starter pack."

"Starter pack?" I regret the question as soon as it's out of my mouth.

"We're creating a Starter Pack. For basic poseurs and social climbers." I note this girl's eyes—blue. They narrow nastily as she speaks. So far we have Sophie, Bracelets, and Blue Eyes, I think. And a fourth one, wearing diamond studs. It's good to keep track of your enemies.

"You know, like pictures of accessories that are the poor person's idea of a rich person," Sophie purrs.

"Like a Mercedes C-Class. Or those pumps you're wearing," Diamond Earrings says.

My chest tightens. My throat constricts.

Don't let them get to you, I think. They're just small-town popular girls. All you're having is a primate status stress reaction. Your monkey brain is willing you to roll over, suck up to them. Don't.

Still, I can feel my heart pounding up into my throat.

"This one's Birkin is her beige flag," Bracelets says, sugar-sweet, all innocence. "Hold up the bag. Let me snap a pic."

This bag has gotten me through a lot. It's the only thing I've carried with me from town to town since I was nine. It's also the only thing I have left from my mom. I thought it would take care of me, be my disguise.

I guess not.

The door to the office behind me swings open. A tall, dark-skinned woman in a gray suit steps out. "Good morning, Sophie Cortez," she says to the mole-lip girl. "Sophie Edgington, nice to see you," she nods at the Diamond Earring girl. "Sophie Vuong, glad to see you're already including our new student," she tells Bracelets.

WHAT?

40

ARE THESE GIRLS ALL NAMED SOPHIE? I wonder, as the principal says, "And Kyra, how's that tennis elbow?"

"Much better, thanks, Principal Annan," the blue-eyed girl says. "In fact, we were just about to invite the new girl to play tennis. Sophie's grandmother heard she's a Riding."

Liar. These girls don't want to hang out with me. They want to haze me.

"Bullshit," I spit, without thinking.

The principal frowns. "Chloe," she says. "Your grandmother said you weren't quite housebroken. Hmm. Follow me."

PRINCIPAL ANNAN SITS at her desk and steeples her fingers. She stays quiet for a long time. At last, she speaks.

"Generations of Ridings have attended Sweet Harbor High. There has been a Riding on our school's board of directors for over a century. But today, I find myself perplexed. How am I to welcome you—and, at the same time, discipline you? You have not only used a foul word. You have used it against the junior class president on your first day of school."

Ugh. I knew this school thing was a bad idea.

"I think we'll start with placement tests." Her eyes gleam. "That will help us figure out your exact grade level, given you've been homeschooled."

"I'm sixteen, so I should be a junior—"

"We offer a very challenging curriculum. It is possible that even ninth grade could be too difficult for you. We may need to send you down to Sweet Middle School."

"What? No!"

"We will see," Principal Annan says. She opens a file drawer and pulls out a thick stack of papers. "Here you go. Ms. Burberry in the front office will set you up," she says. "Don't forget to use a number two pencil. Good luck."

. . .

I SIT at a small desk in the outer office to take the tests. The principal's assistant is clearly a Dog Mom—there are framed photos of her Burberry-sweater-wearing Corgi all over her desk. Every time she catches me looking at them, she says, "Focus on your test."

My dad taught me some math. Gambler's math, really. I'm good at calculating odds for betting. And I know how to count cards in blackjack. But geometry? Uh...

I fill in the answer bubbles randomly, hoping I don't wind up back in middle school. My fingers are aching from writing—I'm not used to holding a pencil—when a girl in a pink sweater walks in. She has long, dark hair and a shy smile.

She gives a note to Ms. Burberry, who reads it and sighs. "Addie Kim. You'd like to be excused from sailing lessons in gym. Again?"

"My mom signed the form," Addie says.

Ms. Burberry studies it, running a finger along the silk Burberry scarf around her throat. "You know, the school's official policy is that Yachting and Nautical Etiquette are key components of a Sweet Harbor High education."

"I know."

"Honey," Ms. Burberry says, voice syrupy-sweet, "if you can't afford the P.E. fees at Sweet Harbor, why not go to Shady Cove High? Don't you think you'd be more comfortable over there?"

Addie's eyes flick downward. She tugs at the hem of her sleeve, twisting the fabric between her fingers. There's a flash of something raw in her face—like she's used to being the punchline and is bracing for it.

"Miss Burberry!" I interrupt. "My pencil broke!"

As she turns, I meet Addie's eyes—and snap my pencil in two.

There's a beat of silence. Then Addie's mouth curves into a grin, shy but unmistakable. The kind of grin you only give someone who just saved you from going under. I'm glad I made her smile—for the first time today, so do I.

CHAPTER 9

TYLER

"We can do more. Gas Station was just a taste," Cy says.

"Yeah," I joke, "a taste of gasoline."

The guys—me, Benny, and our friend Zane—laugh. Burning off his eyebrows by spitting stolen gasoline into a lighter? Classic Cy behavior.

Cy is antsy, spoiling for a fight, because his ex, Deana, just started talking to a new guy. Cy needs to do something or he'll basically explode. I get it.

"We can go bigger. I'm talkin' *Homecoming.*" Cy slams his huge fist down on the workshop table so hard a hammer jumps.

Our workshop is an abandoned pole barn on a scrap of land outside of Shady Cove that everyone thinks is haunted. We're not superstitious, though.

So when we found the old barn while camping a few years ago, we took it over and fixed it up.We use the workshop to fix up cars, bikes, boats. We do a little traffic in salvage, too. If we come across a find, we don't look too closely at the paperwork aspect of it all.

If anyone's parents ever drive them up the wall, they can come and crash out here on the couch. The four of us, we've been friends forever; we'll always have each other. We're basically family, and this workshop is our house.

It's a good place to bring girls, too. When they're willing to come.

"Crashing the Sweeties' homecoming is not a bad idea," Zane says.

The Sweetie Homecoming.

I wish I believed I could find Chloe there.

But she's gone.

Last week, I cut class early and drove by her high school every day and still never saw her. I won myself a Saturday detention for truancy.

Finally, I went by her grandma's extra-large house, even though I knew someone like me would never be welcome there.

A maid in a gray uniform answered the door. She told me Chloe's grandmother had sent her to boarding school in Switzerland. "That's a different country. It's across the ocean," she said, looking down her gray nose at me as if I were some complete ignoramus.

Still, I can't stop thinking of the girl I barely glimpsed... the girl who smells like honey and lemon... the girl who kicked me in the gut and scrambled my brain.

I wonder what Chloe would say if she knew I was planning to disrupt the Sweeties' Homecoming. Probably: "You're an idiot." And she'd probably be right.

But I'd like to think she'd appreciate the loyal gesture to my friend.

Now Benny starts up, always analytical. "The Sweeties' downfall is they are creatures of habit. Every year before homecoming weekend, they have that weird party down at the D&D."

The Dock & Drink, aka the D&D (and, as I prefer to call it, the Douche & Diarrhea), is the Sweeties' favorite hangout.

Technically, the D&D is a regular bar and restaurant. But it runs more like a junior version of the Sweet Harbor Yacht Club. If you've got a boat, you can pull it right up to a dockside bar.

Of course, it has to be the right *type* of boat. Benny's little aluminum johnboat wouldn't cut it.

Anyone, technically, can eat in the restaurant. It's a public place.

They just use a dress code to keep people out.

When I was a kid, the D&D fascinated me. Because it floats. The whole restaurant is like a giant pontoon boat, tethered to an enormous deck.

Back then, it seemed so unfair my family couldn't eat there. But we weren't allowed. Because we didn't have little alligator logos on our shirts—or whatever the dress code was that year.

We could go to the beach next to it, though. The restaurant itself belongs to the Sweeties. But the beach… that's more of a free-for-all.

You never know who you might see there. Shady High kids, Sweet Harbor kids, dockworkers, drunk CEOs, junkie cosmetic dentists, beach bums. There are occasional fights, and, depending who's winning, the cops look the other way.

The cops may patrol the beach, but the D&D openly serves minors inside at the bar.

Sweeties of all ages put their martinis right on Mommy and Daddy's tab.

I'm not a fan of the D&D. But I don't mind hanging out on the beach by a fire pit, listening to the waves, staring into the flames, if that's what's going down.

I bet Chloe would like it there. It's got her vibe—everywhere and nowhere, all at once.

Too bad she's in Switzerland.

But maybe it's kind of a relief she's gone.

It's terrifying to think of what might happen if she were here.

She might destroy my soul. I could wind up like Cy, spitting gasoline and lighting it on fire just to feel alive.

"I've got it," Zane says. "What about that weird ritual the Sweeties do with their school mascot?"

"Yeah," Benny says. "The weekend before homecoming, the Sweeties' dog carries some flowers in its mouth and gives them to last year's homecoming queen at their D&D party."

"Exactly," Zane says. "I say, we take it. Kidnap the dog. Dognap him."

"And then what?" Cy says.

"Walk him," I say. "We keep him nice and fed and tamed until Shady Cove plays Sweet Harbor at the Thanksgiving game. Then, at halftime, we clip him on a leash and walk him across the field."

Cy grins. "That's what we do with Sweeties. We dog walk 'em!"

The boys and I spend the afternoon in the shop, figuring out the plan.

Benny and Zane will come in Benny's boat, blasting fireworks to create a diversion. Meanwhile, Cy and I will do the actual dognapping.

Hopefully, Benny and Zane will get the boat working in time. Benny's been tinkering with the outboard motor. He's good with mechanical work.

But you can only do so much with inferior parts. That's why I fully anticipate finding myself high and dry with Cy the night of our dognapping. What else are friends for?

A FEW DAYS BEFORE THE SWEETIES' party at the D&D, Cy drives up in our dognapping vehicle.

It's his dad's box truck. It used to be a U-Haul moving van. You can still see the U-Haul logo through the sheer coat of white paint covering it up.

Cy's dad bought the truck cheap. He uses it to pick up carcasses. He's a taxidermist. Hunters pay him to mount their kills. Other times he collects roadkill.

The thing with roadkill is, half the time, the animals aren't properly dead when you pick them up. That's why Cy's dad needed the box truck.

Once, he picked up what he thought was a dead bear. He put it in the back of a regular passenger van.

Halfway home, the bear came to and lunged for him in a wounded rage.

Its claws gouged a huge hunk out of Cy's dad's shoulder before he had the presence of mind to slam on the brakes, sending the bear through the windshield. After that, Cy's dad switched to the box truck.

He wanted a wall of solid steel between him and his killer roadkill.

Cy slaps his palm against the hood of the box truck. "This is the perfect dog-napping vehicle. There's no way anything goes wrong."

We all get quiet.

Cy's involved—so the odds something *will* go wrong are pretty high.

But nobody has the heart to say it.

"Ran into Deana at the Dollar General," Zane says, kicking the van's front tire. Of course, he's also kicking at Cy's heart, just by mentioning that girl's name.

I step up to stand between Cy and Zane, just in case Cy sees red and goes after him. But so far, Cy is keeping his cool.

"She gave me some insider info about the D&D," Zane says.

That's right. Deana used to wait tables at the D&D.

I glance back at Cy. His jaw has the tension I associate with an over-tightened screw.

Man, I never want to wind up like him. Heart cracked wide open, with nothing but bad plans to hold it together.

Zane doesn't notice Cy's unease, though. He keeps talking about Deana.

"She told me that the Sweeties keep the big dog in a kennel in the dry storage room, behind the bar," he says. "There's an unused back door that goes right to the parking lot. Just pop that door open with a crowbar and you're in. They hold the dog in there till they let him out to do that parade down on the dock."

"Oh, yeah," Benny says. "My cousin Addie goes to Sweet Harbor. She told me the dog parade thing is at midnight every year."

"So, what time should we get there?" Zane asks.

"Ten," I say, "late enough for people to have had a few drinks and let down their guard. But ten's still early, so people won't have started to leave. The parking lot will be quiet."

I turn on the air compressor, and Cy lays a stencil flat against the side of the van. It doesn't take long to airbrush a logo—Sweet Harbor Restaurant Supply—on the side of the truck.

Nobody will notice a van like that in the D&D parking lot. Not unless they look too close.

Then, after we kidnap the dog, we can paint over the logo. Cy's dad will never know. In fact, his truck will look better with a fresh coat of paint.

After we're finished painting, I gather up a collection of worn towels and rags. I pile them up in the back of the box truck and drape a ratty old pink blanket over them.

"What are you doing?" Benny asks.

"If we're getting a dog, he's going to need a bed," I say. I pat the big cushion I've made. "There, fluffy as a cloud."

"Metal," Benny jokes. "Metal."

CHAPTER 10

CHLOE

"Stop wiggling. You need to look perfect for the clambake at the Dock & Drink," Granny Riding says.

Madame Defarge kneels at my feet, pinning up the hem of a red fit-and-flare sundress.

"Is this seriously what I'm supposed to wear?" I ask.

"You don't like it?"

I stare at myself in the mirror. "I look like I'm going to a sock hop. Like from the 1950s."

Granny sneers. "Perhaps you could've asked Sophie for advice about what to wear. If you had attempted to get to know her. But I understand from Principal Annan that you are quite a loner. That's not acceptable, Chloe."

"It's hard to make friends when the principal keeps you in the office taking placement tests all day," I say. My voice shakes a little. I don't want to get the results of the placement tests back. I didn't know what I was doing. Half the time, I was randomly picking answers.

I can handle myself in the world. But this school stuff? I just hope the results aren't too embarrassing.

And if they are... I don't have to stay here, right? If I could find that safe deposit box key, I could get my dad's money and get out of here, away from this entire School Situation.

But it's hard to even imagine the outside world when I'm Rapunzelled up in Granny's gray house. She won't even give me the Wi-Fi password, let alone a data plan.

"In order to be friends with Sophie, I need to get on social media. For that, you need to give me internet access," I tell Granny.

I've never really had any social media accounts before (my dad always thought they could be incriminating), but I'll do whatever it takes to get some internet access. Including trying to make friends with the Sophies.

"Nonsense," Granny Riding says. "You'll read books in my house. And a good, in-person effort with Sophie and her friends will mean so much more than any of this social media nonsense. Besides, if you're anything like your father, I'd get you an internet connection and you'd be running an illegal pyramid scheme from my house in about five seconds flat. No, thank you."

I sigh. I've been trying to find out more about Sweet Harbor Bank—if I can't find a key, maybe I can find a sympathetic employee to help me open Box 311—but it's impossible without the internet.

I can't even wander around downtown asking directions. Granny lives miles out of town, and my ankle still isn't up to the hike.

Plus, some part of me is curious about Granny, and about this place.

I want to Google her. I want to learn more about her. More about my family. More about what it is like to *have* a family.

But another part of me wants, just as badly, to run away and never look back. And either way, I need money. It's the only way to help my dad.

"I think you look quite nice," Granny Riding says.

I stick out my tongue in the mirror.

"She'd look beautiful if she'd just fix her face. Right, Madame?" Granny says.

Madame Defarge looks up at me from the floor and nods, her mouth full of pins. "Mmm-hmm," she mumbles. The pins wobble between her lips.

Granny's cell phone rings. At least she has a phone. But she doesn't text—she's that old school. She even steps outside of the boutique to answer it.

"Do you know where Sweet Harbor Bank is?" I ask Madame Defarge.

She says something, but I can't make it out because her mouth is still full of pins.

Granny steps back inside, beaming—if a person whose vibe is 100 percent gray can be said to beam. "Wonderful news about the clambake at the Dock & Drink. Kyra will take you."

"Kyra?" I say. The only one of the Sophies who's not named Sophie? The one with the mean blue eyes?

"Her mother owes me a favor," Granny Riding says calmly. "That's why I am sure Kyra will be a very gracious hostess." She sighs. "You're a quick study, Chloe. So I doubt Kyra's leadership skills escaped you. If you can get in Kyra's good graces, you'll be on your way to being a raging success at Sweet Harbor High. By success, I mean National Merit scholar and, of course, prom queen. I expect nothing less."

"Got it. Nothing less than genius prom queen."

"Exactly. That is, if you want to be a member of this family."

"What does being a member of this family mean, exactly?" I say. "Love? Money?"

"Love! Money! Is there a difference?" Madame Defarge purrs in her French accent. "There! I have finished."

"Spin around," Granny says. I twirl, and I can't help admiring how the red silk skirt flares.

Granny leans close to adjust the straps of my dress. A lump rises in my throat as I smell her Chanel perfume. No one has fussed over me like this since my mother left. Granny smoothes my hair into place and pats my cheek.

"That will do nicely," she says at last, and I'm not sure if she's talking about my dress or about me.

As we leave the store, my heart leaps at the sight of a rusty dark-blue Toyota pickup with only the letters YO remaining on the tailgate. I reach up my hand to wave, but Granny raps my knuckles with her fist. "Don't you get any ideas," she says.

"Ideas about what? I was just smoothing my hair," I lie.

"A Sweet Harbor girl is very careful in everything she does. She avoids attracting interest from the wrong sort of young man."

"What young man?"

"The one who I strongly suspect is behind the wheel of that unsightly pickup truck," Granny says. "I don't know how you know him, but from now on, you don't know him. Understood?"

I don't know how Granny knows I was thinking of Tyler. I've never told her anything about the guy in the truck that dropped me off at her house in the middle of the night.

Do I talk in my sleep? Is she recording me? Or am I just that bad at keeping a poker face?

Back at Granny's, Helga is sitting at the kitchen counter looking deadly with a long, silver pair of scissors. She narrows her eyes at me as she snips at a newspaper.

"Something for your scrapbook, Helga?" Granny Riding calls out, pressing a button on the fridge to fill a glass with sparkling water.

Helga gives me a weird gray look and lets the clipped scrap of newspaper fall where I can see it. The headline of the Sweet

Harbor Herald takes my breath away. It says: RIDING HEIRESS RETURNS HOME.

I snatch the clipping off the table. I barely hear Granny Riding's words over the beating of my heart. I skim the article anxiously.

The last thing I wanted was my name in a newspaper. What if those mobsters see it? Will they come after me in Sweet Harbor?

I don't know how much they know about me or about Dad. We've always used fake names, but the mafia isn't known for being stupid. They're not called organized crime for nothing—they're actually organized.

My guess is that the people my dad owes money to have had somebody monitoring Sweet Harbor news for years. They've probably been waiting for him to come home. "When did this paper come out?"

"Yesterday," Granny Riding says. She rolls her eyes. "That vulgar rag. But, when you're Society, you learn to deal with society gossip." She belches quietly and presses her fingertips to her mouth. "Do excuse me. Dyspepsia. Now, it's time for my siesta."

"Wait!" I say. My heartbeat throbs in my eardrums. I feel dizzy and steady myself on the counter. "I know you're angry with my dad. But he's in danger. And so am I. That newspaper article—the one that said I'd returned home to Sweet Harbor—I'm worried that some loan sharks saw it. They might be after me."

"Poppycock," Granny says. "Your dad liked to tell tall tales, too. I bet the moral of the story is your pressing need for cash. Am I correct?"

"Yes. Money would help."

"Your father always ran away from his troubles. I let him. I won't make that mistake with you. If you live in this house, you'll face your troubles head-on. No running. No hiding. No cash. No secrets. Now, I'm off to my nap. Let me sleep in peace."

I sit in my gray room and stare down at the driveway,

listening for the sound of mobsters' giant SUVs, Suburbans, and Escalades. I watch the rain until the light fades.

Once, I think I hear an old truck rattling down the main road —maybe Tyler's Toyota. I wonder where he is. There was something so comforting about his voice, his presence, his raspy smell of green lava soap and warm cedar.

Maybe if he were here, I would feel less afraid.

Whatever.

I've always taken care of myself.

I can take care of myself here, too.

So why does it feel so lonely?

CHAPTER 11

CHLOE

A stylist comes to Granny's to do my hair and makeup before the clambake. It would feel luxurious, if it weren't so stressful.

When the stylist finishes her work, Granny inspects me, tut-tutting in disappointment.

"Oh, give me that," she clucks, seizing the stylist's tweezers. She goes in and yanks out a stray hair from between my brows.

"Ow!" I say.

"Beauty hurts," Granny says, diving in to pluck another hair.

Later, in the mirror, I don't look like myself. I look airbrushed, polished, Instagram-filtered. I'm used to wearing disguises, but this time feels different — if I stay here long enough, pretending to be the Riding heiress, eventually that's who I'll become.

"Do I really have to do all this?" I ask.

"Cheer up," Granny says. "Maybe you can steal Kyra's boyfriend. He's quite the catch."

I've never heard Granny joke before, and I'm trying to decide whether to laugh when Helga drags me out to a long black vintage limo. It's packed with high school queen bees—three Sophies and a Kyra.

I climb into the limo. Into the swarm of Sophies.

Such sharp white teeth they have. Such heavily lashed eyes.

No one will talk to me. No one will even look at me. I'm used to being alone. But that doesn't mean it feels good.

I wish there was just one person I could lean on. Someone who could make me feel safe.

My mind flashes, stupidly, to Tyler—who I'll probably never see again. Because everyone here has made it clear that Sweet Harbor and Shady Cove people have nothing to do with each other.

I take a deep, steadying breath.

OK, if this is what I have to do to get my inheritance—or at least get a cash infusion to help Dad, I can do this. I can brave the mean girls.

Because it could be so much worse! I could be zip-tied in the trunk of a Cadillac driven by a bunch of mafiosos . .. not just iced-out of the conversation by a bunch of Sophies.

To distract myself from my anxiety, I pick a fight.

"Hey Kyra," I say. "How much did your mom pay you to invite me today?"

The Sophies take a sharp, collective breath. The mole above Sophie C.'s lip quivers. Sophie E. twists the diamond stud in her ear. Sophie V. trains her phone camera on me.

"A trip to Cartier," Kyra says, without looking up from her phone.

No one says a thing after that.

It's fine, I tell myself. *I don't have to have fun. I just have to get through this awkward evening without getting kidnapped.*

Maybe it's a good thing I'm going out tonight. Granny's house is isolated. Going to the clambake might actually be safer.

Because who would be bold enough to attack a group of rich kids at a homecoming party?

"Ooh," Sophie E. purrs, staring at her phone, "look at this adorable picture of Sweetiepie."

The girls lunge to gaze at Sophie E.'s phone, going ga-ga over some photos on it.

At last, Sophie C. takes pity on me and fills me in. "Sweetiepie is the school mascot," she explains. "She's a Tibetan guard dog. Do you know what those are?"

"Umm..." I say.

"You should at *least* know about Sweetiepie." Sophie E. condescends to show me a picture of an enormous, fuzzy red dog. "That's Sweetiepie. Isn't she gorgeous?"

"Did y'all hear? Sweetiepie's litter mate just sold for half a mil at a pet auction," Sophie V. says. "The fact that Sweetiepie is the Sweet Harbor High mascot increased the litter mate's value well above market rate."

"If I were a dog breeder, I'd hitchhike on the Sweet Harbor High brand if I could," Kyra says.

Silence falls. Then Sophie C. pipes up, "I don't want you to think we're mean, Chloe. We're not. We just have to be careful who we let in. We have to protect our Sweet Harbor brand. You can see now how our brand impacts the real world, can't you?"

"Right," I say, "if your brand value decreased, so might the price of exotic dogs."

"Exactly," Sophie C. purrs, but Sophie E. gives me a look, like she caught my sarcasm. The other two are too deep in their phones to notice.

WOW.

Granny had a point about Kyra's boyfriend.

He's the first thing I notice at the D&D, apart from the overwhelming aroma of money and steamed clams.

"Stay back," Sophie C. hisses at me. "That's Jackson Devereaux. He's Kyra's boyfriend."

Jackson Devereaux is a tall, gorgeous Black guy surrounded by a crowd of admirers. He has almond-shaped eyes and a sly smile that seems to make everyone around him feel drunk.

Seriously, with that kind of charisma, this guy could have anything he wanted.

And apparently, he wants a nasty rich girl with spiky fake eyelashes.

Trust Kyra to get the biggest piece of cake.

Speaking of cake. I'm starving. I look around the room, searching for the buffet.

The D&D has exactly the our-kids-can-afford-better-but-it's-good-for-them-to-have-a-place-where-they-can-roughhouse vibes I was imagining.

The decor? Classic Crab Shack Chic. The round windows are made to look like portholes, and the whole restaurant floats on pontoons. Water sloshes below me as I ogle the buffet, the piles of clams and crustaceans in serving dishes.

I wish my dad were here. He'd go nuts for all-you-can-eat lobster, then fill his pockets with clams "for later."

I don't know how many times I've opened a hotel mini-fridge to find it sloppy with pilfered oysters. Good old home cooking, Dad called it.

I hope he's okay, wherever he is.

Please, please, let him be okay.

"HELL YES! JACKSON DEVEREAUX!" A crowd of athletic-looking guys around Kyra's boyfriend whoops and cheers. Apparently he's hit a bull's-eye on the dartboard.

When Jackson approaches us, the crowd parts for him. All three Sophies quiver and giggle as he walks up.

Kyra oozes all over him like a jellyfish.

To his credit, he tenses up when she touches him. His body's on to her tricks, even if his brain hasn't caught up yet.

When Kyra slimes off him, he extends his hand and smiles at me. "Hi. I'm Jackson. You must be the new girl. Welcome to Sweet Harbor. What's your name?" There's not a trace of irony in his voice. He sounds sincere.

"Chloe," I say, feeling confused by his bizarre combination of sincerity and hotness.

Jackson asks me bland polite questions—where I've lived, what I think about Sweet Harbor, etc. As we talk, I feel more grounded. His smile doesn't make me dizzy anymore.

He's almost, I realize, too perfect. At least for me.

I like my guys a little rougher around the edges. My mind flashes to that glimpse of Tyler's stubbly jaw, his bristly scent of lava soap.

Kyra grips Jackson's arm and narrows her eyes at me above her toothy fake smile. She clearly hates that he's talking to me, but can't say so without looking like a mean girl in front of him.

"So, Jackson," I say, testing him. "My grandma told me your aunt just got elected governor. Congratulations."

His eyes light up and I get the weirdest impression—he actually *likes* his aunt, like, as a human, and not just to secure his family's ambitions. "Thanks. We worked so hard on her campaign." He slings his arm around Kyra, who coos,

"*I* was in her ads. I was the Face of Now."

"The Face of What?" I ask, cupping my hand over my ear, like I'm having trouble hearing over the music.

"Now," Kyra says. "The Face of Now."

"I don't see it," I say.

"Don't see what?" Jackson asks, innocent.

Guys never get it when girls are fighting. It's like if there's not a knee to the groin, they think we're all sunshine and crumpets.

"That isn't very nice of them to say, Kyra. I mean, I guess your nose is a little cow-like, in the way it's squared-off at the end," I say. "You do have large nostrils. But I would say calling you the Face of Cow is going too far."

When I say *large nostrils,* Kyra covers her nose with a perfectly manicured hand, and I grin.

"The face of *now,* not cow," Jackson corrects me, laughing.

"Ohhhhh," I say, "I'm sorry. I misheard. I'm so embarrassed." I make a big show of hiding my face, so Jackson steps away from Kyra to pat my shoulder comfortingly.

Kyra and the Sophies shoot me about a million eye daggers. I love how easy it is to make them angry.

"Thanks for understanding," I say to Jackson. "And I'm so sorry. It's just really hard to be the new girl. You're so out of the loop on everything."

"Well, you're very welcome here," Jackson says, and while he's looking at me, Kyra hurls her martini glass to the floor, where it shatters into a fury of shards.

Maybe tonight won't be so bad after all.

CHAPTER 12

TYLER

*C*y and I pull up to the D&D and back the box truck into a spot around the side of the building, near the little door Deana told Zane about. If her intel is good, the Sweeties' mascot will be tied up just inside.

I walk around, check the place out. There's no one in the parking lot; all the Sweeties are inside, partying. I can hear their pretentious murmuring from out here. Sweeties are yammering on about "Sophie's PJ."

At first, I think they mean pajamas.

Then I think they mean some kind of Sweetie sex act, which, I'll admit, sounds intriguing.

Finally, I realize that Sophie's PJ = Sophie's private jet.

They're all planning to take it to Tulum for fall break. Someone, Chad or Chazz or something, has a beach house there.

I listen closely, hoping to detect Chloe's voice. But of course, she's not here. She's at that boarding school in Switzerland.

Some Swiss yodeler is probably winding her silky hair around his finger. Offering her a mug of goat milk and laughing at her sarcastic jokes. If he's lucky, she'll kick him in the gut, too.

I look over the parking lot. Our truck, parked in the side lot, doesn't seem suspicious at all. "It looks like we're making an ordinary restaurant delivery. Perfect," I say, and Cy gives me a high-five.

We slide open the truck's back cargo door and drag the loading ramp out of its slot. We line it up with the side door.

"Now it's time to set the trap," Cy says. I play lookout while he makes a path of steaks leading up the ramp and into the truck.

"Looks good," I say. "No dog could resist that trail of steaks."

Now all we have to do is wait for the signal from Ash and Zane. They're planning to pull the johnboat up near the dock and light off the fireworks we stole last summer.

Then, while all the Sweeties are distracted by the fireworks display, Cy and I will open the side door and untie the dog.

She'll smell the meat and run right into our trap. Then we'll pull the cargo door shut and sneak into the restaurant, steal booze and snacks, and drive off with our loot.

But for now, we wait.

CHAPTER 13

CHLOE

Kyra sends Jackson off to fetch her another drink, then drags the Sophies onto the dance floor.

I scan the room, looking for mafia types. Somebody here could be a mafia plant. Or they might send goons in later in the evening, when people are drunk and distracted.

I get my back to the wall, just in case, and glance at the clock.

9:30 p.m. I make a mental note to pace myself on the drinks. I need to keep my wits about me.

So far, I don't see anyone suspicious. Just hunky jocks and girls who look like money—like pale imitations of The Sophies.

Sophie V. circles the dance floor, armed with her phone flashlight. She lunges toward girls, shining the light in their eyes, and ripping off their false eyelashes like she's collecting trophies.

"What is she doing?" I murmur.

Addie—the girl from the school office, in a cute owl-print sundress—is suddenly at my side. "Lash patrol," she says dryly.

"Excuse me?"

"The Sophies all wear eight-millimeter mink lashes. If anyone else copies the look, they rip 'em right off." Addie smirks.

Before I can even react, Sophie V. heads straight for me. Instinctively, I cover my eyes.

"Relax," Sophie purrs. "Your lashes are scanty as panties. You're fine. But quit talking to her." She jerks her head toward Addie.

"Why?"

"Kyra doesn't like it."

"I don't care," I say.

"It's okay," Addie murmurs, but I shake my head.

"It's not okay. I'll talk to whoever I want."

Sophie's fingers—cold as buffet shrimp on ice—graze my arm. "Chloe, you're new. You have potential. But you need to follow the rules."

"Why are you all so obsessed with rules?" I mutter. "I dare you to wear nine-millimeter lashes."

"Why? Eight-millimeter lashes suit my eye shape perfectly," Sophie V. says, but her nostrils have flared, so I can tell I've hit a nerve. "Like I said. I'm here to help. And Kyra will not be happy if she sees you talking to... *that*."

Sophie V. casts her eight-millimeter eyelashes toward Addie, who scratches her nose with her middle finger.

Addie's subversive gesture makes me smile.

"Why? Is Kyra jealous of Addie or something?" My dad always told me powerful people can be insecure. That's why they're so easily manipulated. "Does Kyra's perfect boyfriend have a secret crush on Addie? Is that why Kyra hates her?"

"Ew, ick!" Addie snaps. "Wash your mouth out, Chloe. I hate Jackson Devereaux."

"For once, Addie? You're right. It's disgusting to think of Jackson even looking at you," Sophie V. snaps. "And Chloe, shut up. I'm saying that as a friend."

Sophie V. stomps off. I suppress a giggle.

"I'm sorry," I tell Addie. "I didn't mean to—"

"Humiliate me?" Addie hisses.

I step back, startled by the fury on her face. "Really, it was unintentional. I had no idea there was something between you and Jackson—"

"There's not. There's nothing between us. Nothing."

"Can you accept my apology?" I'm used to faking apologies, but I'm not faking this time.

Addie seems like one of those rare, genuinely sweet people. Plus, I could use an ally—especially one who can get under Kyra's skin.

But Addie's staring at Jackson and Kyra, circling on the dance floor. "I hate him. He's dead to me."

"Okay," I say. "So if he's already dead, I guess I don't have to go over there and kill him for you—"

"Now is *not* the time to joke," Addie spits. Then she softens. "But I appreciate the implied offer to assassinate him. Preferably in the most painful way possible."

"Anytime. Want to go play darts?"

Addie gives me a nod. Good. I'm forgiven-ish.

"So, what grade are you in?" Addie asks, plucking darts from the board.

"Um," I say, trying to avoid the question. I'm really hoping my placement tests put me in some age-appropriate grade. I grab three darts and hit three bull's-eyes in a row.

Addie gasps. "Where'd you learn to do that?"

"I grew up in bars, playing bar games with my dad. Your turn."

She throws her turn.

Addie's... well, let's just say she's no threat to the dartboard.

"Mind if I show you a few tricks? That way you can aim straight for your enemies' hearts," I say.

She laughs. "Am I aiming for the dartboard, or the dance floor?"

We're working on her stance when there's an explosion.

Ear-shattering blasts crack the restaurant's glass portholes. Light stutters across the dance floor. Bright flashes streak across the sky outside.

Everyone rushes outside.

Everyone but me.

I know what this is.

It's a diversion.

The perfect way for someone to kidnap an heiress whose father owes them money.

I duck down behind the bar. With one hand, I reach up and grab a bottle of something—maybe gin? It feels heavy. Good. I might need to smash it over someone's head. I hope it doesn't come to that.

At the far end of the bar, I see a door. As successive explosions rattle the walls, I crawl toward it and scurry through, expecting to find myself in a kitchen.

Instead, I'm in the dark.

It must be a closet. I fumble for a light switch. At last, my fingers find it. I flip it on, but there's no light. I try again. Nothing. It's broken. I'm stuck here, hiding in the dark.

Then I hear, from close by, a low, deep growl.

My breath hitches. My fingers tighten on the bottle.

No one ever tells you that when the big moment comes—the moment when you might need to fight or flee—you don't feel brave. You feel small. Tiny. Cold all over.

I press my back against the wall, holding my breath, hoping whatever is in here with me can't hear the slamming of my heart.

And I wait.

CHAPTER 14

TYLER

*B*enny and Zane's illegal fireworks explode over the harbor. Cy gazes up, openmouthed, at the explosions shattering the sky.

"Come on," I say. But I'm hesitating, too. Awestruck.

This is a *lot* of fireworks.

Last summer we stole the entire contents of a roadside fireworks tent out on Highway Q.

How we did it was, we rented an identical tent for $20 from the U-Can-Rent-It Place, set it up a half-mile from the *actual* tent, and tricked the security guys into guarding the wrong tent while we stole fireworks from the real one.

Luckily, I managed to convince my buddies not to light the fireworks off immediately. Why advertise your location?

But now, months later, it's clear we stole a TON of fireworks that day.

I've never seen the sky lit up like this—not even the Sweet Harbor Yacht Club puts on such an extravaganza.

"We bring the thunder!" Cy says, pounding his chest as fireworks boom and scream and whistle down into the sea.

"Come on," I say again. We head over to the building. The door's easy; one swift move with the crowbar and it pops open like it was never locked at all.

The little storeroom is pitch dark, and the dog inside is furious—snarling, growling, barking.

I shine my phone flashlight. It cuts a narrow path of brightness through the stuffy space, lighting up stacks of boxes. At the far end, I see the kennel. Inside, a huge red dog thrashes against its cage.

"It's okay, buddy," Cy soothes. He presses a T-bone to the kennel door. The dog quiets and sniffs at the meat.

When Cy unlatches the kennel, the giant dog nearly knocks him over as she bounds out, desperate for steak.

Suddenly, a dark, club-like shape flies toward me. I duck just in time.

A bottle smashes against the wall.

The sharp scent of gin fills the room, and someone rushes past me into the parking lot.

Who knew the Sweeties would have the dog guarded?

I figured they'd all be out at the harbor, watching Zane and Benny light it up.

It's no problem, though. My dad made state for wrestling back in his day. He taught me everything he knew.

My body reacts before I can think. I launch myself at my attacker and lock them in a cradle hold.

As we struggle on the asphalt, I'm overwhelmed with the scent of honey and lemon.

Chloe? I think. It couldn't be.

In my split second of divided focus, my attacker twists away and starts running.

No way am I going to let them get away and alert the Sweeties. If they catch us, there'll be hell to pay.

"Start the truck!" I yell.

I take a flying leap and push whoever-it-is into the back of the truck and hop in after. Cy takes off, and I pull the cargo door shut as we race out of the parking lot.

The door locks automatically behind us, and the truck roars onto the highway.

Guess we won't be stealing any lobster rolls from the buffet tonight.

Suddenly, my attacker sneezes. Three cute, high-pitched sneezes.

It's a girl.

I kidnapped a girl. A She-Sweetie.

How could I have missed that? Was my adrenaline blinding me? Oh, God, this is bad.

Kidnapping? This is felony, federal-prison-level, twenty-to-life bad.

"My grandma will give you anything you want. But if you hurt me, you get nothing. She's a stone-cold negotiator, so if you want your ransom, you better listen up."

Hope spikes in my chest. That voice. I know that voice. And her scent, like a lemon grove in summer.

How has fate thrown me and Chloe together again?

Maybe, just maybe, she'll remember me.

She'll remember how I gave her a ride and *didn't* kidnap her that one time.

If she believes this really was an accident, maybe she won't press charges.

Maybe we won't all get felonies.

If I'm lucky.

Or maybe it's better to say nothing. Drop her off, disappear, hope this blows over. If my dream girl presses charges, we're toast.

CHAPTER 15

CHLOE

"*I* mean it," I repeat. "Ransom me. You'll get whatever you want." I make my voice sound confident. Inside, I'm not sure.

Most likely, Granny Riding will turn her back on me when I need her most.

She'll think I was in on my own kidnapping. She always thinks I'm trying to scam her.

But promising a hefty ransom is the thing you do when mobsters kidnap you from a clambake. Right?

My kidnapper says nothing. But even in his silence, I try to get a feel for him.

There's something familiar about him, even in the pitch-dark back of the truck. Where have I seen him before?

I probably saw him in Boston. These guys have likely been tracking me since I fled the Ritz.

I take deep breaths, trying to calm down. I focus on my senses—what I can touch (cold metal walls), what I can smell

70

(cooked meat), what I can hear (the dog, gobbling from a plastic bag).

I shrink up against the far wall, away from the dog—and the kidnapper.

What is the dog even doing here?

The truck bumps over uneven ground. I think I hear waves.

Oh, no. Are they taking me on a boat? I am not ready to trade Louboutin pumps for cement slippers. I burst into tears. I'm not ready to die. I'm not ready for any of this.

Finally, my kidnapper speaks. His voice is warm, strong, soothing. "Hey, it's all right. It's okay. I'm sorry. There's been a mistake. Please let me explain—"

"What is there to explain?" I sob.

"Shh, don't cry. You're okay. It's me. Tyler. From the other night? Do you remember?"

I thought he seemed familiar.

But why is he kidnapping me now, when he could've just driven off with me then?

"Are you working with them?" I blurt.

"With who—"

"You saw my grandma's house. You read the article. Who are you working for? Gardetti Brothers? DiMeo Family?"

"No. Chloe, you're safe. It was a prank. Everything's okay." Tyler hums that ridiculous pizza jingle, and I feel my neck relax —until I remember psychopaths are said to be very charming.

"Don't be scared," Tyler says again. (When someone says that, it's a clue to be VERY AFRAID.) "It's all a misunderstanding. We're not kidnappers—"

"So you threw me in the back of a van because you're not a kidnapper? Right."

"Chloe, believe me. We only meant to steal the dog. We thought you were guarding Sweetiepie."

Hearing her name, the dog stops eating, then dives back into the bag of meat and starts chomping away again.

"That's Sweetiepie?" I say.

"Yeah. We were pulling a dumb mascot prank."

The blood starts thrumming in my veins. I couldn't find the safety deposit box key. But maybe I don't need to. "Sweetiepie is worth half a million dollars. We can sell her. I know someone in Philly. We'll split the money."

"Aren't you super rich? Why do you need money?" Tyler asks.

"My grandma's letting me crash with her. Otherwise, I'm broke. And I need some cash to help my dad. Come on—just take me to Philly."

"No way," Tyler says. He raps on the wall. "Cy, stop the van. Unlock the door. We gotta get rid of the dog."

The van slows. The tires spit sand.

"What are you doing?" I ask.

Too late. The back door flies open. Sweetiepie jumps out, dashing down the beach.

"Sweetiepie! Here, girl!" I call, but she ignores me.

I try to jump after her, but Tyler pulls me back as the door slams shut.

"What are you doing?" I demand, trying to shove him off.

He lets go of me, which leaves me feeling surprisingly disappointed.

"If we steal that dog, it's felony theft," Tyler says. "Sweetiepie would send us to jail."

"We weren't going to get caught—"

"Maybe you wouldn't get caught. But Cy and me? We'd go away."

Tyler knocks on the wall of the truck. "Hey, Cy! Take us up to Harborview Drive."

"No!" I say.

"No?"

"I'm not going back there. My grandmother expects me to be a social success. Coming home early from a party is not okay."

"Okay," Tyler says softly. "You want to... get ice cream or something?"

It's annoying. How can someone be so good-looking, even in the dark?

"It's the least you could do," I say. "And maybe let me ride up front like a human? Where did you even get this kidnapping van?"

"It's more of a dognapping van," Tyler says. "Technically, it's for undead roadkill."

"What?"

"Sweet Harbor's a weird place. Welcome to Sweet Harbor. You'll get used to the weird."

"Well, I'm not sure I'm sticking around," I say, more sharply than I mean to.

"I've got James Dean over here," Tyler teases. "Rebel without a cause."

"Watch it. I'm a kidnapping victim, remember?"

The van hits a rut. I crash into Tyler's arms.

I can feel his heart, beating through his T-shirt. His cheek, rough with stubble, brushes my neck.

As he shifts, my lips barely graze his. A wild flare of electricity shoots through me.

"It's okay," he murmurs, pulling me close. That's when I realize I'm shaking. "We scared you, didn't we? I'm really sorry." He smooths my hair.

"It was terrifying," I say. But I don't feel any terror now. All I'm feeling is the floating sensation of being locked in his arms.

Falling for someone is a losing game. I've seen how that ends. I know better.

Still, just for now, I want to pretend anything is possible. I close my eyes against his chest.

Until I hear the police siren.

CHAPTER 16

CHLOE

I'm lying face-down on the cold steel hood of a police car, wrists cuffed behind me.

My heart surges with fear. The only good thing is that, in the flashing lights of half a dozen squad cars, I can finally feast my eyes on Tyler to my heart's content.

He's every bit as gorgeous as I'd sensed in the dark.

He's handcuffed and sitting on the ground. With my cheek pressed into the car's steel hood, I study his face.

His jaw is set and determined, the sharp line of it catching in the flashing lights. His profile doesn't betray fear or anxiety, not even when the cops find tell-tale, Sweetiepie-red dog hairs in the truck.

Tyler doesn't shudder. He doesn't blink.

He just sits on the ground, his blue eyes vivid and defiant.

Wow, do I love a good poker face. Really, it's a very practical skill to have. Plus, it's hot as hell.

He's smart, too. When the cops ask him questions, he says: "I have the right to remain silent."

"We'll go easy on you if you tell the truth. Besides, your buddy over there in my squad car just spilled the beans," a mustached cop says. He gestures toward one of the squad cars, where two officers are wedging Tyler's gigantic friend—the guy who must've been driving—into the back seat.

My dad always said cops make the best con artists. They know how to manipulate you into confessing, even to something you didn't do.

Their main trick? Tell you your friend already confessed.

But Tyler's not falling for it. He shrugs, which is actually not that easy to do in cuffs. His arms are astonishing. I try not to drool on the hood of the car.

When two of the cops turn to talk to each other, Tyler's eyes twinkle at me, like he finds the whole situation funny. "It's OK," he mouths, through full lips. "Don't worry."

And when he says it, I believe him.

Under his gaze, I can feel my heart melting, the way a prisoner's resolve softens under relentless interrogation.

"Uh-oh," Mustache Cop says to his partner. "I found this ID in the girl's purse. She's Chloe Riding."

The other officer whistles. Then he leans down to speak with me, so close I can smell the grape bubblegum on his breath.

"Excuse me. Are you any relation to Mrs. Riding? Lives up on Harborview Ridge?"

"I'm her granddaughter," I say. "I live with her."

"I apologize, miss," Bubblelicious Cop says. "I'm Officer Tran. Please allow me to take these cuffs off you."

Within a moment, he's freed me. I flex my wrists and look back at Tyler as Officer Tran ushers me to his vehicle.

Tyler gives me a nod. "See ya, Sweetie," he says, with a rough edge in his voice that makes me feel all confused and fluttery.

Officer Tran brushes stale French fries off the passenger seat and says, "Excuse me, it's a pigsty in here. Won't you please have a seat? I'll drive you home."

"Wait," I say. "What about Tyler and his friend?"

"Don't worry about them," Officer Tran says, starting the engine. "Do you need anything? Hot cocoa? Ice cream? Happy to cruise through a drive-thru. It's on me, of course. My treat. I certainly apologize for not recognizing you, Miss Riding. But I understand from the newspapers you've only just returned to town, correct? How was your time away?"

I peek in the side-view mirror for a last glance at Tyler. He looks strong and resolute in the flashing red and blue light of the other squad cars. But I imagine he's dreading what comes next.

As the squad car pulls onto the beach road, I can see that half the police force has turned out to look for Sweetiepie. All down the beach, flashlight beams sweep the beach as the officers follow the half-million-dollar dog's footprints along the shore. With every minute, the steady waves erase the dog's tracks.

I can't help it. I'm rooting for the big, red beast to roam free.

"Tyler did nothing wrong," I tell the officer.

"Oh, no, of course not," Officer Tran says. "Just youthful hijinks. Nothing for someone like you to worry about. We'll get you back to your grandmother, and everything will be all right. I promise."

"Then why won't you let him go?" I ask.

"Oh, we've got procedure to follow. Got to find out where he lives. Who he really is—do you even know that, miss?"

The question makes me feel clammy all over. For a split second, I wonder if Officer Tran is really a police officer—or if he's a gangster in disguise, tricking me into going with him.

But I stop wondering when he pulls the car into the drive-thru lane at Sweet Harbor Doughnuts. Even through the crackling order intercom, the cashier recognizes Officer Tran's voice.

"Two sprinkle donuts and a cup of decaf, officer?" the cashier says.

My stomach growls.

"Make that a dozen sprinkles," Officer Tran says, and he winks at me.

Officer Tran walks me to Granny's door. He knocks until she opens it, even though it's late.

She's wearing her gray silk dressing gown. Her gray silk sleep mask is pushed up on her forehead. The rest of her face is covered with pale, pigeon-colored face cream.

"I seem to remember a young lady insisting that she was nothing like her father," Granny Riding says stiffly. "A police escort home suggests otherwise."

"It's not my fault!" I say.

"She was a victim of mistaken identity here, ma'am," Officer Tran says.

The walkie-talkie at his hip crackles. I strain to listen, trying to catch a word about the guys.

What about Tyler and his friend? Are they okay? Are they on their way to jail?

Granny Riding scoffs. "I doubt my granddaughter has ever been the *victim* of anything. She's far more likely to have been the instigator. Well, come into the house, Chloe. Go upstairs. You've woken me up, and I'll deal with you in the morning."

"It's not like you think—"

"Upstairs, Chloe."

"Fine."

As I head upstairs, Granny calls me back. "Phone," she says, holding out her hand.

"It doesn't even work in here," I say. "I don't have cell data and you won't give me the Wi-Fi password."

"Phone," she repeats. I sigh and place my useless device in her hand.

Upstairs, in my all-gray bedroom, I open the window and peer outside, hoping to overhear Granny Riding's conversation on the steps with Officer Tran.

As I watch, Granny Riding reaches into the pocket of her gray silk robe and pulls out a huge wad of cash. My jaw drops. I make a mental note to check all of her pockets for spare cash the next time I'm sneaking around looking for that safe deposit box key.

Granny passes that fistful of cash into Officer Tran's hand. "For the Police Officer's Ball," she purrs. "A donation."

A sour, metallic taste fills my mouth as he accepts the obvious bribe.

My dad always said that the petty crimes he did—fraud, deception—were no big deal. They were nothing compared to the big-time corruption he'd grown up with in Sweet Harbor. Justice, he always said, was a joke—so do what you want. Have fun. Life is a game.

I rub my wrists, still sore from the bite of the cuffs. Tyler is probably still wearing cuffs, or else in lockup by now.

I wonder about him. Who will he call? What are his parents like? How old is he? He looks at least eighteen. But I hope, for his sake, he's still a minor. This could get serious.

I wish I had some cash. I could bail him out. Stealing the opposing team's mascot really shouldn't be a criminal offense.

But I know I can count on people like The Sophies to treat this light dognapping like the Boston Massacre—and the police will listen to people like The Sophies, and their parents.

I rummage in my Birkin bag. I feel like I'll find some money in some hidden compartment, if I just look hard enough.

But all I find is a handful of poker chips I stole from my dad. They aren't worth a dime outside of Atlantic City.

CHAPTER 17

TYLER

*L*ockup's not so bad when you have a girl to think about. When I close my eyes, I can almost smell her. Chloe. Honey and lemons. Sweet and sharp.

Is it her shampoo? Or her lotion? Something about the aroma feels so distinctively her, that I doubt it. I think that's just the way her skin smells. I remember the brush of her lips against mine — light as a spark, like a match striking in the dark.

When our lips touched in the van, it was like nothing else. I've dated my fair share of girls.

But with Chloe, even that brief, accidental touch felt different, electric, like something out of this world. The heat of it still lingers on my skin, even here in lockup, under cold steel and concrete.

While Chloe's memory etches itself onto my brain, Cy etches graffiti into the wall of our holding cell with a tiny nail he found on the floor.

The nail is obviously contraband. It was left here, like a gift, from some other poor soul who was stuck here. So now I hear Cy scratching, plus the sound of snoring.

The snoring would be Louie, the beach bum. He's in here, too, sleeping it off on his steel cot.

Everybody knows Louie.

Liquor Lou of the Dunes.

One time, the boys and I went crabbing and then had a cookout on the beach. He came and ate some of our food. Told us hilarious stories. He knows where all the good Dumpsters are in Sweet Harbor.

"I live like a king," he kept saying, "I live like a king and I don't spend a dime. Fishing in the trash is better than fishing in the sea, because when I get a salmon, I don't even have to cook it. Listen to me, boys, and you can live like kings, too."

He's a nice guy.

A nice guy with big problems.

On cold nights, he gets himself arrested on purpose. Jail is warm at least. Other times, he gets arrested for acting out.

This time, he got caught messing with some guys' motorcycles, dumping restaurant sugar packets into their gas tanks. That'll wreck an engine for sure—I know. I did a whole apprenticeship fixing motorcycles.

Why would Louie do something like that? He's not a mean-spirited guy. Maybe he was just drunk?

When Cy asked Louie why he did it, Louie told some drunken saga that made no sense. "Beware the Renegades," Louie slurred, then passed out.

Must be some biker gang. Zane's dad took off with some bikers years ago and we haven't heard from him since. For a while, he was with the Zombies, then the Cavalry.

Those groups are always fighting, breaking up, sometimes killing each other as they run drugs and guns up and down the coast. They're always re-forming new gangs with new, macho-sounding names. Like *Renegades*. Please.

Now Louie's fast asleep, sawing logs and enjoying some wine-soaked dreams. He mumbles in his sleep: "Pass the caviar. Yes, first-class to Paris, then on to the Riviera. Mmm, you smell delightful. Is that Chanel No. 5? Oh, a Lambo's fine. But I prefer a Maserati."

Dreaming about luxury, I guess. Good for him. I hope he stays asleep for a long time.

It's freezing in here, and there's not a single scrap of warmth or comfort anywhere. The floor is concrete. The cots are just stainless steel. There's not even a blanket. I'd rather be sleeping out in the shop, even with the roof leaking.

I wonder if the cops have called my mom by now. They're supposed to. I'm seventeen. I'm technically a juvenile. But cops around here don't always go by the book.

Speaking of books. I wish I had one right now. I'm used to escaping into them. Forgetting about the world around me, losing myself in the story. But I don't have a book. Instead, all I have are thoughts of this girl. Chloe Riding.

The way her hair felt, brushing my face. Her breath on my neck. Her body in my arms.

Her soft skin. Her sharp sense of humor. Plus—her courage and daring.

I've never met a girl so ready to leap out of a moving van and chase after a stolen dog to sell on the black market. Talk about hot.

It's pointless to think about her, though. We're from two different worlds. She's a Sweet Harbor girl and I'm from—well, pretty soon it's going to be the federal penitentiary.

How could tonight have gone so wrong?

Cy scratches into the walls with the nail. The noise is so annoying. I tuck my fists into my armpits, doing my best not to punch him. If it weren't for Cy, I wouldn't even *be* in this mess.

I'm seeing red, just blank primal fury, at everything and

everyone, when once again Chloe's face rises to my mind. Dammit.

My life just got a lot more complicated. And now I have a stupid crush.

Even worse, it's a ridiculous crush, a crush on the heiress to Riding Industries, a girl I could never have, a girl whose family owns the company that wrecked my town and ruined my family. The last girl in the world I could ever date.

But for now, just for now, I'll think about her.

Thinking of Chloe helps block out the cold. And the boredom. The rage. The fear. The snoring. The scratching.

"Hey Tyler," Cy says. "Did you make out with her, or what?"

"Huh?"

"That Sweetie. In the back of the van? You guys get it on?"

"Shut up."

"Here I was, the whole time, thinking we'd nabbed some little he-Sweetie. Like some wimpy water boy who was guarding the dog. Turns out we got ourselves a big ol' Sweetie princess. Did you see that cop turn green soon as he found out who she was? Odds are good he'll lose his job for slapping the cuffs on her," Cy says.

"Maybe," I say.

"I hate Sweeties," Cy grumbles, patting his stomach. "I'm starving, and it's all her fault. First, she attacks us, so we don't even have a chance to run in and grab a few lobster rolls. Then she calls the cops—"

"She didn't call the cops."

"How do you know? She probably has one of those phones connected to her watch—"

"She didn't, okay?" My hands are in fists again.

I force myself to take a breath. "There is no way she called the cops," I say, concentrating on keeping my voice steady, my temper under control. "It was dark in the van. I would've seen her phone, or her watch, light up. Besides. You heard the cops talking to each other while we were waiting to get our mug shots. We got caught because the van had a busted taillight."

Which is the dumbest way to get caught. I can't believe I didn't inspect that when I was fixing up the van. Probably I was too distracted, wondering if I'd see this girl who's now landed me in jail.

By now, Chloe's gone back to her grandmother's. But the dog we liberated is still running free. Unlike Cy and me. Sweetiepie's out there somewhere, chasing rabbits. The cops couldn't catch her.

But they did find telltale red dog hair in the van. Which is enough to pin theft of a half-million-dollar animal on me and Cy.

Now that I know how much the dog's worth, I can't even bear to think about what happens tomorrow.

Being charged with felony theft—that's going to kill my mom and my sisters. They need me. I can't go to prison.

"Chloe," Cy spits her name. "Chloe's a Sweetie name if I ever heard one. She's the one that ruined everything. But then, that's what Sweeties do, isn't it?"

"Wreck and destroy," I say. "Then act all innocent."

"They get away with murder," Cy says. But then, when he sees my face, he turns red and apologizes. "I'm sorry, man. I didn't mean to bring up what happened to your dad—"

"It's okay," I say. Even though it isn't. I don't like to talk about my dad. Or what happened to him. Or those responsible. "Let's not talk anymore. We just need to get through the night. Maybe the judge'll let us out in the morning."

"Yeah, and maybe it'll rain champagne," Cy says.

"Champagne isn't champagne unless it's from the Champagne region in France," Louie mumbles, turning over in his sleep. "If it's from anywhere else, it's just a sparkling white." I can't tell if he's talking to us, or still dreaming of luxury.

I close my eyes and think of Chloe. Dreaming isn't such a bad idea. There's nothing else to do—at least not until we see the judge in the morning, and learn our fate.

CHAPTER 18

CHLOE

"Chloe! Wake up." Granny Riding tears open my blinds. Hot sunlight slashes into the gray room.

I wake with a start, realizing I'm snuggled up with my pillow. Fragments of my dream drift by: me and Tyler curled up on a pink blanket.

Canoodling? Is that what we were doing? I muse, trying to hold on to the warm, dreamy feeling of his arms around me.

"You look like you've slept soundly," Granny snaps.

"I always do," I say.

"You'd think a guilty conscience would keep you awake. Apparently you lack even the decency to have remorse."

"I'm just a good sleeper—" I start, but Granny's fierce gaze silences me. She rips the covers off me and throws the blankets on the floor. "Get up."

Uh-oh. This seems serious. "Granny, I'm sorry, I can barely open my eyes. Maybe Helga could bring me a coffee—"

Granny takes the glass of water from my nightstand and

dumps it on my face. While I splutter and wipe my eyes, she says, "I've just heard from Judge Ramachandran. You're being charged with theft."

"What? That's not fair. I was kidnap—" I clap my hands over my mouth. I remember how Officer Tran kicked Tyler's knees out from under him, pinned him to the ground and cuffed him.

Me, on the other hand—he tried to buy me ice cream.

If I talk about the kidnapping in court, they'll believe me.

But will they send Tyler to jail?

Granny Riding gives me a sharp look. "If that's your story, you'd better tell that to your lawyer. He's on his way to meet us at the courthouse right now. So get dressed and we'll drive downtown for your arraignment."

Granny Riding storms out of the room, but I can hear her muttering to herself in the hallway. "It's that double-crossing District Attorney Vasquez behind this. It's got to be her. She's been dying to pay me back for cleaning her out at mah jong—and now she's messing with my granddaughter. We'll see about that."

"Mrs. Riding?" Helga calls up the stairs. "Would you like your blood pressure medication?"

"Buzz off," Granny snaps, and slams the door to her room.

If there's anything I know, it's that a good appearance in court can work wonders. Luckily, Granny bought me all these geeky back-to-school outfits.

A tweedy pencil skirt, a cardigan, and a sensible ponytail should do the trick. If only I had a pair of glasses.

I scrub every trace of makeup off my face. I secure my hair in a low, demure ponytail and top the clean girl look off with the faintest layer of Chapstick.

There. I'm the picture of innocence. But Helga still refuses me breakfast.

"Nothing for thieves," she says, unplugging the toaster as soon as I insert a piece of bread.

When I reach for the coffee, she intercepts me. Helga pours

the coffee down the drain. As aromatic steam rises from the sink, I feel like crying.

I miss my dad. Sometimes he had to go to court. When I was little, he'd had no choice but to take me with him, so he'd always make a treat of it. *When in doubt, make it fun*—that was his motto.

So on the way to court, we'd stop at Starbucks and he'd order me a 90/10 hot cocoa. (That means a cocoa that's ninety percent whipped cream, ten percent cocoa.)

Dad.

I wonder where he is now. I hope he's OK.

I scrub away a tear, and then swallow my feelings.

Sad feelings lead to bad outcomes in court. Dad taught me that much. So it's essential I get my mood up.

If I'm going to help my dad, I need to stay in Granny's good graces—and out of juvenile jail.

Granny drives us into town in her Land Rover. She's so tiny it looks like she can barely see over the steering wheel. When a rusty pickup cuts us off, Granny gives me a dirty look. "Friend of yours?"

"I don't know what you're talking about," I say.

"Keep it that way. I could turn you over to foster care, young lady. Cut you out of my will. I told you to make friends at the clambake. Not steal the damn dog with a pack of ruffians."

"I didn't—" I say, but I stop, because I don't know what will incriminate Tyler.

"Better to keep your mouth shut than lie to me," Granny says. "I know everything, Chloe. You remember that. I've got eyes in the back of my head."

At the courthouse, we wait for Granny's lawyer.

"Ah. There's Jules now," she says, as a blue Lamborghini slides into a parking spot out front. A tall, elderly Black man in a bespoke suit steps out. His shoes and briefcase shine. "He's a miracle worker," Granny Riding explains. "Not that you deserve it, Chloe."

Granny Riding gives Jules air-kisses when they meet. He tells her how much he likes her hairdo. She holds his wrist as she inspects his new watch, admiringly.

"Oh Jules," she coos. "A new watch. How lovely of your fraternity to honor you in that way. Is it a Patek Philippe?" Her laugh has a fluttery tone, and her eyes have changed from gunmetal gray to warmer, fuzzier, pussy-willow gray.

Watching her flirt, I can't believe she's the same person who ripped the covers off me so sternly this morning.

The two of them walk ahead of me, murmuring to each other. At one point, Granny tosses her head back and nods her chin at me. "That's Chloe. The *defendant*."

Jules stops and takes both of Granny Riding's hands in his. He gazes into her eyes and says, in a reassuring tone, "We'll simply request that Chloe's tried separately from those Shady Cove rascals. Then there should be no trouble at all. Judge Ramachandran bought a summer place just across the way from mine, and when her tennis court was being resurfaced, she played on mine. We're old pals. So no fretting about today. And, another time, let's talk, the two of us, about that other thing…"

Granny Riding giggles in that horrible, flirty way again, and I follow them both into the courtroom.

The thing about Tyler is he even looks good in prison orange.

It's not a shade that's flattering to human beings.

But Tyler can pull it off. He wears that ugly jumpsuit the way other guys would wear a football uniform. Proud. His jawline could cut glass, and there's something magnetic about the tilt of his smile.

In the bright sunlight, he looks even better than he did in the middle of the night. The stubble on his chin has grown out to glorious five o'clock levels. His sandy hair looks adorably tousled after a night in jail and his sleepy blue eyes match the harbor just outside the window.

There's a restless energy to him, the kind that draws your eyes without you even realizing it.

His lawyer, however, looks like a hack.

The guy has toilet paper stuck to his shoe and coffee spilled down his shirt.

Meanwhile, Tyler's friend—the hefty, baby-faced guy who drove the van—keeps sweating, literally. In fact, he's perspiring so much he looks like he's melting. His prison jumpsuit is slowly turning a darker shade of damp orange.

When the driver lets out a shuddery sigh, Tyler gives his buddy a friendly nudge with his elbow.

It seems to calm him, but it also makes me realize something.

Tyler and his friend aren't just wearing orange. They're actually *shackled*, at the wrists and ankles, like they're violent criminals.

Why? They're just kids pranking kids at another high school —in one of the safest towns in America.

It hits me that this could be a deciding moment for their future. And who's here to help them?

I study their lawyer, looking for signs of hidden brilliance. The lawyer opens his briefcase. It's empty, except for one sad-looking breakfast burrito.

Uh-oh.

Jules nudges. " Don't say anything until I tell you to." His breath smells like orange Tic Tacs and confidence.

Still, my nerves tense as the pant-suited prosecutor—Ms. Vasquez, the woman who lost at poker to Granny Riding—lays out the charges.

Just as Tyler predicted, the fact that an expensive dog was stolen made them level up the charge to a felony.

It's so unfair. Tyler didn't even know the dog was worth money. I'm the one who wanted to take advantage of that.

I shiver. Just that word, *felony*, scares me. Not even my dad has been charged with a felony, though he's definitely committed a few.

I dare myself to look over at Tyler as the charges are read. His deep blue eyes meet mine. He holds my gaze for a minute, then he looks away, out the window, toward the boats scudding along in the breezy harbor.

Have I ruined his life?

Am I ruining it, right now, with my fancy lawyer?

Is his punishment going to be worse because I'm about to be set free?

My dad always told me never to stick my neck out for anyone. Always look out for number one. And I know that's exactly what I should do in this situation. I should do everything I can to make Granny forgive me, keep me in the will, let me stay living at her house.

But when Jules stands up and asks the judge to try me separately from my "co-defendants," something inside me snaps awake, sharp and stubborn.

I stand up. "Objection!"

Behind me, Granny Riding sucks in her breath. "Chloe," she hisses, warningly, but I keep talking, even though I can feel my armpits starting to sweat.

Jules furrows his brow, and says, "Chloe, I advise you to sit down."

"No. I'm a human being. No different from these guys. I want the same treatment as those two."

The judge purses her lips. She looks around the courtroom. I don't dare look at Tyler and his friend.

They might think I'm giving them charity. But I'm just trying to do the right thing. Without even knowing exactly what that is. All I know for sure is that the pressed cotton fabric under my arms is getting damp, and I feel shaky.

"In my chambers," the judge growls, and the lawyers—Jules, the guy's lawyer with the burrito, and the DA who plays mah jong with my granny—all disappear through a small door next to the judge's bench.

I dare myself look at Granny. "I'm sorry."

Her mouth is a narrow gray line. She shakes her head at me.

"I know you think I'm just like my dad," I say.

"No," she says, fishing a tissue from her purse. "Right now you remind me much more of my other son. Your uncle. And frankly, that's worse." Her breath hitches, and she dabs at her eyes with her Kleenex.

I was expecting anger, and I got tears. My throat feels narrow. Every time I take a breath, it's like trying to swallow a stone.

The story is, my uncle disappeared without a trace when my dad was my age. For a while they thought he ran off and joined the Army. But the military never found records of him. And that's who I remind Granny of?

Granny Riding blows her nose and wipes a tear.

I may not know what grade I'm supposed to be in at school, or what subjects I'm skilled in.

But I guess I'm pretty good at causing drama.

CHAPTER 19

CHLOE

*T*he judge returns.

The guys' lawyer whispers to them. I watch them out of the corner of my eye until Granny snaps her fingers in my face. Jules, my lawyer, wants my attention.

"The D.A. is dropping all charges, except for a misdemeanor—disorderly conduct. The judge has agreed that if you three plead guilty, she'll let you all off with community service. She understands it was just a prank," Jules whispers to me.

I let out a shaky sigh. I glance over at Tyler. He's not looking at me, but his shoulders drop slightly, like a weight has slipped off them.

"Loyalty is commendable," Jules says quietly. "But be careful who you show loyalty to in Sweet Harbor. Be strategic."

Granny doesn't speak on the ride home. Not even when I make a joke about how much she resembles the Queen of England when she's driving her Land Rover. (Tiny woman, huge vehicle, prim driving gloves — it's uncanny.)

Granny scoffs. "Liz Windsor? Heaven forfend. Her Highness, may she rest in peace, never met a designer she couldn't offend." She cuts me a sharp look. "You are not to talk to any of those boys again."

"I'll try not to," I say.

"Try? No. Just don't."

"But we have community service together," I say. "We're on beach clean-up duty."

Granny's hands tighten on the wheel. "Figure it out. You're a Riding. Act like one."

COMMUNITY SERVICE STARTS at six a.m. Saturday. It's headache-early, eye-burning early when Helga drops me off.

"You may under no conditions speak to those unruly males."

"Got it," I say. "Only speak to ruly males."

"Chloe—"

"I won't talk to them. I swear."

I walk down the beach, delighting in the roar of the waves. The sun warms my skin, the breeze tugs at my black-and-white striped romper (Granny calls it my Jailbird Suit), and the salt air stings my nose.

It feels like maybe everything's going to be okay.

Until—oh no. There he is.

And he's not wearing a shirt.

Sunlight gleams on Tyler's bare chest; water drips from the frayed hems of his cutoffs. Saltwater runs down his tanned legs as he tosses a football down the beach. In the distance, Cy leaps to catch it.

His whole body seems to sing when he smiles. And when he jumps, his pants slip just enough to flash the waistband of his boxers.

A whistle blows. A redheaded woman in a neon vest stabs a beach umbrella into the sand.

"Hey! Convicts!" she shouts. "I'm your supervisor, Marcy. Come sign in."

Marcy hands me a trash picker, a vest, and a blue plastic bag. "Head north," she says. "And don't forget the dog poop."

I'M STABBING at a styrofoam box stuck in some seaweed when Tyler taps me on the shoulder.

I jump, dropping my trash picker.

"Hey," he says, voice soft, almost blending with the waves. For half a second, I imagine I can feel his breath on my skin.

"Hi."

He pulls a tube of sunblock from his pocket, handing it to me. "Marcy said to give you this."

"Thanks."

"She needs it back," he adds, burying his hands in his pockets. The move makes his shoulders shift, muscles flexing under the vest. I glance away, pulse thumping.

I squirt sunblock into my palm and begin to apply it. "I bet I'm getting white streaks all over my face," I joke, hoping for a compliment.

"Yeah," he says, noncommittal.

My stomach dips. Not exactly the swoony moment I was hoping for.

Tyler's friend Cy jogs over, glowering. "Ty, what are you doing talking to the Sweetie?"

Tyler raises a hand. "Cy."

"We don't need your charity," Cy mutters at me.

"I never said you did," I snap.

"Dude, that's my sunblock," Cy huffs. "What are you doing giving her my sunblock? It says right on the label, *Not for Use on Sweeties.*"

"Shut up, Cy," Tyler says, firm this time.

As Cy trudges away, my heart does backflips. Because clearly, Tyler borrowed the sunblock just to have an excuse to talk to me!

"Don't worry about him," Tyler murmurs.

"I'm not," I say. "I'm worried about ultraviolet radiation."

He grins. "Good thing that's SPF 50."

"I would expect no less."

He mock-bows. "I do my best."

My body vibrates like it's tuned to a frequency only Tyler can touch.

Without thinking, I blurt, "Can you get my back?" The words land between us like a dare. It's a cliche dare. But still. My pulse skitters.

His fingers glide across my shoulder, and for a second I forget the sun, the sand, the whole world. My skin burns where he touches it, in the best possible way.

"Oops," Tyler says, tugging at my reflective vest. "Might've gotten some sunblock on your, uh, beautiful uniform."

Laughter bubbles in my chest. I can't remember the last time I laughed like this—giddy and helpless.

A wave rolls up the shore, pushing a glass bottle toward us.

"I call bottle!" Tyler shouts, trash picker raised like a spear.

As the retreating wave drags the bottle back out, he lunges into the surf, vest flapping, feet kicking up white spray. When he emerges, soaked and triumphant, bottle held high, my heart gives one stupid, romantic little lurch.

Is that a love letter in a bottle? Please, universe, don't play with me like this.

CHAPTER 20

TYLER

I wave to Chloe, standing on the beach, and hold up the glass bottle in triumph. Another wave comes, lifting me off my feet, and I let it push me toward shore.

Chloe runs to the water's edge. She plucks the bottle from my hand. "I'll take that," she says, moving to tuck it into the trash bag dangling from the waist of her safety vest.

"Wait," I say. When I reach for the bottle, I accidentally close my hand on top of hers. "I think there's a message in this bottle."

She laughs but loosens her grip. A wave climbs up on shore, the water hissing and swirling around our ankles, then retreats. I take the bottle from Chloe.

I wasn't lying. There's a little slip of paper tucked inside. Probably somebody just got bored, peeled the label off their beer, tucked it inside, then fastened on the bottle cap.

It's nothing to get excited about. Not really. But when Chloe's dark eyes meet mine, something flickers through me, and I lead her around Maiden Rock — this enormous pile of boulders that looks like a reclining woman — and we sit down in the sand to fish the paper out of the bottle.

I shake the bottle like a ketchup bottle, but the slightly damp paper inside doesn't budge.

"Maybe it's a treasure map," she says.

"What do *you* need with treasure?"

"I told you," she says. "I'm broke. I need money for my dad."

It's hard to believe someone who lives on Harborview Drive needs anything. But I nod. "Treasure's cool with me."

"Do you know anything about—" She stops, biting her lower lip in this adorable way.

"What?" I ask.

"Sweet Harbor Bank?"

"What, you want to rob it?"

"NO!" she squeals, punching me playfully. The feel of her knuckles against my arm sends a jolt through me.

I tell myself to settle down. The last thing I need is a girl-friend, let alone a Sweetie. I've got too much going on for that level of chaos.

"I just mean, have you ever been there?"

"Yeah. It closed a while ago, though."

"It closed?" Chloe looks out at the water, her lips a straight, tense line.

"You okay?"

She stares at the ocean for a long minute. "Can you keep a secret?"

"Sure."

"My dad had a safe deposit box there. He left something in it for me. But if the bank's closed…"

"Oh," I say, glad I can actually help her with something. "They merged with First American Bank. I've been there a million times. My aunt works there. She used to always give me extra free candy. My guess is the safe deposit boxes transferred over to First American."

"Really? Your aunt works there?" When Chloe's eyes light up, they dazzle me like Christmas lights used to when I was a kid.

"Can I tell YOU a secret?" I ask.

"Sure." Chloe She leans close. The wind blows a strand of her silky hair against my cheek.

"Sometimes I still go to the bank, just to get candy," I whisper.

She leans even closer. "What. Kind. Of. Candy," she whispers back. The mock-serious tone she uses nearly kills me.

I lean closer. Our lips are almost touching. But not quite. "Reese's. Peanut. Butter. Cups."

Our lips are so close, a breeze couldn't slip between them. Chloe shuts her eyes and I stare for a second at her lashes, hypnotized.

"Tyler," she breathes. "Do you have your truck here? Could you take me to the bank?"

And just like that, something slams shut in my chest.

Was that what all the laughing and arm-punching was about? Needing a ride? Asking me to ditch court-ordered community service—and risk *jail*—to drive her around?

But then she looks up at me, and there's shadow in her eyes. A darkness that reminds me of how frightened she seemed when I found her on the road, skittish and cornered.

She's afraid of something. What, I'm not sure. Maybe her dad. Maybe something else.

And that's the thing—there's no way to know if she's playing me. No way to know if the desperation in her eyes is real or if she's working me.

I think about how she acted that day in court. Insisting that we all be treated the same. She stuck her neck out for me when she didn't have to.

So I want to believe her, even though they say that if a Sweetie is moving their mouth, they're lying.

But I want to trust her. And that's dangerous as hell.

"Yeah," I hear myself say, like the complete idiot I am—the

complete idiot who accidentally kidnapped an heiress and a half-million dog—"Of course I can give you a ride."

We hike up the rocky side of the beach and double-back to the north parking lot. Apparently Chloe's maid is spying on her. But if we take the long route, she won't see us.

As we walk, Chloe holds the glass bottle up to the light. The sun shines through it, casting a white blob on the sand. "If we find tweezers, I bet I could get the message out," she says.

"Or we could just smash the bottle," I say.

"No!" she says, hugging the bottle to her chest like it's a teddy bear. "This is our treasure from the sea. We can never destroy it."

When Chloe climbs into the truck, I remember hauling her into this truck on that foggy night when I picked her up on the side of the road. It feels like forever ago—and like a second ago, all at once.

Chloe bounces a little on the seat. The holes in it have been duct-taped together, and it has a broken spring. But she smiles and looks comfier than you'd expect the Riding Heiress to be in a rusted-out Toyota pickup.

She hesitates, turning the bottle over in her hands, so light flashes on her long, bare legs. I pull my eyes to the road.

She lets out a shaky sigh. "I don't know why I feel like I can trust you, but I do," she says.

And my heart sinks. When people tell you right away they trust you, it's a sure sign you shouldn't trust them. My mom told me that, and she's been right every time.

Once upon a time, she trusted the Riding Industries lawyer—with his shiny shoes, his flashy watch. He laid out a pile of manila folders all around him. Clicked his Montblanc pen. It seemed like he knew what he was doing. But trusting him was a big mistake.

"*Can* I trust you?" she asks, turning her eyes on me.

I keep my eyes on the road. "To a degree," I say, finally.

She laughs. "That's an honest answer. OK. I can trust you. My dad is a complicated person. He's basically on the run these days, from some people he owes money to. Bad people. Seriously bad people."

Something about the way her voice quivers makes me want to punch a wall or wrap her up in a blanket—maybe both at once.

"If I can get some money together, I can help him. Keep him alive, at least. That's why I need to get into that safe deposit box."

I'm not sure what to say. All I can come up with is, "That's intense."

She laughs again. "Yeah. That's my life."

"Can't your grandma help him out?"

"She could. If she wanted to. But she doesn't. She's sick of his crap. But I don't think she realizes how serious it is. Or else she really has quit caring."

We fall silent as I turn onto the highway into town. At last, I say, "People's families can get messed up."

"Yeah," she says. "Would you believe my dad ditched me in a hotel? He left with nothing. Just a note about a safe deposit box five hundred miles away."

Once again, I'm not sure what to say. Finally, I joke, "Did the hotel at least have a pool?"

Luckily, she laughs.

We drive slowly through the picture-perfect little town that is Sweet Harbor. A town where there's a flower in every window box, and a sweater on every dog.

"Here we are," I say, parking in front of First American Bank. "Ready for your Reese's Peanut Butter Cup?"

"Yeah," she says, "and I'm ready to get my money."

Something about the way she says it makes me uneasy, in a way I can't explain. But we're here—no use turning back now.

CHAPTER 21

CHLOE

"Can you reach in the glove box?" Tyler says. "I've got a T-shirt in there." It's a crime against humanity to hand this boy a shirt, but I pass him a soft white cotton tee anyway.

"I think there's a pair of flip-flops under the seat, too."

While my heart is still racing from the fact that Tyler drives barefoot, he rummages under the seat and pulls out book after book after book.

At last, between Dostoyevsky paperbacks, he finds his flip-flops.

Hot and hyper-literate?

It's too much.

WE STAND in line in the bank, and I do my best to focus on the task at hand. *Keep your eyes on the prize and your hands off Tyler.*

When we reach the front, the teller eyes us up and down. I'm sure we're a strange sight—me in a silk romper and Gucci shoes,

Tyler in cutoffs and a threadbare V-neck—but I marshal my best adult voice and say, "I'm here about safe deposit box number 311."

Tyler reaches into a large fishbowl filled with complimentary candy. He pulls out a mini peanut butter cup. He puts one perfect finger on it and slides it down the counter to me.

I pick at the foil wrapper while the teller, a slight, gray man, examines the key. He turns it over in his hand. I swallow.

Behind us in line, I hear little kids. "Mom! Peanut butter cups! I want peanut butter cups!"

"Candy! Candy! Give me candy!" they squeal.

At the same moment, Tyler and I turn to look at the kids. We are so on the same wavelength.

The poor mom has an entire flock of kids—six of them at least—and two of them are climbing up on her like they're pigeons and she's a statue. "Just be quiet, wait in line," the mom says, floundering in her purse. "Mommy has to deposit her paycheck."

"But I need a snack!" one kid wails.

"Look at me, look at me!" another kid says, prancing around.

Tyler rubs his mouth with his hand, like he's trying not to laugh. When our gazes meet, his blue eyes sparkle into mine. For a second, it's just us in this whole bright, noisy world. I'm hypnotized. The teller has to clear his throat twice before I turn to face him.

The teller gives a sour smile. "Do you have a key?"

"Well," I say, giving him my glitteriest gaze, "the box was originally at Sweet Harbor Bank, but I understand there was a merger and—"

"All box holders were issued new keys."

"But I wasn't," I say.

"You were," he says.

"I wasn't."

The teller looks past me. He waves at the guy in line behind us. "Next?"

"Wait just a minute," Tyler says, planting his palms on the counter. "Is Susan working today? She's my aunt."

"It's her day off. Next?"

"Is there a manager we can speak to—" Tyler starts to say, but I shush him, because just then, Judge Ramachandran walks in.

She's wearing her tennis whites, not her judge's robe, and she bobs around like a plump ghost, grabbing a deposit slip and greeting people in line.

I squeeze Tyler's arm, pulling him down close to me. He's tall enough I have to get up on tiptoes to whisper in his ear.

"We've got to get out of here," I hiss. "That's the judge over there! The one who gave us community service. You know— where we're supposed to be *right now.*"

Tyler's sapphire eyes lock on to mine. For a beat, I see something flicker there—like he knows we're about to cross a line together. But then his grin slides into place.

As if in slow motion, I see him reach for the fishbowl filled with candy. He mouths the word "Go!" silently.

I don't know why I trust him, but I do.

I turn to run out the door. Tyler heaves the fishbowl off the counter.

"CANDY!" he yells, swinging the fishbowl through the air.

Dozens of gold-wrapped peanut butter cups fly into the air.

The second they hit the floor, those six kids go wild. They shriek and scramble after the scattered candy.

The kids crawl on all fours, pawing at people's ankles, squealing, "Mine! Mine!" Like it's like an Easter egg hunt.

As I push my way out the door, I glance back and see Judge Ramachandran, hands in the air, braced for chaos. A little girl, chasing a rolling peanut butter cup, has crawled right between the judge's legs.

"Oh, my!" Judge Ramachandran gasps, as the little girl grabs the hem of the judge's tennis skirt, using it to haul herself back up. "Eeek!" the judge squeaks, as her skirt slides down. I see a flash of hot-pink judicial underwear before the judge manages to tug her skirt back up.

In the commotion, Tyler rushes unseen past the judge. He runs out the side door. I take off running and meet Tyler at his truck.

I wrench open the passenger door, hop onto the seat—avoiding the broken spring—and collapse into laughter.

Tyler jumps in and starts the engine. We take off with a roar and we're two blocks away before I realize he's laughing, too. He runs his hand through his sandy hair, making it stand on end, and sighs with relief. It's adorable.

"I can't believe we made it," I sigh, between fits of laughter.

Tyler just shakes his head, but a broad grin stretches across his face.

He turns onto the highway and speeds up. I gaze out the window, feeling the warm sun, the rushing wind.

Suddenly, something hits me. Tyler is showering me with fist-fuls of Reese's peanut butter cups. He's cracking up, too. He has an amazing laugh.

"I didn't see you steal these," I say, grabbing a peanut butter cup and throwing it back at him.

"Well, maybe you're not as observant as you think you are," he says.

"Shut up." I unwrap a Reese's peanut butter cup and stuff it in his mouth. "There. That'll keep you quiet."

I like his football-on-the-beach smile.

I like his narrow-escape smile.

I even like his "my mouth is full and I'm trying not to laugh" smile.

Oh, no. This is bad. Not just crush-level bad. This is spiraling-out-of-control, can't-afford-to-feel-this bad.

I can't fall for him—not now. Not with everything else going on in my life. I've got a dad to find. And if I can't find him—if he's not okay—then I've got an inheritance to tend. I can't upset granny too much, without risking the only stability I've ever had.

Tyler parks on the far end of the beach, past the boulders. The tide has receded, leaving a stretch of wet, slippery rocks between us and the sand.

Tyler proceeds expertly, his bare feet gripping familiar stones. But I slip and slide in my Gucci sandals.

Tyler stops. He offers me his hand without really looking at me, but his fingers twitch just slightly.

My heart stops. I take his hand. We walk toward the beach.

I wish I could enjoy holding hands with him more. But I'm focused on not falling on my face. When we finally reach smoother terrain, he drops my hand instantly.

Which is fine. Totally fine. It's safer this way. For both of us.

The only reason I should talk to him is to see if his aunt will help me with the safe deposit box. That's it.

As if reading my mind, Tyler says, "I can introduce you to my aunt sometime."

"Thanks," I say. "I'd like that."

He shoves his hands in his pockets and stares out at the rolling surf. "We should get back. Marcy might be looking for us."

"Right," I say.

We grab the trash pickers we stashed by the boulders and head toward Marcy's umbrella.

Tyler walks a couple of feet ahead of me all the way back down the beach. His shoulders are tighter now, not loose and laughing like before, and I wonder if he's feeling the same knot in his chest that I am.

He stays so far out front that sometimes the waves wash away his footprints before my feet can reach them.

Which is fine. Better, even. It's best if it doesn't look like we're walking together, in case Helga is watching.

So it's all good.

At least, that's what I tell myself. But the truth is, I can't afford to fall for Tyler. Not when Dad's life is on the line. Not when Granny's watching. Not when this whole house of cards could crash down around me

Can I? As I contemplate it, Marcy flags me down. "Your grandmother's maid called for you. She said she can't pick you up today. She suggested I drive you."

"She did?"

Marcy rolls her eyes. "She assumed I had nothing better to do. Which is false. Can one of you boys take her home?"

CHAPTER 22

TYLER

I ditch Cy without thinking twice and jump to offer Chloe a ride home. Fifteen minutes ago I promised myself *not* to get involved with her. To stop holding her hand for God's sake.

But here I am, on Harborview Drive again. I can't tell if it's a comfortable silence in the truck, or an uncomfortable one.

I guess if you have to ask, it's uncomfortable.

"What—what happened to your ride?"

"Helga had to get a wart burned off on her foot." Chloe's voice is neutral, but the corner of her lip twitches with a smirk.

"Helga?"

"The maid."

Right. Helga was probably the woman who told me Chloe was in Switzerland. Now it's my turn to smile, thinking of her warty foot. That's karma.

"Helga," I say. "That's a perfect name for her."

"What?"

I feel the heat of embarrassment, creeping up my chest. The last thing I want to do is let Chloe know I stopped by her place.

""That's a perfect name for a maid, I mean." We fall into silence. "Do you ever think you'd be different if you weren't named Chloe?"

"No," Chloe says. "My parents called me Beatrix for two entire years when we were running this scam in London. It made no difference."

"You lived in London?" I say. "I feel like I can hear it in your accent."

"Really?"

"Yeah. Just the way you say certain words. It pops out now and then. Like you don't say either. You say eye-ther. Not either."

"Listening closely, huh?" she teases.

"I'm known for being observant."

"Anyway," Chloe says, "Helga's out getting her wart burned off. And Granny's at the club, playing mah jong. So you can come in and hang out at the house. It will be just us."

Just us. Alone together. Alone in a house with a bedroom. Alone in a Sweetie mansion on Harborview Drive.

I shake my head. Never thought this would happen. Or that it would feel so easy, so natural.

I turn down the long, curving driveway. We pull up to the immense house. "Which window is yours?" I ask. There are at least a dozen in the front.

"That one," Chloe says. "The corner."

I note the climbable trellis leading up to her bedroom window.

"Maybe park around back, just in case," Chloe says, guiding me to a parking pad behind the five-car garage. We cut across a large stone patio overlooking the vast, gleaming bay.

A fresh, salt breeze blows over us, making wisps of Chloe's silky dark hair dance around her head. She reaches up to smooth it, tucks it tightly behind her ear.

We enter through the patio doors, and Chloe leads me into the largest kitchen I've ever seen, bigger even than the restaurant kitchen at Shady Pizza.

"Did we just step into a black-and-white movie?" I joke, because everything in here is shades of gray.

"I know, blah, right?" Chloe says.

"Right," I say. But *blah* is not what I'm thinking.

I've never been inside one of these old-school Harborview Drive mansions before. It's so quiet. Outside, I could hear the water, the wind in the trees. In here, it's like wearing noise-canceling headphones. I guess they can afford some pretty good insulation.

"Want a tour?" Chloe asks.

"Sure," I say.

"Maybe while I show you around, we should look for that key. The safe deposit box key my dad hid has got to be here somewhere."

"Okay," I say. "You want me to just rummage around in here? Basically, case the joint for a future robbery?"

Chloe laughs. "Why not? Granny's insured."

"Naw," I say, "I wouldn't." Somehow I feel protective of the old lady. Even though she was giving my eyes like a staple gun in court, she's important Chloe.

Still, I don't mind pulling open the drawers in the butler's pantry. Chloe stands on a stepladder above me, rummaging in the china cupboards, looking for the key.

As we search, I try to be respectful, but can't help glancing up, looking at where Chloe's silky legs vanish into her shorts. I reach out, touch her smooth skin, slide my hand up her calf, over her knee.

She glances down at me. "Thought you could use a spotter," I say, as I wrap my arms around her bare legs.

"Thanks," she says. She dusts off her hands. "I think there's no key in here."

In the large, cathedral-like front room, I flip over a gray, zebra-striped painting to see if a key is taped to the back of the frame. As I do, my heart skips a beat. The painting is a signed original. "Chloe? This is a real Alberto Faviolo," I say. "It's probably worth way more than Sweetiepie."

"Good to know," Chloe says. "How do you know so much about art?"

"Eh. I read a lot. I like to know a bit about everything. Jack of all trades. Master of none."

We head upstairs. "This is my grandmother's bedroom," Chloe says. "We better search it now, while she's gone."

The huge gray room smells like strong floral perfume. And it feels weird to be in here. Chloe points out the deep jacuzzi tub.

"Care for a soak?" she teases, and I look away, because I want to say yes, *hell yes, I'd get in a bath with you*—but the last thing I need is to get busted in a jacuzzi by an octogenarian.

I busy myself with the photos in silver frames on the bedside table. Two young men stare out of the black-and-white portraits. One looks like Chloe; the other seems familiar, too—maybe just because they're related.

"I give up," Chloe says. "There's no key in here. You want to see my room?"

I swallow and say "Yes" at the same time, so the word comes out sounding strangled. But I really, really mean it.

Chloe takes my hand and leads me to her room. She glances back at me, laughing, her silky hair cascading down her shoulders, her eyes teasing. It's impossible, how perfect she is. It's impossible how much I want this.

We perch on the edge of her gray bed. The gray covers are all pulled super tight, folded with hospital corners.

"Did, ah, Helga make this bed?" I guess.

Chloe laughs. "It looks uptight, doesn't it?"

"Yeah. Maybe we should mess it up a little."

Her eyebrows shoot up.

"Oh, I didn't mean—I just meant—" I grab a fluffy gray pillow and whack her playfully with it.

She jumps up on the bed and says, "Look out, I have a down body pillow."

"Uh-oh, the big guns," I say, as Chloe chooses a huge, silk-covered pillow that's almost as tall as I am.

She slides it over me, pinning it in place with her body. It's almost like we're hugging, but the pillow is between us.

Something beeps. Chloe jumps back, and the pillow falls to the ground. "The security system!" she says. "Someone's here!"

She cracks the door to listen. Footsteps scuttle crablike across the marble floors downstairs. "It's Granny," she says. "Quick, I'll distract her and keep her in the living room. You—"

"I'll climb out the window."

"It's a long way down—"

"I'll be fine," I whisper, even though I'm not sure I will be.

Suddenly Chloe throws her arms around me and hugs me for real, pressing her warm body the length of mine.

We could be interrupted any moment, but I don't care. I pull her close, then lean back to cup her beautiful face in my hands.

Her eyes flash with something raw, something unguarded, something that tells me: she's just as scared as I am. I lose myself in the amber-dark depths of her eyes and then kiss her, a long kiss that deepens until time stops.

Her lips taste like they imagined I would—like honey and lemon. Her body softens in my hands, and I can't get enough of her. I push her up against the wall, pressing against her, getting as close as I can, wanting more and—

"CHLOE!" the grandmother's voice shrills.

And all of a sudden Chloe's gone, vanished, running down the stairs. I make for the window, planning to climb down that trellis I sighted on my way in.

When I open the screen, I notice there's something loose about the window frame. As footsteps plod up the stairs, I test the frame with my fingers—and a silver key pops out. I pocket it and scramble out the window, onto the trellis. It sways under my weight, but I hurry down it.

When I reach the ground, I look back up at the soaring mansion. My stomach flips over to see the height I scaled. Not bad, I guess.

The only thing is, I left dark muddy boot prints all down the white trellis.

Hope no one notices.

CHAPTER 23

CHLOE

*O*n Monday, Principal Annan gives me my course schedule. To my surprise, I did okay on the the placement tests. I'm a junior in every class except math, which is better than I expected.

But going to school is even weirder, and harder, than I thought it would be.

First, there are The Sophies and Kyra, who seem to have decided that I wanted to kidnap Sweetiepie. So everybody stares at me and mumbles things like "Dog-napper" and "Sweetie-snatcher."

Being shunned feels terrible. I try to remind myself I'm a citizen of the world, not some would-be high school queen bee.

But the sting is real, sharper than I expected. Especially when I was, technically, kidnapped, too! But I can't say that without risking getting Tyler in trouble.

Then there are the classes. Which are a) hard to find and b) boring.

Plus, all I can think about is Tyler.

That kiss. It left me dizzy. Even remembering it now makes my skin flush scalding hot, makes my cheeks and throat and chest tingle. I keep imagining the feel of his fingers, brushing along my neck, my collarbone, when he pushed me back against the door to my closet, kissing me.

I've never been kissed like that before.

How am I supposed to concentrate on school?

It's a relief when the bell rings for lunch.

I've been to Japan. I've eaten sushi there. But the sushi lunch here at the Sweet Harbor High cafeteria rivals that.

I sit at a carved oak table in the open-air lunchroom, enjoying my meal and staring out at the sea. The glass garage-door walls are rolled up, admitting fresh, salty air. Sunlight streams in through the skylights. I could get used to the peace, the luxury and the—

Uh oh. Here come The Sophies.

Three of them circle me like a pack of rabid dogs. Correct that. Rabid hyenas. (They're all wearing coordinated leopard-print dresses.) There at three of them today. Kyra is nowhere to be seen.

"Where's your leader? Did she leave school early for some modeling audition her parents bought her?" I guess.

The Sophies gasp. I grin. Looks like I guessed right. My dad always taught me the importance of reading people.

Sophie C. asks, "How did you know?"

"Turn the camera off, Sophie," Sophie E. snaps. "Don't record this."

Sophie V. obeys.

I turn to Sophie E. "So. I'm curious. If Kyra winds up leaving to become a model, will you finally be the one in charge?" I smile sweetly.

The three girls' six chemically-plumped lips open and close. They look like matching fish in the principal's aquarium. No one ever talks to them like this. They can dish it out, but they can't take it.

"Whatever, dognapper!" Sophie C. says, finally.

Then she goes full toddler. She grabs some food from her plate and shoves it in my face.

Which would be funny.

Except, have you ever had a huge wad of super-spicy wasabi go up your nose?

It's like setting your head on fire. My vision tunnels, my ears ring, and the next thing I know, I'm blinking up at someone pouring milk down my face.

"Hold still. Tilt your chin up. Let me irrigate your sinuses."

I blink and look up. The guy who's speaking is about my age and 100 percent gorgeous. Wild curly black hair. Coppery skin. Chiseled jaw. Emerald eyes.

As he leans over me, his T-shirt slides on his broad chest, and I can see a pair of collarbones like you wouldn't believe.

Good googly moogly, I think, as he shoves the spout of a cardboard milk container in one of my nostrils and begins to pour.

One of the guy's friends, a redheaded girl who looks like Ariel the Mermaid, takes me to the bathroom to clean up. She even has a spare T-shirt in her purse.

"My purse is like a bag from one of the Magic Academy movies," she says, "you know, with a whole shopping mall inside of it? I always like to be prepared." She introduces herself as Jessa and invites me to sit with her.

"Don't mind The Sophies. They're not all bad. Just territorial," she says. "They'll get used to you, eventually."

She pulls out lip gloss and applies it in the mirror. "I think you know my friend Addie," she says, lips pursed. "She eats second lunch, or I'm sure she'd be joining us in here."

"I met her at the Dock and Drink," I say. Then I ask, "Why are you being so nice to me? I thought everyone was mad because of what happened to Sweetiepie."

"What *did* happen to Sweetiepie? You didn't murder her, did you?"

"Of course not," I say. "I think she's still roaming free."

"I wish I were roaming free," she sighs. "This place is a prison."

"Hand towel?" From out of nowhere, a restroom attendant in a pink uniform materializes. "Moisturizer, ma'am? Mint? Spritz of Annick Goutal or Chanel No. 5?"

I haven't been to school in a long time, but I don't remember schools having bathroom attendants. I glance at the attendant's silver tray, mostly out of habit—looking for something that would be easy to swipe.

Next to cut-glass bottles of expensive perfume and jars of diamond-laced hand cream, I see a series of syringes, each with a long, sharp needle at the end.

Catching me looking, the attendant says, "Squirt of collagen? Your upper lip is looking a wee bit thin."

"Is that even safe?" I ask.

"Trust me. I'm a nurse."

"Nurse Mimi is the best," Jessa says. "I know someone who once had truly volcanic acne. Mimi fixed it with a swift injection of cortisone."

"So... the bathroom attendant is an actual nurse? How much are they paying her?" I muse aloud as Jessa leads me back to the cafeteria.

Jessa shrugs. "Enough to lure her away from Sweet Harbor's second-best dermatologist. Welcome to Sweet Harbor High, where every lip is chemically plumped and every pimple is professionally popped."

When we reach the cafeteria, the gorgeous guy is still at the table, eating sushi.

"I'm Micah, the guy who, ah, milked you," he says.

"Chloe."

"So, the Riding Heiress. We meet at last." He stirs wasabi into his soy sauce. "Sorry, I hope seeing wasabi isn't triggering."

"It's fine."

"Micah's a Leland," Jessa says.

"Jessa," Micah says warningly.

"What? I like having friends in high places," she purrs.

She studies my baffled expression.

"Don't you know? The Lelands and the Ridings have been business frenemies for years. You're practically—well, not *related,* but it's like you're royals from neighboring countries. Allies one day, rivals the next. England, meet France. France, meet England. Now marry each other and produce an heir so we can avoid a war."

"Chloe, if you and I got married today, my parents would literally die with happiness," Micah says. "Hmmm... Presuming fatal levels of parental delight, let's get married."

"Micah!" Jessa says, punching him. "You don't really hate your parents."

"I do right now," he says. He pulls a circular seaweed wrapper off his sushi and offers it to me. "Do you accept this ring?"

"I won't wear any ring a fish wore first," I say, and he pops the seaweed in his mouth. "What do you need revenge for?"

"I like someone that I'm not allowed to date."

"Oh," I say. "Who is she?"

"He," Jessa corrects.

"Sorry. My bad," I say. Honestly, high school is new to me. Being around a lot of people my age is new, too.

"No worries, I'm bi. It could be she," Micah says, his eyes twinkling. He plucks a piece of pickled ginger with his chopsticks.

"So... are your parents homophobic? Is that the issue?" I ask.

"No, of course not," Micah says. "But the guy I like... his mother is a judge. She ruled against my family in court."

"I see," I say. "Is his last name Ramachandran, by any chance?"

"Yes. It's Rajiv Ramachandran. Do you know him?"

"I'm acquainted with his mom."

"Look," Jessa says, showing Micah her phone. "Benny just liked my comment."

"Stay away from that boy," Micah says.

"You know that just makes me like him more," Jessa says.

Micah looks at me. His green eyes dazzle. "The tragedy is that Jessa has terrible taste in guys, but she can date whoever she wants. I, however, who have impeccable taste, am not allowed to indulge it."

"Pity, pity," I say, starting to figure out Jessa and Micah's way of talking.

"So, should we get married, Chloe? Please say yes. Only my parents' death by happiness will ensure my freedom," Micah says.

"Maybe," I say. "We did just have quite a meet-cute over there, with the nostril irrigation and all. But I do have an idea. We don't have to date. But we could pretend to."

An idea sparks before I can stop it—reckless, maybe brilliant. If we fake-date, we both win.

Micah's eyes sparkle.

I keep going: "From everything you've said, my grandmother would also perish with pleasure if we were to pair up. We could meet, go out and go our separate ways. You have a boy to woo, and I have other things to do."

When I say "other things," my mind immediately goes to Tyler, showering me with candy in his pickup.

But that's not right. My focus should be on getting into that safe deposit box. Retrieving the cash, if it exists. Saving my dad. I need safety and security, not a bad boy boyfriend. Right?

"Sounds great. It's a date," Micah says.

Then he gasps with horror.

"What is that?" he asks.

"A flip phone," I say. "My grandmother gave it to me this morning. For emergencies. Give me your number."

CHAPTER 24

TYLER

I can't wait to see Chloe's face when I tell her I found the safety deposit box key she's been looking for. I want to watch her eyes light up. I want to feel her throw her arms around my neck, the way she did in her room.

I tried to go by her house, but her grandmother has installed a new gate and security cameras—maybe because of my boot prints on the trellis.

I tried to find her at school, but her grandmother had already picked her up in that Land Rover. Which is basically an armored car.

I couldn't even text Chloe to tell her about the key, because her grandmother doesn't let her have a phone or Wi-Fi access.

Chloe is more or less a prisoner, and the only time she's free, ironically, is court-ordered beach cleanup.

On Saturday, waiting in the beach parking lot, I turn the empty glass bottle over in my hands. The slip of paper inside—whatever message someone tried to send—rolls back and forth.

I've thought about opening it, shaking the message out. But it seems wrong to do it without Chloe.

I came to the beach early to read. It was too noisy at home. My little sister had a sleepover last night, and the place is still packed with adorable, shrieking tweens.

My mom isn't doing so well, but she insisted on throwing my sister a birthday party anyway. It was chaos—but good chaos.

This morning, though, Mom looked exhausted. When I offered to help her make breakfast, she shooed me out the door, telling me, "This is a good day. I'm feeling fine. I got this. Please. Get out of here. Go and be a kid for once."

I never know whether it's a good idea to believe her or not.

She's not always honest about whether she's feeling okay.

Sometimes she fakes it, pretending everything's normal. But then she collapses—and needs a trip to the hospital.

The early morning light is gray. As the sun rises, the light sharpens. The words on the page I'm reading come into focus. I look out through the windshield as the sun surges up over the sea.

As I watch the sunrise, a dolphin leaps in to the air, and arcs back into the water.

I wish Chloe were here to see it with me.

I wish I could stop thinking about her.

I touch the safe deposit box key, which is dangling from a thin silver chain around my neck—a chain I hope she'll wear.

I'm doing my best to concentrate on Kerouac when I hear the crunch of tires over gravel. I look up and see the Ridings' Land Rover pull up near the stairs leading down to the beach.

Chloe steps out, her long dark hair blowing in the ocean breeze. I jump out of the truck and jog to catch up with her.

As I pass the Land Rover, the driver leans out the window to yell something at me. And guess who it is? Chloe's fascist maid.

I ignore her and hurry to Chloe. It takes everything I've got not to pull her into another kiss, but Chloe steps away, her movements tight and nervous.

"Helga's watching me today. I think they're suspicious—they put up a security gate," she whispers.

I nod and hang back, keeping a safe distance, even though all I want to do is scoop Chloe into my arms and race with her into the glistening waves. I can almost taste the salt on her skin, feel her laughter against my mouth.

The waves wash over our bare feet as we walk down the beach. She shows me her new phone—a flip phone.

"It's a *classic antique*," Chloe says, doing an excellent imitation of a posh Sweet Harbor voice.

But before I can get her number, Marcy blows her whistle.

"Hustle up, lovebirds," Marcy calls. She hands out our fluorescent yellow safety vests, trash picker sticks and garbage bags. "Tyler, you head south," she says. "Chloe, you go north."

Chloe and I lock eyes. Marcy waves a trash picker between us like a sword.

"Go on, *git*," Marcy shoos.

With a toss of her silky dark hair, Chloe skips off down the beach, leaving a trail of adorable footprints in the sand.

"Be careful, Tyler," Marcy warns. "A fellow could get diabetes."

"What do you mean?"

"She might be just a little too Sweet for you," Marcy says. "Where's Cy?"

"Benny is dropping him off."

"You work with him today," Marcy says. "If you take my advice, you'll leave Chloe be."

"She's different," I say. "She's not like the others."

"Hmph." Marcy shakes her head. "I've heard that one before."

"What's that supposed to mean?"

"A leopard doesn't change its spots."

"You say that like there's something wrong with her." My

heart starts pounding—my usual sign to take a breath, count to ten.

"You really got it bad, huh, hon?" Marcy chuckles softly. "Look, she seems like a good kid. You're from different worlds, that's all. Don't underestimate that. Besides. This is community service, not *Love Island.* Now get to work."

When Cy shows up, we work together, and I keep one eye on Chloe, watching her move down the beach with her trash picker.

As the sun climbs higher, it gets hot. Cy and I strip off our shirts and splash in the waves to cool off.

Then the storm clouds darken the horizon.

Metaphorically, that is.

A few Sweetie girls jog down the beach—matching silver running outfits, matching bouncing ponytails.

Cy whistles. "Check that out."

"I thought you didn't like Sweeties."

"They're only good for one thing," Cy says.

"Gross," I say. "Don't be a pig."

"Shopping," Cy grins. "I meant *shopping.*"

Cy can always make me laugh. But something about these girls makes my skin prickle. They pause when they reach Chloe, circling her like hyenas. She looks so alone when she's surrounded by them.

My bare toes dig into the sand. My body winds tight, ready to spring.

But before I can move to defend Chloe, the Sweeties jog away.

I smile. I guess Chloe can hold her own.

When Marcy blows the whistle for lunch, I head to my truck, grab my backpack—and the bottle.

Maybe Chloe and I can read the message inside.

On my way back to the beach, I notice the Ridings' Land Rover parked on the overlook. A tinted window rolls down—and that awful maid leans out.

"I saw you, Tyler Court. Mrs. Riding has given strict instructions. You are to have no contact with Chloe Riding. Is that clear?"

"Look," I say, "you can tell Mrs. Riding to mind her own damn business."

The maid grabs my arm. "Tyler," she hisses, "how's your mother doing?"

My heart stops. How does she know who my mom is?

"Your mother. Coralee C. Court. Date of birth June 12, 1983. How's her health?"

My mom's cancer is none of her business.

I yank my arm away, but her nails dig in.

"I hope she's getting good medical care. It would be a shame if something happened with her insurance coverage. Riding-Leland Health, isn't it?"

I'm so stunned, I barely notice when the maid releases me, rolls up the tinted window, and locks the Land Rover doors.

I'm angry my ears are ringing and my body feels like wildfire blazing down the stairs to the beach.

At the bottom of the steps, I almost crash into Chloe. For a second, I barely recognize her; my rage blurs everything.

"Tyler," she says, smiling. "I wanted to catch you—"

My fingers clench around the bottle without thinking. My body's buzzing, tight with adrenaline. And then—without really planning it—I haul my arm back and hurl the bottle into the sea.

If that bottle ever contained a love letter, the ocean has swallowed it whole.

"Wait! Hold on!" Chloe says, grabbing my sleeve. But I shake her off.

"Not now, Chloe," I mutter, my voice raw. My chest tightens; my heart pounds like it's trying to break free. It's not her fault—but if I let her in right now, I'll fall apart.

I can see the hurt flash in her face, but it barely cuts through the red fog around me.

"Tyler?" Chloe's voice wavers. Her hand brushes my wrist, tentative, almost scared.

"I wonder what message was in the bottle," Chloe whispers, staring out at the sea.

"Who cares? It doesn't matter. Words can't change anything," I snap. I start to walk away, but Chloe moves to block my path.

"You said I'd always know where you stand. But I don't know what's happening. Why are you upset?" she says, voice trembling.

My fists are clenched and my every nerve is sparking like a live wire.

But when she looks at me like that—like she sees past everything, to the heart of me—I break.

I take two steps toward her and crush her against me, my mouth finding hers in a kiss that's not quiet, not gentle, but all need and ache and fury and love. Her fingers curl into my shirt. My heart pounds against hers.

For now, that's everything.

For now, that's enough.

CHAPTER 25

CHLOE

I've escaped gravity.

Tyler is kissing me and my feet haven't touched the ground since his hands found my waist.

His soft, warm lips, and his rough, stubbled chin wake my body up. Wherever his mouth goes—my lips, my cheek, my neck, my throat, my shoulder—my skin comes alive.

Up in the parking lot, a car horn blares, but I stop hearing it when Tyler brushes aside the strap of my romper to taste my shoulder. He murmurs "Mmm, fruity," and kisses my strawberry-shaped birthmark.

The car horn blares and blares, like it's a car alarm, a robbery. It's quickly eclipsed by the sound of my own heartbeat, of my breath, quick and shallow, and the distraction of our mingled lips and hands and tongues.

Suddenly something pokes me, hard—right in the butt. "Ow!" I say.

"Sorry," Tyler murmurs.

But it wasn't him. I know where his hands are and—

OW!

I pull back, open my eyes. The real world careens into view. The angled sea, the steaming beach.

And there is Helga, standing on the beach, holding my poky trash picker-up stick like a lance. She prods me with it again.

"OW! Stop!" I say.

"Whoa, sorry, I didn't mean to do anything you didn't want to," Tyler says, opening his eyes now, setting me gently on my feet.

"It's not you," I say, "It's—"

"WHAT exactly are you doing?" Helga demands, shaking the trash stick.

"What does it look like?" Tyler snaps. He pulls me close and I can feel both the heat of his anger, and the heat of his feelings for me.

"You're playing a dangerous game, young man," Helga says. "I would have thought after what happened with your father, you'd have learned your lesson."

What happened to Tyler's dad?

Tyler's grip on my arm tightens, almost painfully.

"Don't talk about him," Tyler says.

"Tyler," I whisper. "Don't grab me so hard."

"Sorry," he murmurs into my hair, relaxing his grip.

"There a problem?" Marcy says. "There better not be. I'm not getting paid enough to leave my sunshade."

"This young man was harassing my employer's granddaughter," Helga says, high and mighty.

"These young people are under *my* charge right now," Marcy says. "You go on back to your vehicle. Or I'll have the law on you for interfering."

"You wouldn't dare," Helga hisses.

Marcy doesn't blink. She stares Helga down. When Helga flinches, Marcy shifts her attention to me and Tyler. "Get back to work, you two," she growls. "Tyler, you head south. You leave her alone. After your shift is done, you two can do what you like. But there is no kissing on my watch, got it? This is a love-free zone."

Tyler leans in for one last quick kiss, but I turn my face so he catches my cheek. It's not that I don't want to kiss him. It's that if there is any way to avoid a showdown with Granny, I need to take it.

It's like reality started existing again as soon as he set me down, as soon as my feet touched the ground. What was I thinking, to make out with him, right in the open where Helga or anyone could see?

I glance back toward Tyler as I walk north on the beach. Marcy's leading him by his elbow, but he's turned back, looking at me with those dazzling blue eyes, grinning.

It gets hotter and hotter as the afternoon progresses. The seaweed starts to steam and stink on the sand. I rake it up. I can feel my shoulders burning, and I'm desperately thirsty.

When Marcy blows her whistle, it's afternoon break. We crowd into the scrawny shade beneath her umbrella. "You guys did a good job," Marcy says. She opens her cooler. Lets us each take out a bottle of soda.

"It's starting to feel like an armpit out here," Cy says. "Can we take the afternoon off?"

"Ha!" Marcy scoffs. Then she sends us back out, to the stilled breeze, the scorching heat, the sweaty humidity.

Picking up trash, the sand burns my feet. Even the sea breezes feel sweaty. I wish I could run off somewhere with Tyler, somewhere icily air-conditioned, like a movie theater, and collapse into a heap of scorching, melting kisses.

But when I look up at the parking lot, I see the glare bouncing off the Land Rover's windshield. Helga is in there in the air conditioning blasting, watching me.

I shade my eyes with my hand and look down the beach. Cy and Tyler are having a great time. They're staying cool, splashing in the water. They even fill up a plastic bag with sea water and douse Marcy with it. I can hear her rasping guffaw from here.

"You rapscallions," she scolds.

Rapscallions. I haven't heard that word since my dad used to tell me bedtime stories. **I almost laugh. But instead I bite my lip.** The thought of my dad instantly blurs my eyes with tears.

What I am doing, fooling around with Tyler when my dad is on the run? When I need to find some money to help him?

The last thing I should be doing is upsetting Granny when I need her help. When she's offering me the only home I've ever had.

I should tell Tyler no… or wait. Or at least be more discreet.

I've lived my life running from place to place, never getting stuck before. But now I feel trapped, boxed in, torn between my feelings for Tyler, and what I need to do to survive—and to help my dad survive.

I make angry X's in the sand with my rake, piling up raggedy seaweed. *Stay away from Tyler,* I vow.

I'm raking furiously when I hear shouting on the beach. When I look over, Tyler, Cy and Marcy are crowded at the water's edge, kneeling in the sand. Waves crash around them; Marcy almost gets knocked over and has to grab on to Cy to keep from falling.

Curious, I walk over, dragging my rake behind me so it scores a trail in the sand.

When I get close, I drop my rake. I can't believe my eyes.

There's a dolphin beached on the shore.

Waves roll and hiss around the dolphin's tail, but he's too far inland for the surf to carry him back out to sea.

His sleek body sinks into the wet sand.

How strange, for a creature who's never known gravity, to find himself stuck.

"Oh, the poor thing," I say, sinking to my knees. The animal trembles, helpless and afraid.

"He can't be that heavy," Cy says. "Tyler, you and me should just pick him up and throw him back—"

"No!" I say. "He might be sick. We need to get a vet."

"Whatever," Cy says, squatting low and preparing to lift the dolphin.

"Don't," Tyler says. He elbows Cy. Cy falls out of his squat and lands on his butt in the water. I resist the urge to laugh; I can already tell Cy is suspicious of me. And after the way the cops treated me, versus him, he has a good reason to be.

"Chloe's right. This animal needs professional help," Tyler says.

"It is so cute," Marcy says, pulling out her phone. She leans down to snap a selfie with the dolphin. She tosses her red hair and pooches her lips into a pout.

"Marcy! Your hair's in its blowhole. It can't breathe!" Tyler says. His tone is decisive. "Everyone, get out of here. Cy, here's the key to my truck. You and Marcy go into town and get Dr. Kai, the veterinarian on Market Street. Chloe and I will stay here and take care of the dolphin. Now, go!"

Tyler speaks with so much authority that even Marcy, who's supposed to be supervising us, runs back toward the parking lot with Cy.

Now the two of us are alone with the stranded sea creature. The waves rush and roar, and my heart is pounding.

I'm an independent person. I flew to Paris by myself when I was six. I navigated the souk of Marrakesh at twelve, haggling with the vendors, scoring deals on fake jewels and fresh spices.

I always know what to do. But here, in the real world, where the laws of gravity apply, and where there's this real emergency and this real guy, I feel helpless.

CHAPTER 26

CHLOE

"Chloe, here's my water bottle. Keep filling it with seawater. We can pour it on the dolphin to keep him cool," Tyler instructs.

I run into the water, splashing up to my knees, and bend down to scoop up water. A wave crashes over me. I splash back to the dolphin, my wet silk romper clinging to my legs, and kneel in the sand.

Tyler cups his hands around the dolphin's blowhole, protecting it from water. I empty the water bottle on the dolphin's back.

"Do you think he's going to be okay?" I ask.

Tyler nods. "I think so. Dr. Kai will know what to do. She does a lot of marine rescue. Plus, Cy has my truck, so if we need to carry the dolphin into the animal hospital, we can."

"Do you think he's sick?" I ask, patting the dolphin's smooth, wet back.

"Most of the time, if a dolphin gets beached, there's something wrong. But maybe not," Tyler says. He gives me a funny look. "Fine. I watch a lot of nature videos, ok?"

"No judgement," I say. "I'm just worried about the dolphin."

"Don't be. This isn't the first time this has happened. There are a lot of dolphins in these waters. Dr. Kai will know what to do."

"I hope so," I say, as a tremor runs through the animal. His fear trembles up through my fingertips and into my chest — a tight, helpless feeling I know too well.

The fact is, human beings are terrible. They lie and cheat and betray you. They dump toxic chemicals in the ocean, for money and for fun.

Did you know cruise ships empty their toilets right in the ocean? I've seen it done.

But this dolphin never hurt anyone. He doesn't deserve to be stranded on shore, stuck here in Sweet Harbor, shaking and afraid.

I get up and fetch more water. Then I sprinkle it on the dolphin's fin and down along his back. I kneel next to Tyler. "The poor thing must be so scared. He must feel so alone."

Tyler reaches out and takes my hand. "It's okay. We're here to keep this dolphin safe and cool until help arrives. Dr. Kai knows what she's doing. We're going to do everything we can for this dolphin."

His fingers wrap around mine, steady and sure, and for a second, the ache in my chest eases — not just for the dolphin, but for myself.

Then I remember. I'm trying not to touch Tyler.

"We probably shouldn't let anyone see this," I say. "We need to be more discreet. My grandmother—it's a complicated situation."

Tyler squeezes my hand then lets it go, giving me the kind of smile that makes me regret telling him we need to be discreet.

I switch focus, sprinkling water on the dolphin, until Tyler's truck barrels down the beach, spitting sand. The veterinarian hops out. She's wearing pink scrubs and carrying a medical bag. Marcy and Cy climb out after her.

"Move," the vet barks. Tyler squeezes my hand one more time before letting go. Then we make way for Dr. Kai.

Wavelets soak her scrubs, which are printed with kittens, as she crouches down with a stethoscope.

I wonder what a dolphin's heart sounds like.

For the first time, I consider what it would be like to be a vet. I've never expected I'd have a career. We always lived moment to moment.

But watching Dr. Kai, I wonder what it would be like to belong somewhere — to have a role, a purpose, not just drift from one disaster to the next. Watching the veterinarian tend to the dolphin, I feel a sharp, unexpected ache to know what it's like to *matter.*

With practiced movements, Dr. Kai slides the stethoscope down the dolphin's side. Waves kiss at the tip of her long, dark-brown ponytail, but she doesn't appear to mind. She's in the zone.

While Dr. Kai listens to the dolphin's heart, mine pounds, because Tyler is standing next to me. Our hands, at our sides, are almost touching. If I moved my pinkie a fraction of a centimeter, it would brush against his.

I'm so focused on the space between our fingertips that I barely hear a car door slam in the distance. I don't fully register Helga, walking down the beach steps, until it's almost too late.

Dr. Kai steps out of the water, draping her stethoscope over her shoulders. From the beach steps, Helga shouts, "Excuse me! What exactly is going on here?"

Everyone turns to look. It's funny to see her, in her maid's uniform, standing on the beach with her hands on her hips. The wind ruffles her apron, and a sudden gust sends her maid's cap askew. She looks out of place.

Dr. Kai beams, patting the dolphin's side. "Wonderful news! This girl is pregnant!"

Helga gasps, one hand flying to her mouth.

Possibly with twins," Dr. Kai adds cheerfully, giving the dolphin another pat.

Helga stalks over, leaving heavy orthopedic footprints in the sand. She grabs me by the arm. Her nails dig into my flesh.

How can a housekeeper have such long nails? Shouldn't they have been worn away with scrubbing?

"Your grandmother is going to be so upset," she said. "Pregnant?"

"Not *me*," I say, pointing to the dolphin. "The *dolphin*."

Helga exhales loudly, releasing my arm as if she's just defused a bomb.

"Right," Dr. Kai says. "It looks like there are six of us. That's good. It takes at least six to lift a dolphin. I have a special tarp in the truck. It's got fin-holes cut out. We'll just slip it under her and carry her out to sea."

"Hold on," Helga says. "These shoes are prescription. My doctor says I can't get them wet."

I drop to the ground and begin unlacing Helga's shoes. "Take them off!" I say. "When are you going to have another chance to rescue a dolphin?"

Dr. Kai tags the dolphin's fin with a GPS chip, so we can keep track of her and make sure she's safe.

Then, working together, we slip the tarp under the dolphin. She trembles and thrashes with fear, but we soon hoist her into the air.

Even with six of us, the dolphin is incredibly heavy. I glance over at Tyler, who's carrying more than his fair share of the marine mammal. His expression is tense, but steady.

Dr. Kai counts to three, and we lift the dolphin, walk into the sea. My arms ache. I grit my teeth and keep going. My feet sink into the sea floor and I struggle to move forward. My arms shake with the dolphin's weight.

"You got this," Helga gasps, encouraging me. Or maybe encouraging herself. Her face is bright red, straining with the dolphin's weight.

At last, the water grows deeper; the dolphin begins to float, making our burden lighter.

When we're waist deep in the water, Dr. Kai tells us to drop the tarp. No sooner do we let go than the dolphin, sensing her freedom, takes off into the water. Her fin streaks toward the horizon. As soon as she reaches deeper water, she dives and disappears completely.

"Well," I say, "that's that." But my voice cracks, almost with tears.

I can't understand the knot in my chest. I'm happy the dolphin is free. But some part of me aches — maybe because I wish I knew how to break free, too.

Break free of the debt that's chaining my dad to the mafia.

Break free of the family dispute that's driven my grandmother and dad apart.

Break free of the social rules, the fear of losing my inheritance, that are keeping me from Tyler.

As the dolphin swims away, I find myself wishing we could have kept caring for her, just a little longer — even though I know wild things aren't meant to stay.

We stand in water, up to our waists, gazing out at the empty horizon.

"Goodbye, darlin'," Marcy croaks. She wipes a tear under her eye. Even Helga sniffles and wipes her eyes.

Just then, the dolphin breaches. She leaps from the water and arcs into the air, doing a dazzling flip.

It's like she's saying thanks.

A tear comes to my eye. Tyler looks at me. I hate being caught showing my feelings, but his eyes are so kind it almost makes me really start crying.

Then, under cover of a rising wave, Tyler's hand finds mine beneath the water, his fingers squeezing gently, like a promise.

He mouths the word "discreet" at me, and I laugh.

When the wave recedes, he lets me go. We both pretend like nothing happened. Together, the six of us walk, dripping and exhausted, to shore. I do my best not to run around and glance back at Tyler.

"Hey Tyler," Cy says, "Your pants are falling down."

I whip around just in time to see a flash of plaid boxers as Tyler hikes up his dripping cut-offs.

We all laugh, but as the sound fades, a hollowness creeps into my chest.

I glance toward the horizon where the dolphin disappeared, wishing I could follow her — wishing I could be that free.

But I'm not.

And tomorrow, everything I'm running from will still be waiting.

CHAPTER 27

CHLOE

"Guess what," I tell Granny, "I have a date."

The kitchen falls silent. Helga freezes with her hands in the soapy dishwater. The room is so quiet I can hear Granny swallow her iced tea.

"With whom?" Granny stirs her drink with a long spoon. The ice clinks in the glass.

Helga sneaks me a look. She's been noticeably nicer to me this week. Dolphin rescuing is, apparently, a bonding experience.

Helga even told me that if I agreed to stay away from Tyler in the future, she wouldn't tell Granny what she'd seen—a big step for her.

"Micah. Micah Leland," I say.

Granny drops her spoon. It lands on the newspaper she's reading, blurring the ink. "Chloe, I'm astonished. I can't believe it. You've actually... made me... *proud.*"

"I appreciate those low expectations, Granny. But what I'd really like is permission to go out on Sunday night."

"A school night? Well, if it's with Micah, of course. Where are you going?"

"To the Sirloin Club," I say. "Micah says they have amazing popovers."

"Well, they're more known for their steak," Granny Riding says. "But regardless. I hope the two of you enjoy yourselves. Do you need a new dress? Some spending money? I'm sure he'll offer to treat, but I know the modern young lady likes to pay her own way."

"Money," I say. "Thanks, that would be great."

And for the first time since I arrived, Granny Riding opens her big purse and starts doling out the cash.

MICAH and I have an iron-clad plan. He's going to pick me up at six and drive me to the Sirloin Club.

We will skip dinner and immediately order crème brûlée and tarte tatin. We'll Latergram ourselves eating dessert, and then split up.

He'll go see his secret boyfriend.

I'll go to Tyler's and meet his aunt, who has plans to join the family for dinner. I've got to find out what the deal is with the safe deposit boxes that used to belong to Sweet Harbor Bank.

At the end of the night, Tyler will drive me to meet up with Micah, who will take me home. Micah and I will spend fifteen minutes in his car in my driveway, just long enough to make Granny wonder if we're making out, and say goodnight.

I've thought a lot about what I want to achieve tonight. It's always important to set clear intentions and be strategic. When I texted Tyler, I made sure to keep it short and professional.

Sure, we kissed.

We held hands on the beach—but that was a unique circumstance. A marine mammal was in danger.

None of that means I can depend on Tyler the way I need to.

If life has taught me anything, it's that you can only depend on yourself—and cash, if you have it in hand.

I need to remember: Tyler's sweet, but he's not a plan. And if I am going to give up what Granny is offering me—a home, security, an inheritance, and just maybe, help for my dad—I need more than just feeling safe in Tyler's arms.

I need real security. Which is why I'm going to try to keep things light with Tyler. Keep the focus on my strategy. I need Tyler's aunt to help me find my money and save my dad.

The week passes quickly. School is not so bad. As soon as Micah became my fake boyfriend, people started treating me differently.

Now nobody calls me a dog-napper. Even the Sophies and Kyra ignore me—not politely, but at least they've stopped harassing me.

On the day of the date, Granny Riding drapes a gleaming strand of silver-gray pearls around my neck. "You look marvelous," Granny says. "Why don't you borrow this necklace for the night?"

I study my reflection in the mirror. Granny picked out a gray satin bandage dress for my date with Micah. Ordinarily, that's a style I associate with mummies, but the lustrous fabric makes up for it.

For a second, twirling in the mirror, I glimpse the girl Granny wants me to be—shiny, sleek, harmless. And for one reckless heartbeat, I wish I could just be that girl.

"Wow," I say, "thanks." I unclasp the clutch. The sequins cast rainbow lights in the gray foyer. "It is a really fun bag."

Under any other circumstance, I'd love it. But all I can think about now is that without my big purse, I'll have no way to change clothes before going to Tyler's. I'll have to show up for his family dinner wearing a satin Herve Leger dress.

Tyler's family's going to think I look exactly like every other

Sweet Harbor Sweetie—stuck up, overdressed, and condescending. Great.

MICAH and I do an excellent job of following the plan. He picks me up. Then we drive to the restaurant, skip dinner and go straight to dessert, which we document with selfies.

We go our separate ways in the parking lot.

"You going to be all right?" he asks, climbing into his Tesla.

"Yeah," I say, glancing around the parking lot. It's filled with luxury vehicles. There's not a rusty Toyota pickup in sight. "I'm sure Tyler will be here soon."

"Okay," Micah says. "I'll meet you back here at eleven."

"Great."

The Tesla starts silently. The black car glides out of the parking lot.

Where's Tyler?

A band of warm yellow light flows out through the Sirloin Club's window; inside, I can see smiling couples at round tables, clinking glasses and gazing into each other's eyes. Their happiness makes me feel lonely.

But then again, are they really happy? Their relationships might all be as fake as my date with Micah.

In fact, they probably are. No one is as lovey-dovey as they look. Everyone's all about their image. Especially in Sweet Harbor.

I stand on the asphalt, shivering in my satin dress. What if Tyler doesn't show up? What if I'm stuck, standing here in my Granny-mandated dove-gray pumps for the next three hours?

It doesn't help my nerves that a slow black Escalade with New York plates drives past me three times. I tell myself it's probably tourists, but my chest tightens anyway.

Could they be looking for me? For my dad?

"You're just being paranoid," I tell myself. "Wouldn't those gangsters have come for you already, if they were going to?" But the back of my neck prickles.

And what if Tyler never shows up? What if he met someone else, or stopped caring, or—

At last, I hear the familiar rumble and rattle of Tyler's truck.

As the Toyota's headlights sweep over me, I feel embarrassed about this dress. Is he going to think I'm showing off? Flaunting my grandmother's wealth? Playing the part of the heiress, slumming it in Shady Cove?

Sure enough, his jaw drops when he sees me, and he raises his eyebrows.

My stomach sinks. He probably does think I look like a Sweetie. Like I'm flaunting his grandmother's wealth.

The wind lifts a curl off my shoulder. For a second, I almost wish I could disappear.

"Whatever," I think. Who is he to judge me? He doesn't even know the full story.

"You're late," I growl, hopping into the truck. I'm trying to sound firm, but this satin dress is so slippery, I slide across the bench seat and crash right into him, and in an instant, we're kissing.

So much for keeping things light.

CHAPTER 28

CHLOE

*M*ist and fog melt into rain as we drive through curving country roads. The truck's windshield wipers squeak.

I'm breathing shallowly. Maybe because my silver dress is too tight. Maybe because I'm nervous about meeting Tyler's family.

Tyler's sure his aunt can help me access the safe deposit box my dad left for me—and that's what I'm officially here to do: get access to that box. Get the money inside it. Help my dad, and whatever comes next after that.

But I don't really know much about interacting with families. I wonder what Tyler's family will think of me.

I know how Cy sees me. He looks at me like I'm a bubblegum-flavored garden slug.

I doubt Tyler's mom will approve of me any more than Granny would approve of Tyler.

"You okay?" Tyler asks, placing his hand on my knee. His warm touch makes me shiver all over.

"Yeah," I say. "Just nervous to meet your family."

"They'll love you. How couldn't they?" Tyler says. But his words don't reassure me. I imagine Tyler's mother will want to protect him. She'll want to investigate me.

But can I pass her tests? Do I even deserve to?

I've never had a boyfriend or even a real friend before. We moved around too much.

I don't know how to act. I don't what I'm doing. I don't know how to avoid hurting Tyler, or myself.

Sometimes, this dating thing feels like slowly peeling off the bandaid that's been holding my bloody heart together. And now, I'm dragging Tyler into my mess, into my dad's secrets.

And if I *do* find the safety deposit box and get the money to help my dad— then what?

Would I have to leave Sweet Harbor?

I can't imagine Granny Riding would want much to do with me if I connected with my criminal dad.

Tyler pulls off the road and we bump along a dirt lane. We pull up in front of a yellow bungalow with a sagging porch roof.

A chicken pecks in the gravel between a pair of rusted-out old pickups. Pea vines climb a faded picket fence. Pumpkins grow in a lacework of leaves along an uneven flagstone walkway.

"Home sweet home," Tyler says, and I follow him through the yard. Raindrops prickle on my bare shoulders, and I'm careful not to step in the wild sprawl of pumpkin plants—the last thing I need is a silver stiletto stuck in a squash.

"My sisters grow those," he says. "They sell them around Halloween."

"Cool," I say. I never lived anywhere long enough to grow a pumpkin. I would've loved to, when I was a kid. I wonder if my parents ever imagined me in a place like this—normal, rooted.

"Watch out for the broken step," Tyler says, as we climb onto the low, sagging porch. As he opens a squeaking screen door, I smell cooking—something savory on the stove.

I'm worried I'll feel out of place in Tyler's living room, standing there in my satin cocktail dress, clutching my sequined bag. But when I step into the room, no one notices me. There's too much chaos.

Two little girls with springy blonde curls are chasing a fluffy collie who's chasing a tiger-striped kitten who's chasing a wind-up car across the floor.

"Hey, everyone!" Tyler says, over the sounds of barking and giggling. Through the doorway into the kitchen, I can see the corner of a fridge. The fridge door swings open as I watch, and I swallow, imagining Tyler's mom.

Instinctively, I tug on the hem of my bodycon dress, trying to inch it closer to my knees. I want to disappear.

"Hey, this is my friend Chloe," Tyler says.

The girls look up from their spot on the rug. The younger of the girls smiles at me with gapped front teeth. "Are you a princess?"

"Why are you dressed so fancy?" the older girl asks, her expression serious.

The lie comes to me easily. "I dressed up because I wanted you to like me," I say. As soon as the words are out of my mouth, I realize that, at least on some level, they're true. These girls are adorable.

"Can I try on your shoes?" the older girl says.

"Mia," Tyler says, warningly, but I say,

"No, no, it's fine." I kick off my heels and Mia steps into them.

The littler girl eyes me suspiciously.

"The little one's Nevaeh, the bigger one's Mia," Tyler explains.

I set my sequined clutch down next to Nevaeh. The little girl's big blue eyes grow wide at the sight of rainbow sparkles.

"Look. It's really fun to open and close this purse," I say. "See these two pieces of metal? You snap them together to open and close, like this. It's called a kiss clasp."

"Oooh!" Mia says, clomping around in my heels, "K-i-s-s-i-n-g." She glances meaningfully at me, then at Tyler.

"Tyler?" a woman calls from the kitchen. "Can you give me a hand in here?"

"Come meet my mom," Tyler says, taking my hand and leading me into the kitchen.

Tyler's mom stands at the stove, stirring a pot of chili. She's barefoot and so thin she's swimming in her jeans and flannel. She's wearing a gorgeous sapphire-blue batik scarf wrapped around her head.

When she turns to look at me, I'm struck by her eyes. They match her scarf and are as blue as Tyler's. She's so thin that her eyes have grown deep-set, which gives her gaze a powerful intensity.

I step back as she takes me in. I brace for her judgment, ready for her to make some crack about my dress, like that it probably cost about as much as it would to fix her leaking roof.

Instead, she walks right up to me, takes both my hands in hers, and gives me a warm smile. "Chloe," she says. "I'm Coralee, Tyler's mom. It's so nice to meet you. I've heard so much about you."

"Really?" I glance over at Tyler, curious what he's told her, but he's peering over the chili pot intently.

"Of course. I hear you're new in town. I was the new girl once, many years ago. I remember how tough it was. I hope Tyler has been welcoming." She squeezes my hands. Her fingers are thin and frail-looking, but warm.

"Oh yes," I say, "very." I wonder if Tyler's mentioned picking me up on the side of the road. Or kidnapping me. Or going to court with me.

Whatever he's told her, his mom beams at me. Why is she being so nice? What's her motivation?

Coralee turns to Tyler. "Honey, will you grab some red

pepper flakes from the spice cupboard? I think the chili needs a little more kick."

When he opens the cupboard, an avalanche of paperback novels spill out. I stifle a laugh. It reminds me of Tyler's truck. Every time he brakes, books slide out from under the seat.

"Sorry about that," Coralee says. "I'm always reading about ten books at a time. I seem to stash them wherever I go." She bends down to pick up the books, but Tyler says,

"No, Mom. I've got it. Please, sit down." He pulls out a spindly chair and Coralee takes a seat at the kitchen table. Tyler picks up the books. Then he doctors up the chili with spices and tastes it.

"Aunt Susan's going to be a little late, Ty," Coralee says. "Got held up at the bank."

"Held up at the bank?" I say, picturing bank robbers in black ski masks. "Literally?"

Coralee laughs. "That's a good one. No, she's just delayed by a bit of paperwork. We can keep the chili warm on the burner for her, but the girls are hungry. Might as well eat."

My pulse jumps. Aunt Susan. The bank. The safe deposit box. It's all about to crack open.

So why does the thought of it make my stomach hurt?

Tyler calls into the living room. "Nevaeh? Mia? Dinner."

He ladles chili into bowls and pulls a pan of cornbread from the oven. Mia troops in, wearing my high heels, twirling on the cracked linoleum floor before taking her seat.

"Oh," I say, "we're short a chair."

"No we're not," Nevaeh says, climbing into her mom's lap, snuggling. "Mom is my chair."

Tyler pulls out a chair for me and I sit down. "That's our dad," Mia says, pointing to a framed 8x10 photograph on the wall. It's a picture of a handsome older man. He looks like a brown-eyed version of Tyler.

"He's dead," little Nevaeh says.

"Nevaeh," Mia says, "Don't say it like *that*." She sprinkles shredded cheddar on her chili as she explains. "Nevaeh doesn't remember our dad. I do. So does Tyler."

"I'm sorry," I say.

I didn't know. How could I? Tyler never said anything.

But it occurs to me that even though he knows all about my family—my con artist dad, my fancypants grandma, even my control freak maid—he hasn't been as open about his own family.

Or maybe I was just too self-absorbed to ask.

What happened to his dad? How did he die? And is Coralee okay? Is she just regular thin? Or is she . . .sick?

A bit of dry cornbread sticks in my throat as I wonder if I've been too wrapped up in my own story to see his.

Coralee coughs—a little, dry cough at first, but it turns into a deep, gasping cough that shakes her thin frame so much Nevaeh slides off her mom's lap and runs to Tyler, who lifts her up and puts her on his knee. The little girl buries her face in Tyler's chest until Coralee's coughing subsides.

"Chili okay?" Tyler asks me, as if Coralee hasn't just about hacked up a lung.

"Yes, it's delicious," I say.

That might be true. The chili could be scrumptious.

But I can't taste it.

I can barely swallow. My throat feels tight. I'm worried about Coralee. I'm worried about all of it—about this fragile, warm, messy family, and about whether I have any right to bring my own chaos into it.

Soon, the front door opens, and a short, stocky woman—this must be Susan from the bank—joins us in the kitchen. She grabs a dish towel from the oven door and uses it to rub the rain off herself, all the while chattering nonstop.

"Nevaeh! Have you lost another tooth? Let me see your smile. Coralee, did you finish that book I loaned you about the dragons? Tyler, how was that math test? Mia—why, Mia."

The little girl in heels has leaped from her chair and flung her arms around her aunt's waist. Susan smoothes Mia's curls affectionately, and when Mia releases her hold, I notice she's left a mouth-shaped imprint of chili on the front of Susan's cream-colored blouse.

I catch Tyler's eye; he's covering his mouth, amused.

And to my astonishment, Susan's not even angry. She just goes to the sink, squirts a little dish soap on the stain, then dishes herself up a bowl of chili.

Something in the center of my chest breaks, cracks. I've never been around people like this before. They're so warm. So relaxed with one another.

I don't want this dinner to end. I don't even want to ask Susan about the safe deposit box. I don't want to do anything to disrupt the cozy peace of this place.

But my dad's the only family I've known.

And if I don't look out for him... who will?

CHAPTER 29

TYLER

*I*t's not that I don't like cake. I do.

In fact, I have a huge sweet tooth.

But there's something embarrassing about carving up a discount, bakery-leftover sheet cake—one with Happy Birthday misspelled on it—in front of the Riding Heiress.

Aunt Susan brought it back from the Save-Rite Bakery. The girls love it. They'll do anything for cake.

"I get a rose!" Nevaeh insists.

"What do we say to Aunt Susan for bringing us a cake?" Mom asks. She sounds more hoarse than usual.

"Thank you!" my sisters chorus.

I'm proud of my family. Dad hauled waste for Riding Industries, trusting their safety rules. After he died, the settlement paid off the house—but when my mom signed the agreement, she signed away her right to any further lawsuits.

A year later, she got sick too. The doctor says maybe it was from washing Dad's clothes.

At least we own the house. Sure, the roof leaks. Sometimes the electricity gets cut off. But no one has a right to judge us. We're survivors.

Still, I can't take my eyes off Chloe. I have to admit it. But I'm worried what she'll think—about the leaky roof, the messy cake.

So many Sweeties have looked down their noses at us. When will Chloe start doing that too?

AFTER DINNER, Mom goes to lie down, and I send the girls to play Candyland. I help Chloe unclasp the chain she's wearing—the one I gave her—and hand the safe deposit box key to Susan.

Susan inspects it. "Old model. We moved those boxes when we merged with First American. We told people to come clear them out."

"But I didn't," Chloe says softly. "I mean—my dad didn't clear it out. He left me this key."

Susan frowns, turning the key over in her hands. "So where would Chloe's stuff be?"

"My guess is... still in the old bank."

"Aunt Susan," I tease, "are you telling Chloe she needs to rob the old Sweet Harbor Bank?"

"Tyler, don't joke," Susan whispers sharply. "I'll keep your secrets for now. But if you step one toe out of line..."

Her threat silences me. My mom doesn't know anything about the night I spent in jail. Susan covered for me. Neither of us wants to stress my mom out.

"Sorry, Susan," I say. "If you want to rob a bank, Chloe, I'm afraid you're on your own."

But even as I say the words, I know they're not true. The way Chloe's looking up at me—trusting, hopeful—I'm already lost. I'd follow her anywhere, even into a heist.

.   .   .

"Chloe, what about your mother?" Susan asks. "Why isn't she helping you figure this out?"

"Can I eat the last piece of cake?" I interrupt, trying to change the subject. I told my family Chloe's a Sweetie. But I haven't told anyone she's a Riding.

How could I? I can barely look my dad's portrait in the eye.

As I sweep a blue frosting rose into my mouth, I think—it's one thing to date a Sweetie. Another thing to date this Sweetie.

My mom's always telling me, don't judge people so harshly. Sweeties are human too.

But how would she feel if she knew I was dating the heiress to Riding Industries?

"Chloe, want to see my shop? I can show you around," I offer.

"Sure," she says, glancing uncertainly at her plate. "Should I… clean this?"

It occurs to me she sincerely might not know how to wash a dish. "I'll get it later," I say.

We head outside, dashing between raindrops. The shop's only a quarter mile if you cut through my neighbor's cornfield. When we hit a deep mud puddle, I splash through, then glance back.

She's barefoot.

"Where are your shoes?"

"Mia's still wearing them." Chloe shrugs. "No biggie."

"Well, don't go through that puddle barefoot." I scoop her up. She nestles under my chin, warm and weightless, and I realize the problem—I don't want to put her down.

When we reach the shop, rain plinks on the metal roof. "Careful—broken glass," I warn. "Might be better if this is a full-service tour. No walking required."

"Carry on." She grins up at me.

I carry Chloe to the aluminum johnboat under its dustcloth. "I'm afraid my hands are full," I say. "If you lift the cover..." She leans, whisking it off—and I realize, horrified, my pants are sliding down.

I flex my quads, trying to keep my jeans up, as she runs her fingertips up my neck.

"Parts are expensive," Chloe teases. "Where do you get all this without, you know, a little light-fingered recreation?"

"Junkyard mostly. Scaling fences. Outwitting dogs. Only slightly illegal," I manage, clenching my butt to hold my pants up.

An idea hits me: the vise on the workbench. I spin playfully, easing close, hooking my belt loop around the handle of the vise.

Chloe laughs. As she tilts her head back, I dip, scrunch, and feel my jeans slide back into place. I let out a quiet sigh.

She looks up, eyes sparkling. "Tyler," she whispers, "can I ask you a personal question?"

"Anything."

"Did you just scratch your butt on that vise?"

I toss her onto the old Ford bench seat with a yelp. "Madam," I say dramatically, "how dare you accuse me of rump rubbing?"

We're both laughing. I hold her fast, grinning as she wriggles. "I swear—it was just, my pants were falling down."

"Liar, liar," she teases.

"No, sincerely, watch!"

I hop off and do a set of jumping jacks. As I do, I feel my pants slipping down. Chloe bursts out laughing.

"No plaid boxers this time?" she asks.

"Huh?"

"Your shorts were falling at the beach when we rescued the dolphin. I saw them."

"So you were looking at my underwear instead of saving marine life?"

"Not exactly," Chloe giggles. She pats the bench seat. "Come sit down. Tell me about this upholstery."

I hitch up my pants before sitting. "Found an old leather couch the right color. Skinned it, stitched it to the bench."

"What car is it for?"

I point to my great-granddad's 1950s Ford. Engine's retooled, body's repaired, primer's on. Just needs paint.

"Won't it break your heart to sell it?" she asks.

"Yeah. But we need the money. It's what my dad would want."

She brushes hair from my face, voice soft. "Is your mom gonna be okay?"

I swallow. "I don't know. She's not as sick as Dad was. So... maybe."

"Is it cancer?"

"Yeah."

"Your dad, too?"

"Yeah."

She wraps her arms around me. I feel her warm breath through my t-shirt. "I can't believe they both had it. That's so hard."

I hold her tight, murmuring into her hair. For a moment, I let myself just be here.

I don't want her to know my dad died because of her family. Or that my mom's sick now so Mrs. Riding could buy Chloe silk dresses.

I just want this, whatever it is, to be about us.

"It's not fair," Chloe whispers. "But you're doing an amazing job. Your sisters—you're so good with them. How are you getting through this?"

"I'm fine," I say quickly.

"How can you be?"

It was a relief to be honest, but now she's edging toward truths I don't want to face—not yet.

So I do the only thing I can. I lift Chloe's chin with my fingertips. She holds my gaze. Her lips part.

I lean in, and kiss her.

CHAPTER 30

CHLOE

"*M*mm, a delicious strawberry," Tyler murmurs, nuzzling the little strawberry-stain birthmark on my shoulder.

He tugs down the strap of my satin dress with his teeth. "I think I should call you Shortcake. You know I got a sweet tooth, don't you?"

His lips feel fantastic on my skin, and I close my eyes, relaxing into his touch, his kiss.

Then the shop door creaks open and three guys walk in, laughing and joking. I jump away from Tyler, pulling the straps back up on my dress.

Tyler sits up straighter and puts an arm around me protectively as his friends file in. I recognize Cy from the beach, but I don't know the other two. One's impossibly tall; the other's giving Ponyboy, rebel-without-a-cause vibes.

It's not lost on me that Tyler hangs out with an entire pack of well-above-average-on-the-hotness-scale guys.

Tyler is, in my opinion, the hottest. But seriously, what's in the water here? You never see a crew this gorgeous all together—not in Monaco, London, or Hong Kong.

The room suddenly becomes still, and all eyes are on me. I put my hand on Tyler's knee, feeling vulnerable in such an unfamiliar place.

"Looks like someone brought a little Sweetie in here," the Ponyboy-looking guy says.

The beanpole sniffs. "Oh yeah, I can smell the sugar."

Tyler jumps to his feet, hands balled into fists. "What's that supposed to mean?" He stands tall, taking up space, looking ready to fight if he needs to.

The Ponyboy guy shrugs and leans up against the boat.

"She's with me," Tyler says. "And if you've got a problem with that, we can step outside. Are we gonna have a problem?"

The room falls silent. My heart's beating so hard, I can practically hear my satin dress rustling.

Everyone exchanges uncomfortable glances. Tyler steps closer, fists tight. "Well?" he asks, voice sharp. I can feel the tension rolling off him.

The Ponyboy-looking guy cracks a grin. "Whatever, man, we're just busting your chops." He winks at me, pinky crooked. "Hi. I'm Benny."

"Hi," I say, standing. The shop floor feels gritty and cool under my bare feet.

I want Tyler's friends to like me. I try to look confident, stand tall. I remind myself I have more in common with these guys than they know.

"Everyone, this is Chloe," Tyler says, pulling me close. Instantly, I feel bolder, stronger. Tyler is like confidence juice.

He points around. "You know Cy. And you just met Benny. That giant over there is Zane."

"This is a great place. I really like the boat."

Silence falls again. The guys shift their weight. Cy shrugs. Zane rolls his eyes and puts a case of beer in the fridge.

"What are you, a narc?" Benny says.

"No," I say. "I'm a person with an eye for stolen merchandise. And I know a few good fences in Philly and New York. If you ever need to move something without the law noticing, let me know. I'll hook you up."

"What?" Benny says, dark eyes flashing, intrigued. "How do you—"

"Told you she wasn't an ordinary Sweetie," Cy says. "She's a Sweetie. But with a twist."

"You picked that up even from way down the beach, huh?" I say. Cy grins. I guess he likes it when I give him crap.

"You know, it doesn't take a genius to figure out a girl like me," I add. Cy grins even wider. Benny gives me a look like he hadn't expected this.

"We got ourselves a Maven of Mayhem over here," he says, half-sarcastic, half-amused. When he chuckles, I know I've won. "You want a beer?"

Zane puts on music, and things start flowing. We're all drinking, laughing, joking. Tyler slides his arm around my waist, breathes into my ear. "I wasn't expecting them tonight. If you want it to be just us, we can go."

"No," I whisper. "I want to know your friends."

He gazes into my eyes. "That means a lot. These guys have been like my family. Through thick and thin."

"You have a great family," I tell him. "Your mom, your sisters, these guys. I've never seen anything like it."

"You'll get used to it," he says. My heart swells. God, I hope so.

THE DOOR OPENS, and in walk Addie and Jessa—the only two girls at Sweet Harbor High who've been remotely cool to me. What are they doing here?

The guys roar a greeting. Benny high-fives Addie, saying, "Hey, cuz."

My jaw drops. Sweet, quirky Addie is Ponyboy's cousin?

Jessa tosses her long red hair, bats her eyes at Benny, who gives her a nod, then turns away, grabs a wrench, and busies himself with his boat.

"Chloe?" Addie says. "I wasn't expecting to see you here."

"Oh my god," Jessa says. She grabs my hand and Addie's, dragging us into a corner by a banged-up old Coke machine. "You're dating Tyler? He's so hot. And he and Benny are like best friends. Can you find out if Benny likes me?"

"Jessa!" Addie squeals.

"I know, I know," Jessa says. "It's just…"

"What?" I say.

"Benny's my cousin," Addie explains. "I love him, but he's not ready for a girlfriend. And Jessa—you're my best friend. You deserve someone who can actually show up."

Jessa sighs. "But I like him. And maybe with me, it'd be different from his other—"

"Crash-and-burn relationships?" Addie finishes. No wonder she wears owl-print dresses. She's got that wise vibe.

"Okay, okay," Jessa says. "So don't find out if Benny likes me. Definitely do not do that. If there's one thing you shouldn't do, Chloe, it's ask Tyler to ask Benny about me. Got it?"

"Got it," I say.

"Come on," Jessa says. "This is my favorite song. Let's dance."

BACK WHEN I was shivering in that restaurant parking lot, an impromptu dance party on a shop floor was the last thing I expected.

But as Tyler twirls me, dipping me so low my hair brushes the pickup's vintage hubcap, happiness blooms in my chest.

I never expected to find someone like Tyler. And he comes with *friends*. And a family. Things I've never had.

"Doing okay, Shortcake?" Tyler whispers as we dance close.

"Yeah," I breathe. "I'm doing amazing."

CHAPTER 31

CHLOE

*a*t home, Granny Riding waits up for me, doing Sudoku in the big, gloomy great room. "Well? How is it?" she asks. She wears ashy gray eye shadow, but her cheeks are pink, as if she's excited for my date.

I don't even have to lie. "It was wonderful."

I must look like I'm floating, because Granny says, "You're walking on a cloud. That's a relief. I worried you'd have your father's taste in partners."

"What's that supposed to mean?" I ask, but I feel too shimmery to fully mind the insult to my mother.

Granny clicks her tongue. "Who knows who your mother's family was? I could never get a straight story from that woman, never. She and your father were peas in a pod, and that's not a compliment. Sometimes I wonder... if he'd picked a respectable, honest woman, if his life would have turned out differently."

Beneath the sharp edge of her voice, something trembles—something like heartbreak.

"I wonder where he is," I say.

And I wonder where my mom, is too. But I don't say that part. Because I don't want to hear heartbreak in my voice that I hear in Granny's.

Granny takes my hand. Her fingers are warm, and the three-carat sapphire on her ring glitters.

"I've been wondering where your father is, and how he's doing, for over twenty years. It never gets easier. But now we have each other. We can wonder together, at least." She laughs dryly.

"Granny," I say. "If we could pay his debts, maybe he'd be able to come back—"

Granny sighs. "My child, I've paid his debts more times than I can count. He never comes back. Not really. Not to stay."

"But—"

"He likes his way of life, Chloe. He chose it. He likes the danger. Likes the risk. He gave up his fortune. Raised you in who knows what conditions. But now you have a chance, Chloe. You have a bright future."

"But—"

"I'm very proud of you, you know," she says. Her voice softens, and something shifts in my body, near my throat, like I might cry. I swallow. I don't know the last time anyone said that to me.

"For what?"

"Oh, making friends. Doing so well socially... Micah Leland, he's a catch."

"Because he has money?"

"Not just that... I know his family. They're respectable people. They play by the rules. And there is no way Micah would be just using you for your money. He has plenty of his own. That's important. Do you think you'll see each other again?"

"Oh," I say, "I think so."

The truth is, Micah's date with Rajiv went well, too. Micah

and I already have plans to make more fake plans. I could tell Tyler didn't *love* the "custody exchange" with Micah in the parking lot. But he'll get used to it—it's what needs to happen, if we want to be together.

Still. I feel guilty about lying to Granny, now that she's opening up to me like this.

"What do you like about him?" Granny means Micah, but all I can think about his Tyler.

"His eyes," I say, and Tyler's eyes flash through my mind—mischief, hunger, heat—and the memory of his hands sliding over my satin dress makes my skin tingle.

"What are you thinking about?" Granny Riding teases, and I yank my mind out of the gutter.

"I like him," I say.

"Do you two have a lot in common?"

"Yeah."

"Like what?"

We're both convicted dognappers, I think, but say, "We both like to read."

"I've never seen you with a book," Granny says.

"You don't know me that well."

"That's what I'm learning. Please use my library as much as you like. Now. You must be tired. Off to bed."

"Good night," I say. When I stand, Granny looks smaller, like the weight of the evening, her emotional confessions, has caught up to her.

On impulse, I reach down to hug her. To my surprise, she hugs me back. It's awkward—I have to twist my neck at a weird angle—but I don't pull away.

That's when I see, tucked inside her Sudoku book, a letter in my dad's handwriting that begins *Dear Chloe*.

My breath catches.

What is Granny hiding from me?

That night, when I hear Granny snoring her gray snores, I

sneak out of her room, down to the living room. I find her Sudoku book. The letter is just where I expected it.

It's written in my dad's handwriting. The paper is soft with wear, the edges smudged. My stomach drops.

There, across the bottom, are fingerprints—dark, rusty red. Blood.

CHAPTER 32

CHLOE

*T*he letter says everything you'd expect a ransom note to say.

My dad says he's alive, but not for long. His kidnappers are demanding a ransom: one million.

I'm supposed to text a WhatsApp number when I have it.

A million dollars is more money than even Dad ever scored in one go. How am *I* supposed to get it?

"It's not just me I'm worried about," Dad writes. "If you don't move a little more quickly, honey, these guys are going to come for YOU. Act fast and stay safe. Get that money however you can. If these guys get to you, they'll start sending your fingers to your grandmother, one by one, until she gets them their money."

The skin on the back of my neck prickles, and I look out the window, into the dark driveway, into the dark woods. We're all alone in this big house, shaded by so many trees. Anyone could be hiding on the property.

I wish Tyler were here. I think about texting him, asking him to come over, but Granny would just kick him out. She'd maybe kick me out, too, for bringing Tyler around.

And then where would I be?

I tuck the letter in my pocket and go up to bed, but I can't sleep. Just a few short hours ago, I was dancing with new friends at a party. Everything felt wonderful.

Now it all feels like an absolute mess.

My dad, kidnapped somewhere.

Mobsters after me.

Clearly, Granny's not going to do anything about this. She probably thinks my dad's faking it, trying to get the money for himself.

But he wouldn't lie like this—not to me.

He wouldn't want me to feel afraid.

I'm going to have to act fast, and get the money however I can.

My only hope a disused bank I'll somehow have to break into, to try at least to find the safety deposit box.

There's nothing you can do about this tonight, I tell myself. So I let my thoughts pull me in the most comforting direction. Tyler.

I close my eyes, trying to remember the feel of his hands, the taste of his lips. At last, I fall asleep.

IN THE MORNING, I wake up to a text from Tyler.

> Hey Shortcakes, you were in my dream last night.

> Me: What happened?

> It's hard to describe… I might have to show you
> ;)

I'm just starting to text back when Helga marches in with the laundry basket. "Hey! Ever hear of knocking?" I say.

She rips the covers off my bed and stuffs them in her basket. "Laundry day," she says. "Besides. You're late. Time for school."

HELGA DRIVES me to school in the Land Rover. My stomach feels like I swallowed hot charcoals. I think it's just worry, about my dad.

When I think about Tyler, it eases the pain. Like medicine.

Images flash through my mind, memories: Tyler lying down with his head in my lap, me running my hands through his silky hair, listening to him talk about *The Catcher in the Rye*, which he loves and hates. I traced his jaw with my finger. When I brushed his lips with my fingertip, he bit me—just a little.

Suddenly, a string of Harleys roars by us on the road, cutting us off. Helga has to slam on the brakes to avoid hitting a biker in a black leather jacket.

"Great," Helga says. "We're stuck following him now. He needs a muffler tune-up."

I notice there's a twisted, upside-down cross, embroidered in blood red, on the back of the biker's jacket. It's familiar, but I can't quite place it. But that anxious feeling returns.

I check the side-view mirror, looking for vehicles resembling the ones those mob guys were driving. It's nothing but drop-off line Lexuses and BMWs.

I TRY to focus on the present as Helga pulls up outside of Sweet Harbor High.

But staying focused isn't easy—not when the Make-out Memories and/or Kidnapper Panic take over.

In math, Dr. DeAngelo snaps her fingers under my nose. I jump, startled. I'd been thinking about Tyler.

"Earth to Chloe," Dr. DeAngelo says, snapping her fingers.

"Sorry," I say. "Guess I fell asleep."

"You kids need to turn off your phones at a reasonable hour," Dr. DeAngelo scolds. "Kids need ten hours of sleep. At least. Now come up to the board and solve for x."

At the board, I fumble and drop the smart marker.

This is unacceptable. How am I supposed to keep a cool head —key to surviving in a hostile environment—if I'm constantly bombarded with fear, and lust, and love?

I grit my teeth and face up to the math problem.

"Good," Dr. DeAngelo says. "Now you're getting the hang of it."

Maybe. For the moment.

BUT IN THE HALLWAY, it happens again. I fall into another daydream.

This time it's about something that hasn't happened yet.

It's me and Tyler, breaking into the abandoned Sweet Harbor Bank. He's wearing all black, for the heist.

In my imagination, he's even rubbed eye black under his eyes, like a football player. It looks great on him.

He wraps his sweatshirt around his hand to smash the window. Then he helps me climb through it, saying, "Ladies first."

Sophie V.'s whine pierces the fog of my daydream. I come to with a start.

"She didn't even look at the camera!" Sophie V. shrills.

That's when I realize I've successfully walked through the gauntlet of the Sophies without noticing them.

Wow. I didn't absorb any of their negative energy. I didn't hear their stupid voices. I didn't care that they were taking pictures of my outfit. I was protected by the Cloud of Tyler.

DURING STUDY HALL, I finally receive my school-issued iPad. At last! Wifi!

I check my email. I find a message from Archie, one of my dad's London associates. Opening it makes my throat go dry.

"Hello, love. Got word from your dad. Sounds like the guys who took him put out a contract on you. Look out for the Renegade Motorcycle gang. They're bad eggs, all of them. So until you can cough up the ransom, you had better look alive. The Renegade symbol is an upside-down cross. I know you can handle yourself. But be careful."

I reach out to touch the tiny safe deposit box key on a chain on my chest, and immediately I look up the address of the now-closed Sweet Harbor Bank online. I plot it on a map.

I'm going to break in and find my dad's safety deposit box.

I just need to figure out how.

My flip phone vibrates. It's Tyler. Even when he sends me stupid memes, it makes me feel all melty... melty and planning a break-in.

Archie, my dad's London gangster friend, is right. I know how to handle myself.

I can walk and chew gum at the same time.

I can with Tyler and break into a bank building, too.

CHAPTER 33

TYLER

*T*iffany, the lunch lady, slaps an extra-large slab of glop on my tray. She gives me a huge smile. Silver fillings glimmer in her front teeth.

Ever since it got out that me and the boys were the ones who kidnapped Sweetiepie, it's like we're kings of the school. Sure, the lunches here are a horror show. But now the lunch ladies give us double portions.

The freshmen swarm us like gnats, begging to carry our books or jackets. The teachers give us special treatment, too. Mr. G., the librarian, saves newspaper clippings for us, stapling them to the bulletin board. It's now covered with headlines like:

Sweetiepie Spotted at Rocky Isle

High School Sailors Capsize Cruiser in Unsuccessful Sweetiepie Rescue Attempt

Outdoor Gala Ruined by Mysterious Marauding Mammal. (An anonymous source says the beast "could have been" Sweetiepie, but "it was safest to assume it was a bear. Guests fled while the beast made off with the game hens.")

I'm checking my phone when a bottle of Coke rolls down the cafeteria table toward me. I catch it just in time, looking up to see Coach Maloof taking a swig of his own Coke.

"Keep up the good work, sport," he says, thumping me on the back.

As if I play a sport. Which I don't.

But apparently, the dognapping has earned me an honorary spot on the football team.

Never underestimate how much Shadies hate Sweeties.

Still, I'm pretty sure no one will roll free sodas at me if they find out I'm texting Chloe Riding. It felt good seeing my boys warm up to her last night, but I can tell—they're still watching her. And me.

Cy plops down at the table, shoveling in his double dose of glop.

"Not too bad," he says. "Lasagna?"

"Maybe," I say, poking at it with my fork. "There's definitely tomato involved."

"Right," Cy says.

My phone buzzes. My pulse leaps. It's Chloe. It's got to be.

I force myself not to check it. The last thing I need is Cy seeing her name light up my screen. He doesn't have to know I'm *completely* gone for her.

But the truth will have to come out sometime.

"So, what do you think of Chloe?" I ask.

"Cute," he says, mouth full.

"She's more than that."

Cy belches. "She's cute. But be careful. She might be like an M&M."

"An M&M?"

"Hard on the outside, pure Sweet on the inside. Melts in your mouth, not in your—well, maybe she melts in your hand too." He grins.

I kick him under the table. "Come on."

"Alright, alright," he says. "I get it. And hey—if she makes you happy, there's nothing like it. The way I felt with Deana... worth it, even with the heartbreak. So if you really like her, go for it."

"I do," I say. "I really do."

In biology, my phone vibrates again. I sneak it out for a peek. Every buzz lights up my chest like a string of firecrackers.

There's a frog cut open on the table in front of me, but all I can see is Chloe's face. All I can feel is the pull of the phone in my pocket.

The room reeks of formaldehyde. I barely notice, because Chloe and I are plotting how to get her away from her grandma's house. I'm proposing a rope ladder, and waiting, watching her little texting dots, for her reply.

> A rope ladder? I like those Rapunzel vibes. But I'm working on a deal with Micah.

>> The guy from last time?

> Yeah.

>> You sure he's not into you?

> Totally sure.

I'm not totally sure, though. It felt like a knife, watching her get into that Sweetie's Tesla the other night. Watching him take her home.

I kept my face neutral—no jealousy. My last girlfriend was jealous of everything, and it drove me away.

So now, I hold back.

But Micah?

I don't trust him.

I text her again.

> We could distract your grandma. Maybe send her some phony invites to a Rich Lady Party.

> She'd fall for that. Especially if she were getting an award.

> What for? Best shoes?

> Grayest lifestyle?

> LOL yeah, I've seen her house.

> But seriously—we'll figure this out. You don't have to deal with Micah.

> Micah's cool with the fake-date plan. I got this. Saturday?

> ME: You sure? Because I don't mind scamming.

CHLOE DOESN'T REPLY.

The bell rings. I swallow the frog in my throat and pick up the actual frog from the table.

"Stop!" Ms. Brewster calls. "Save the frog!"

"Huh?"

"District cut our frog budget. Double up on amphibians. Save that critter for the next class, okay?"

"All right," I say. "Reduce, reuse, recycle."

Ms. Brewster laughs. I can always make teachers laugh. Comes in handy when you skip as much school as I do.

But inside, my chest feels tight, like a hand's squeezing it. I keep thinking about Chloe, the fake boyfriend, the private school world. The world where everything is easy, shiny.

What do I have to offer her?

Nothing.

That nothing-nothing feeling wraps tighter around me, a knot I can't loosen.

SEVENTH PERIOD, I keep one hand in my pocket, waiting for her reply. It doesn't come.

I picture her laughing in that palace of a school, surrounded by kids who don't even know what it's like to worry about money or cops or a broken-down truck.

How can I compete with that?

The idea hits me like a slap.

If you have nothing, you have nothing left to lose—and that's something.

I SNEAK my phone out and text her: *Want to rob a bank on Saturday? Find out what's in your safe deposit box?*

Her reply is instant: *YAY!!!!!!!*

I stare at her text. It should make me smile. But instead, the knot pulls tighter.

The bell rings. Everyone files out. Ms. Morales claps the erasers, chalk dust rising like smoke.

"Tyler?" she asks. "You okay?"

"Yeah," I say, voice rough in my throat.

Wasn't that what I wanted from Chloe? A big, excited *yay*?

But even as I stare at the phone, I realize: What I wanted was for her to say no.

Because if I get caught, I don't know what happens to me. Or to my family.

When I did a low-key dognapping, they charged me with a felony. This is hardly a regular bank robbery. It's an abandoned building. But who knows what kind of charges they'd file, because it *used* to be a bank?

171

What's wrong with me? One kiss from a rich heiress, and suddenly I'm ready to wreck my life?

Risk prison. Which would mean abandoning my family. For her.

I stare at the screen. My own words, my own dare.

It was my idea, proposing the bank job.

I'll keep my word.

But God, I hope she doesn't hold me to it.

CHAPTER 34

CHLOE

On Saturday, Micah's black Tesla slithers up Granny's winding driveway. I slick on some lip gloss and lace up my hiking boots.

They're brand new. Granny got them for my "hiking date" with Micah. It's really an excuse to wear jeans instead of a cocktail dress.

Because I'm going to meet Tyler.

We're going to the bank.

"Show her the picnic, Helga," Granny says, and Helga shoves a worn-in frame backpack into my hands.

I peek inside, and Helga rattles off the contents. "Caviar with Brie and Swiss water crackers. Prosciutto-wrapped melon slices. Pâté en croûte—"

"That's goose liver spread baked in a little pie," Granny coos. She smooths my hair, tucking a stray strand into my ponytail. Her fingers feel a little like crab claws, but the gesture warms my heart.

"Thanks," I say, giving Helga a warm smile. "I appreciate you packing us a lunch."

Helga scowls. Granny beams.

"Have an excellent hike," Granny says. "The view from Red Ridge is astonishing. Do enjoy."

"I will!"

I hurry out to the Tesla and hop in. "I brought you goose liver goo," I tell Micah. He sticks his tongue out and throws the car into reverse.

"I'm vegetarian."

"Sorry. So, how are things with Rajiv?" I ask, shielding my eyes from the sunlit dazzle of the harbor.

He licks his lips. "Very good. But on the other hand, my family has another case before Judge Ramachandran. It's not looking like we'll win. So the odds of me ever being able to come clean to my family about Rajiv are getting slimmer by the day."

Micah runs his hand through his hair and sighs. "My dad needs to cut it out with these frivolous lawsuits. He's trying to harass the Sweet Harbor Yacht Club into giving him a better slip for his boat."

I snort.

"That's my dad," Micah says. "He'll spend a hundred thousand dollars on legal fees to walk ten fewer feet of dock." He rolls his eyes, but his voice is affectionate.

I get it. My dad's a freak, too. But I still love him.

Micah doesn't know what my plan is with Tyler, and I'm not telling him we're going to break into the old Sweet Harbor Bank. Instead, I say we'll just go to the beach, sit in the truck, make out.

He sighs. "Hooking up in a truck sounds so hot. Maybe I should get one."

"A truck?"

"Yeah. Like a Toyota Tacoma or something. I think Rajiv could get into that." He laughs. "Maybe I'll even score us some Bud... what's it called, BudWizard?"

I laugh. "You need a refresher course on your basic beers. It's called Budweiser."

"Really? Because it makes you wiser?"

As MICAH FILLS me in on his plans for his date with Rajiv, I lose focus. It's hard to think of anything other than my date with Tyler. Half romance, half potential felony. I shift in the seat, tapping my heel against the Tesla's floor mat.

What if we get caught? It's just an abandoned building, right? Barely even a crime... right?

I miss most of Micah's reply, but I do catch the last words:

"We're going to this supposedly haunted hotel with this supposedly haunted restaurant."

"Seriously?"

"Yes. It's on the edge of the Shady Woods. Crazy old place. They say the ghosts make people fall in love."

"What are you talking about?"

"Everyone who goes there winds up hooking up. The rumor is there was once some sort of business convention there. It turned into a mononucleosis super-spreader event."

"Mononucleosis?"

"Mono. The kissing disease. Oh, come on. You've had to have had it." Micah gives me a knowing look.

That happens when you're very sophisticated. People make assumptions about you.

The truth is, I haven't kissed that many people. Just Tyler and some kid I met playing Skee-Ball in Daytona Beach. *That* kiss doesn't count, though. Because my lips were 98% numb from blue raspberry Icee.

I don't want Micah to know all that, though. It's better if he thinks I have some secret glamour.

I decide to distract him. "I wouldn't know if I've ever had mono. I've never been to the doctor," I say.

"Really?"

"Never been sick enough."

"Not even for checkups?"

"What's that?"

Micah laughs. "I think you may be an actual neglected child. I've read about them in books but never expected to meet one in the wild. You really round out my friend group."

A motorcycle zips by us. I let out a shaky breath.

"Okay?" Micah says, patting my knee. His touch makes me wonder ... is this what it's like to have a friend?

"Yeah, I'm fine," I say. "Just... thinking about some stuff with my dad."

The passing motorcycle is a Gold Wing—the royal chariot of the American retiree, my dad always said. Phew. Not a Harley, ridden by a Renegade with a knife and plans for my pinkie finger.

Micah turns into the beach parking lot.

There is Tyler, tall and well-built, leaning up against his pickup.

"Hey! Wait till I stop the car!" Micah yells, but I've already hit the pavement and am running toward Tyler and jumping into his arms. I wrap my legs around him and he twirls me around, kissing me, before tossing me into the truck.

TYLER DRIVES ONE-HANDED.

He has to.

I'm holding his other hand.

When he brakes, a set of burglar's tools—a pair of crowbars, some welding equipment in case we have trouble with the key—slide around, clanking in the bed of the truck.

"This is a good date," I blurt.

"I don't normally bring welding equipment on a date," Tyler says. "But then again, I don't normally date girls like you."

"I'm one of a kind."

Tyler smiles, then takes a breath. "Are you sure you want to do this? We don't have to."

The rattle of the truck—it could use a new set of shocks—matches the anxious uncertainty I'm feeling in my stomach, which feels more full of moths than butterflies.

I think about the person Tyler must think I am.

A girl who's been everywhere. Seen everything.

A girl who hitchhikes in Louboutin pumps. Who smuggled diamonds in Antwerp and counted cards in Monte Carlo.

A fearless girl.

That's the girl he likes.

So that's the girl I'll be. Not the girl who maybe would rather check out a haunted restaurant—or any restaurant—rather than break into a building right now.

Because Tyler is the one who asked me on this breaking-and-entering date. So he must want to go through with it.

And besides. I have no choice, if I want to get that money for my dad.

Last night, I overheard Granny on the phone with one of her fancy friends who used to be the president of Sweet Harbor Bank. They were talking mah jong.

Maybe if I just opened up to Granny, told her about the safe deposit box, her friend would help me out. We wouldn't have to break any laws.

But Granny would handcuff me to the radiator to prevent me from getting all mixed up in my dad's sleazy deals again.

"Are you sure you want to do this?" Tyler asks again, gazing into my eyes.

"Of course." I press my sneaker against the truck's floorboard, pushing down just to feel something solid. "This is going to be fun." My lips stretch into a painful smile.

Tyler steers us into the alley behind the boarded-up bank.

"Ooh," I say, mustering all the enthusiasm I can. "Good. They're doing some construction on the building next door. We can park behind the construction dumpster. That way, no one will see your truck."

"Smart," Tyler says, but he doesn't sound happy about it. The gears grind as he throws the truck into reverse. A faint metallic clatter from under the truck echoes into the empty alley. Even the truck sounds uneasy.

As we park, I pull a tube of red lipstick from my purse and draw on a bright smile. There's nothing like a red lip to create a mood.

We get out, and Tyler climbs up on the dumpster and pries a sheet of plywood off a window with the crowbar. I hug my arms tighter to my chest, heart thudding against my ribs. I glance up and down the alley. No cops. No cameras. Nothing.

Still, we should have done more advance recon. My dad and I never attempted something this bonkers. He always operated by trickery—not by robbery.

And the thing about trickery is plausible deniability. That's how you avoid jail. You create a situation where people can believe it was all a mistake.

Burglary—that's different. You're obviously committing a crime. Are there special laws about breaking into a bank? Or would this just count as another abandoned building? Is this a misdemeanor or a felony? A jittery shiver ripples up my spine.

Why didn't I think about this before?

Maybe it's not too late to stop. Maybe we can still turn around, get back in the truck—

The plywood makes a cracking sound. Tyler wrenches it away from the granite facade. "Now, to break the window," he says, raising the crowbar.

The glass shatters. It falls into the alley, sparkling like diamonds. Tiny shards skip across the pavement, pinging against the dumpster and my shoes.

Tyler offers me his hand.

"Ladies first," he says, as if taking his cues from my daydreams.

I grip the rough edge of the dumpster, the chill of the metal seeping into my palms as he hauls me up. In a hot second, he's heaved me up onto the dumpster. I follow him through the smashed window and into the bank.

CHAPTER 35

TYLER

"Can you shine your phone flashlight?" Chloe asks. "This phone my grandma gave me is so ancient, it doesn't even have one."

"I left my phone at Benny's to confirm my alibi if I need one," I say, whipping my dad's old Eveready flashlight off my utility belt. I've got everything I need, just in case: lock puller, crowbar, battery-powered drill, wrenches, ratchets.

Every tool for a job I really don't want to do.

But it's clearly what Chloe wants.

I click on the flashlight and send a beam through the vast, dim space.

"Good planning," Chloe says.

Normally, the praise would make me happy, but right now I've got a bad feeling. When I was a kid, Zane told me every piece of gum I swallowed would stay inside me forever, forming a hard glob, big as a softball, in my gut—it feels like that.

Against my instincts, I keep going, walking through what

seems like a back-office area. As my eyes adjust to the darkness, I see we're in a labyrinth of cubicle walls.

Our footsteps rustle in the dried-out leaves of overturned potted plants. Clearly, someone kicked them over on their way out. Then the plants died here, of thirst.

"They really left this place a mess," I say, stepping over a fax machine, abandoned in the middle of the floor.

A twig snaps beneath us, from a dried-out old office tree. Chloe jumps, and I take her hand. Her fingers squeeze mine, small and tense. I squeeze back, maybe a little too tight.

"Alright?" I ask.

"It's really dark in here. Do you think they have those—infrared cameras? Detecting us even in the dark?" Chloe squeaks.

"No way," I say, with more confidence than I feel. I want her to feel safe. But I don't know if we are.

I sniff. "It smells like something died in here."

I flip open the lid of a Xerox machine. It's full of baloney. Literal baloney.

Apparently someone had been Xeroxing slices of lunch meat, and just left it all to rot.

Yuck. That's obviously why it stinks in here. Who would do that?

I slam the lid before I pass out from the stench.

"Eek! I think a cockroach just ran over my shoe," Chloe says.

"You okay?"

"Yeah. I'm fine. Just not a bug person. You know, I think I know why this place was left in such a mess. I overheard Granny talking about this on the phone. Apparently, the bank president's own kids did a hostile takeover. Sold this bank out to First American Bank. So the president wasn't very cooperative when it came to moving out. Maybe that's why things were left in such a mess."

"So… why couldn't you just ask your grandma to help get you into this bank?" I hear my own voice snap sharper than I meant.

But does Chloe really not understand the risk I'm running here?

Does she think I break into banks for fun?

Sure, I take some calculated risks sometimes. Other times, I've had no choice but to do some gray-area things. But who does she think I am?

Does she see me as just some bad-boy caricature? Does Chloe even care about the real me, about my family, my life? Is this what Cy meant about M&M's?

The truth is, I'll do anything for her.

I just want her to care about me, too.

"I didn't want Granny to know I was coming here—" she starts.

"Why not?"

"I just don't think my dad would want me to. This whole thing, it's kind of between me and him."

"But your dad ditched you. He abandoned you in a hotel. He left you no money, nothing. Why do you care what he wants?" The words come out of my mouth before I can stop myself.

Chloe drops my hand. "Don't talk about my dad." Her voice is so cold I can almost see her breath.

"There's no need to. You talk about him enough for the both of us," I snap.

Instantly, I regret it.

I know better than to talk smack about people's parents. Even Benny would kick my ass if I tried that with him—and his mom spends her whole life butt-glued to a barstool.

But even though I know better, I feel my temper rising.

"You talk about your dad like he's some kind of hero. But if he really were a hero, he wouldn't be leaving you puzzles and clues. He'd be with you. And yet you shape your whole life around him. You sacrifice everything for him—"

You sacrifice ME for him, I'm thinking—but I don't say that part.

Chloe storms away from me, marching through the glass doors leading into the bank's lobby.

So this is robbing a bank. Or breaking-and-entering-a-bank. No glamor. No glory.

Just broken office supplies, rancid baloney, and a fight with your girlfriend.

Oh, and lest I forget the cherry on top of this diarrhea sundae.

Jail.

The probability of jail.

This girl's going to be the death of me, I think, as the flashlight in my hand goes cold and heavy.

And then I hear her scream.

CHAPTER 36

CHLOE

*M*y scream echoes in the huge, dark lobby.

"Hey! Hey, pipe down!" a man growls. "I'm the one that should be screaming. Here I was, just taking a nap, and you come along and step on my hand."

I stumble back, heart hammering. Under the pile of newspapers I just stomped through, something moves — a hand, not paper.

My stomach flips. It wasn't just trash. It wasn't just old clothes.

It's a man.

A man covered in hair, rising up, snarling.

No wonder I'm screaming.

In a flash, Tyler barrels into the room, flashlight beam slicing across the marble floor. He's between me and the guy in two steps.

"Get away from her," he says, protective.

My chest is still thudding, but somewhere in the swirl of fear,

I notice — Tyler didn't even hesitate to come to my side, even though he was clearly angry with me.

"Come on, get up. Get out of here," Tyler says, taking a fighting stance before the pile papers, the grown man crawling out of them.

"Chill, dude," the man says. "I was just minding my business. Catching a few z's. Then she steps on my hand. Chill. There's plenty of room in here for everybody."

As the man talks, I notice Tyler's body relax. He lowers his fists. "Louie?" he says.

"Oh," the guy says. "I know you. We shared a cell one night, down at the county lockup."

"Yeah. And another time—"

"Oh, right, from the beach. You and your friends were grilling down at the beach. You shared your food with me. Or I should say... you gave me crabs." He chuckles at his own joke.

Tyler laughs. "Ha. Yeah. You got crabs from us."

"I did." Louie guffaws. The sound of his laugh fills the lobby. It's joyful.

Huh.

I didn't know you could be joyful with no money and no hopes of getting any.

"You're a good egg, kid," Louie says.

"Thanks," Tyler says. "Let me introduce my girl — my, uh, friend, Chloe. Chloe, this is Louie. I think we may have broken into his house."

"Naw. This is the People's House. You can't break into the People's House. It belongs to everybody."

A weird warmth flickers in my chest. Tyler knows this guy. Tyler *helped* this guy, even though he clearly didn't stand to get anything out of it.

Maybe he's one of those mythical unicorns — an actual good person.

My heart softens toward him. Maybe he didn't really mean all that stuff he said about me and my dad.

"Chloe," Tyler says. "Meet Louie."

I shake Louie's hand. His fingers are warm, for someone who's been sleeping on cold marble.

I'm not sure what to say. "The floor looks hard," I say. "There's carpet in the back office. Why don't you sleep there?"

Louie laughs. "What, is your nose broken, girl? It stinks in there. The floor might be hard out here, but at least it smells fine. Besides. I've got me a nice bed."

He kicks away a layer of newspapers. "These are my blankets. And here is my mattress." It's a huge, snowy heap of white deposit slips. He picks one up and hands it to me.

"They had cases of them in the back. Just left them here, like they were worth nothing."

"They're all printed with Sweet Harbor Bank," I say. "They had no use for bank paperwork after the merger, I guess."

"Now let me ask you something, young lady. What's the difference between one of these deposit slips and a hundred-dollar bill?"

"A hundred-dollar bill is worth a hundred dollars?"

"Yes, but why?"

"I don't know."

Louie laughs again.

"Of course you don't," he says. "Because you can't see it. A hundred dollars is worth a hundred dollars because *they* decide it is."

"They?" I ask. I glance at Tyler out of the side of my eye. This is drifting into tinfoil-hat territory.

"Money isn't real. It's the biggest magic show in the world. As soon as people question the value of money, then every last dollar in that vault over there becomes worth bupkis. Squat. Zero. Zilch. But as long as people believe it has value, they'll keep trading and killing each other over these useless pieces of paper."

Louie points toward the service counter, and I look past it to the huge, circular door leading to the vault. It's open.

"Wait," I say. "Are you saying there's still money in there?"

By the time I hear Louie's laugh ring out, I'm scrambling over the counter and racing toward the vault. That's wher the safe deposit boxes might be.

I STEP through the circular doorway of the vault. The interior of the steel chamber emits a low, steady buzzing sound. The rear wall is slotted with safety deposit boxes, but I can barely see them over a mountain of cardboard cartons.

It's like someone turned this bank vault into a recycling bin. I rifle through boxes as I try to make a path toward the rear wall.

Who knows — maybe someone left some cash in one of these cardboard boxes?

Louie's big guffaws echo through the marble lobby. He's laughing at me, but right now I don't care.

I know what it's like to be broke, and unlike this Louie guy, I don't take some sort of sick pleasure in it.

I'll take whatever cash comes my way, and I won't ask questions, either, because this money could rescue my dad. It could save me.

I shake each box and throw it behind me as I work. My hands are sweaty, and my heart is pounding like I've been running.

Why isn't Tyler helping?

If he really cared, wouldn't he be trying to help me move these boxes?

At last, I hear Tyler crunching toward me over discarded boxes. "Did you find the safe deposit box?"

"I thought you didn't want me to."

"Why would you think that?"

"Because you hate my dad." The words burn in my mouth

even as I say them. I know they're not exactly true — but they slip out anyway.

Tyler sighs. "That's not it. I just want good things for you, and for me. And — being here, it just didn't feel right. But we're here now. So I'm game. Let's find the safe deposit box."

My chest tightens — he's words not enough, but it's something. For now.

"Help me move this trash," I say, still mad, but I calm down as we work together to clear out the space.

For a moment, as our hands bump over the boxes, I feel us moving in sync — until the world shifts beneath us.

Tyler and I are so busy moving boxes, we don't notice the vault door grinding shut — until it's too late.

CHAPTER 37

TYLER

*I*t's the kind of thing you dream about. Trapped in a small space, like an elevator, with the hottest girl in the world. Nothing to do but make out.

But in real life, it's not cool.

For one, this bank vault stinks — it's musty, like a basement, like some of the paper in here has gotten wet.

Also, Chloe isn't exactly clinging to me in delicious terror, gazing into my eyes and asking me if everything is going to be okay.

She's still mad that I dared to criticize her dad, and if I'm honest with myself, I'm mad at her for getting me stuck in a bank vault.

I shine the flashlight on the door to the vault, testing the handle. It's stuck. Behind me, Chloe's on a mission, digging through boxes to reach the wall of little steel safety deposit boxes.

Seriously.

We're trapped in here with no obvious way out — and Chloe's scrounging for cash.

We might not have enough air to breathe, but she's still chasing that money. She may not have grown up in Sweet Harbor. But she's a Sweetie, through and through.

"Tyler, help me move this box. It's heavy."

"Um, Chloe? Don't you think we'd better focus on finding a way out?"

"I'm sure there's an emergency hatch. There's got to be. It'd be a huge liability risk otherwise," she says. She shoves a large cardboard box. "Come on. Help me."

I watch her. She's not who I thought she'd be. She's not one of us. She's one of them. And yet, watching her grit her teeth and strain and shove the box until it slides across the floor makes me smile. Never seen a Sweetie work so hard, get down in the dirt. Maybe she's more than the label I gave her.

Because Chloe's unstoppable.

She turns to the wall of safety deposit boxes. "Ok, here we go. 307, 309, and… 311." She slips the key in the lock. Then she stops.

"Oh no, Tyler. I really screwed up. I can't believe I got you into this mess for nothing."

My heart softens. "What's wrong? Doesn't the key work?"

"It does," she says, "but I'm an idiot. I can't believe I forgot this one crucial and extremely basic detail."

"What?"

"It takes two keys. The bank has a key, and the customer has a key, and without them both, the door won't—"

"Oh, I came prepared," I tell her. "Hold this."

Chloe aims the flashlight while I get to work setting up a lock puller. A few spins with the drill, some measured turns with the ratchet, and I've levered out the lock. Then all it takes is a couple of quick twists with a screwdriver and the door pops right open.

"Whoa," Chloe breathes, "I'm impressed." And when she pulls

me into a long kiss, it's like every inch of anger drains from my body.

Then, beneath the soft sounds of our kisses, I hear it — faint at first, but growing stronger and stronger, closer and closer: the whine of a police siren. I tense up, and, as if she can read my fear through my body, Chloe pulls me tighter and says, "Oh no. Tyler, I'm so sorry I got you mixed up in this. I'll do everything I can to get you out of this. I'll say I kidnapped you, I'll say anything—"

She's saying exactly what I needed to hear. But I tell her to be quiet. Because the cops are here.

I hear the sound of boots on marble floors, and the crackle of a police walkie-talkie. One of the cops says, "They must have gotten in through a hole in this plywood."

Then I hear another officer shouting, "Got him!"

I try to place their voices. They sound familiar.

Then the other guy speaks. "That's not a bank robber. That's just Louie. Louie, what're you doing in here?"

Louie's low laugh echoes in the big room. "Welcome to my humble abode, Officer Tran. Officer Forest. Nice to see you, gentlemen."

Officer Tran and Officer Forest were the guys who arrested me and Cy the night we kidnapped Sweetiepie. I thought I recognized their voices.

"Come on, Louie. Let's go back to jail," Officer Forest says.

"Of course, officers. Please accept my wrists, to be cuffed. Allow me to ask you, however, just what harm have I caused here?"

"We got a report of breaking and entry," says Officer Tran.

"And what would be the problem with that? The building is abandoned. I am doing no one any harm."

In the lobby, Officer Forest says, "Come on, Louie. Enough philosophy. Where's your friend?"

"My friend?"

"We got a report of two people breaking in. Now, where is your buddy?"

"Ah! But alas, officers, I am friendless. That is why you pity me — my loneliness — is it not?"

"Forest, search the premises," Tran says. I can hear Forest's boots thumping over the floor. As his footsteps near the vault, Chloe takes in a sharp breath.

Outside, Officer Tran cajoles Louie. "Come on, Louie. You know Officer Forest is gonna find your friend wherever he's hiding. But you can save us some time. You tell us where your buddy is, and I'll take you to Burger King on the way to jail."

My stomach knots. Louie's going to sell us out for a cheese-burger. And why wouldn't he? He's probably starving.

I hold my breath, waiting for Louie to spill his guts.

But he's keeping his mouth shut.

Officer Forest calls out, his voice echoing in the lobby. "Back office is clear. Restrooms are clear. Louie's telling the truth."

"What about the vault?"

"Oh, that's locked," Louie says. "You think I didn't try to open it?"

"Check it out," Tran says.

As Forest's footsteps get closer, I can feel Chloe's heartbeat pounding fast against my chest. Mine's not doing much better.

The vault door clanks, and I swear my heart stops.

"Yeah, it's locked," Forest confirms. "Let's get out of here."

Silently, Chloe's body relaxes against mine. I feel her melting into me, the tension sliding out of her muscles. My hands smooth down her back on instinct.

"Funny thing about bank vaults," Louie says. His voice is louder than the officers'. I can hear every syllable clearly. "Bank vaults are all built with an escape mechanism. You can't break in, but you can break out. That's like the money system. Did I ever tell you boys about the value of the dollar? You think you're putting me in jail, fellows, but you're the ones who are locked up... in your minds."

"Yeah, yeah, Louie."

"We still going to Wendy's?" Louie asks.

Their voices fade as they exit the building. The silence of the lobby settles around us.

We're free.

We made it.

Louie covered for us. The cops are gone. There's an emergency hatch somewhere — we can escape.

Everything's going to be all right.

I'm so happy I pick Chloe up off her feet and spin her around in the middle of the empty bank vault. The light from my flashlight wheels around us as we spin. For once, it feels like we're spinning out of trouble, not into it.

CHAPTER 38

CHLOE

*M*aking out in the bank vault, our bodies crush paper so there's little rustling sounds underneath the sounds of kisses and caresses.

Finally, I pull away from Tyler, saying, "We're going to run out of air—"

"Maybe you need some mouth-to-mouth—"

"TYLER—" It takes all my strength to hold him back. My laugh cracks through the panic still fluttering under my ribs. "Just let me see what's in that safe deposit box, and I'm all yours."

I shine the flashlight into the box Tyler so artfully dissected. I'm not sure what I'm expecting to see. Rolls of cash? Blue Tiffany's boxes? Dragonlike heaps of gold coins?

But there's nothing.

It's empty.

A hollow opens in my chest.

I understand why my dad lies.

I just don't understand why he'd lie to ME.

"Chloe? You all right?" Tyler asks.

I give a tiny nod, faking I'm okay. The tears prickling behind my eyes feel hot and stupid. And what guy wants to see that?

"Talk to me," Tyler says, rubbing my back.

I squirm away, sticking my hand into the safe deposit box, feeling around for gold dust, really just trying to get some breathing room from him.

I'm used to coping with things on my own. I don't know how to be emotional around someone else. Let alone a boyfriend. (Is he even my boyfriend?)

My fingers brush something hard and plastic. I seize on it. "A flash drive. I found a flash drive!"

"Great," Tyler says. "Let's get out of here."

The stone in my throat dissolves a little, like rock candy. I can breathe more easily around it. "Of course. There's got to be information on here that can lead us to whatever my dad wanted me to find. Money, maybe. Or maybe it's Bitcoin passwords, or who knows?"

Tyler takes a beat, and when he speaks, his tone is businesslike. "Chloe, can you stabilize this stack of boxes? I'm going to climb up and work on opening that escape hatch."

While we work, he says, "I know you don't have a computer at your grandma's. Do you want to come over to my place? I only have a janky old school laptop, but you might at least be able to open some of the files on there."

"Yes, please," I say. Gratitude softens the edges of my voice.

I tuck the flash drive in my pocket and hold the boxes steady as Tyler climbs up. When he reaches the top, I shine the light toward the ceiling so he can crank the wheel and open the escape hatch.

The wheel squeaks and squeaks and then, with a final push, Tyler forces open the rusty hatch — and at that exact moment, his pants fall down.

I'm laughing so hard the flashlight beam shakes on his polka-dot boxers.

"It's this utility belt," he says, "my tools are too heavy. Always dragging my pants down."

I scale the boxes, and when I reach the top, I call to him. "Tyler. Help me out."

He pokes his head back down through the hole in the ceiling. "Keep your pants on," he teases, then reaches out to help me through.

Hand in hand, we run through the deserted bank. When we reach the stinky back office, Tyler reaches over and pinches my nose shut with his fingertips, protecting me from the stink.

"Such a gentleman," I squeak, through my closed nose.

"It's just basic courtesy, ma'am," he says, imitating Officer Forest's voice, and my laugh snorts out through my pinched nose.

Soon, we're climbing back out through the broken piece of plywood, crawling over the dumpster, and hopping into Tyler's Toyota truck.

Once we slam the truck doors shut, a zingy, elastic kind of silence falls between us. Neither of us say anything. Without speaking, Tyler starts the engine.

I smile at him, but he's not looking at me. He stares straight ahead. His lips are a tense line, but I sense a sparkle in his eye.

"This is always when people get caught. They get sloppy when they think they've gotten away with something."

"But we're not sloppy."

"No. We're meticulous." His face is dead serious, but his eyes sparkle at me. "The Meticulous Marauders. The Diligent Duo. The Careful Couple."

Couple.

My heart does a little flip I pretend not to feel.

He pulls into the alley, ever more precise and intentional, and we drive down Main Street. We're so quiet that when I hear the "tick" of the turn signal, I jump. Tyler reaches over and squeezes my hand. One quick squeeze. Then he promptly puts his hands back at ten and two, the model of responsible automobile use.

Tyler drives exactly the speed limit — I know, I watch the needle — all the way out of town. He keeps the needle steady until we've crossed the Sweet County line.

As soon as we enter Shady County, the black paved road turns to gravel. It clinks against the belly of the truck. Tyler turns to me. He raises one eyebrow, and floors it.

The little truck leaps forward, kicking up a cloud of yellow dust. We roar through the green and rolling hills, tearing up the road, gravel spraying, and suddenly we're both laughing, scream-laughing, with relief.

We're free! We got away with it! We're free!

Tyler pulls the truck over to the shoulder of the road. Then he nudges the truck down into a green ditch. He cuts off the engine, turns toward me, and pulls me close.

The movies are right. The hiding-from-the-cops kiss is a pretty good kiss. But the just-after-escaping-from-the-cops kiss — that's the best kiss.

"What, is a random ditch the Shady Cove discount version of makeout point?" I ask, when we come up for air.

"Something like that," he murmurs, and I'm pretty sure I'm going to have the shape of a seatbelt buckle imprinted on my bare back.

But I don't care, because the windows are steaming up and apparently I love making out in a truck.

We don't stop until Tyler's watch starts beeping.

I laugh. "You wear an actual watch?" I ask between kisses.

"Only when I leave my phone behind to further my criminal activities. I have to go home and cook supper. You're welcome to stay for dinner and check out the flash drive. How do you feel about spaghetti?"

My lips are too raw from kissing to eat, but I hear myself sigh, "Spaghetti. Yes. Spaghetti."

CHAPTER 39

CHLOE

*T*wenty minutes later, we're driving down the gravel road to Tyler's. I've slid right up next to him, and am holding one of his hands—the non-driving hand—with both of mine. I trace the shape of his perfect fingernails with my fingertips.

Check me out. I have Tyler and a flash drive.

But for some reason, the thought of seeing what's on the flash drive makes me feel as I've swallowed a stone.

I'm just psyching myself out, right? Because whatever's on that flash drive doesn't have to change any of the good things in my life.

I could get my dad's money, bail him out, and still stay here in Sweet Harbor—all without granny knowing a thing about it.

I could still date Tyler.

It's just money, I tell myself.

Money buys freedom. Choices.

And when I have money, I'll have freedom to do what I want.

Q: What could be better than Tyler?

A: Tyler—plus an escape hatch.

WHEN WE REACH Tyler's house, there's no easy way to get to a computer and figure out what's going on with the flash drive. His sisters demand all of our attention.

Tyler's sisters are wearing a pair of his sweatpants. By that, I mean Mia's in the right leg, Nevaeh's in the left.

"Look at us walk!" Mia shouts, and hops forward, nearly crushing the cat, who skitters out of the way.

"That's why your pants are always stretched out," I tell Tyler.

"Shut up," he says, brushing his lips against mine. Then he turns to his sisters, who are now tangled up with the pants and the cat. "Ten more minutes, girls."

Tyler's mom is napping, so Tyler and I make dinner. He turns on the water, twisting the faucet to hot.

He puts a big pot under the white, steaming water. "The trick for perfect spaghetti is to start out with hot water."

"Oh," I say, pretending to be interested.

But I don't know how to cook. Not at all. Dad and I always ate out.

Sometimes I'd eat leftovers from the hotel mini fridge. But that was about it.

Tyler gives me a quizzical look. "Next, of course, we add the onions to the water," he says.

"Umm," I say. I didn't know there were onions involved in spaghetti, but how would I? I've only ever eaten it at restaurants, like in Rome, and once out of a Dumpster behind a Sbarro in Scranton. "However you usually make it is fine."

"I see," he says, holding my gaze, eyes twinkling. "How about sugar? Do you like a lot in the water, or a little?"

"Oh, a lot," I guess.

"How much would you say?"

"The normal amount."

"Two cups, then?"

"Yeah. Do you need help? Where do you keep the sugar?"

I roll my sleeves up and brush my hands together as if I'm dusting them off—as if I know my way around a kitchen.

"You don't put SUGAR in SPAGHETTI!" Nevaeh pops out from under the table, grinning. She's missing another tooth; that makes four.

Mia skips in from the living room, arms and pigtails swinging, and crashes into me. She flings her arms around my waist and squeezes me tight, the way she'd hugged her Aunt Susan.

A tight, stony feeling, like a knot of tears, rises in my throat.

"Hi Mia," I croak.

She gives me a squeeze before climbing on a chair to open a cabinet. She pulls out a yellow box and shakes it. "We are having spaghetti," she announces.

"Chloe wants to put sugar in the spaghetti," Nevaeh tattles. Mia shrieks.

"Sugar! In Spaghetti! That's disgusting."

"Not if it's breakfast spaghetti," Tyler says. "I'm sure Chloe knows a special recipe."

He carries the pot to the stove and turns on a burner. Then he puts his arm around me and whispers in my ear. The warmth of his breath sends a tiny shiver down my spine.

"You don't know how to make spaghetti, do you?" he asks. I shake my head, and when I do, his lips brush my earlobe.

He whispers, "In that case, tonight will be a revelation in pasta."

"I'm looking forward to it."

"WHERE ARE YOUR SHOES?" Mia asks.

"My shoes?" I glance down at my hiking boots.

"Yeah," Nevaeh says. "Your pointy shoes."

"I left them at home."

Mia sticks her lower lip out. "Too bad. I wanted to wear them again. I don't want to wear those ugly boots."

"But I do," Nevaeh squeals, showing off the gap in her teeth.

I bend down to unlace my boots. Tyler puts his hand on my back. His warm touch travels straight through my shirt to my skin.

Seriously. I can't live like this. How is it that his slightest touch can derail my every thought?

I'm like one of those stupid moths, flattening myself up against a neon sign. This level of distraction could be fatal.

But I'll think about that later.

Right now, it feels good to be with him. Good to be with his family. They're so warm, it's easy to pretend that they could become my family.

I OFFER NEVAEH MY BOOTS. She steps into them, balancing herself against the table.

Tyler steers me toward the stove. He ties an apron around my waist and says, "Hold out your hand."

I do, and he adjusts it with a light touch, saying, "That's right. Hold it just like that."

Then he pours salt into my hand. The streaming white grains fill my cupped hand, covering up the lines in my palm. For a second, it feels like time stutters.

I get a sudden flash of memory: my mom, tracing my palm with her long fingernails, saying, "That's your lifeline, that's your headline, and that, poor girl, is your love line."

I don't remember where we were—in my mind's eye, all I see is candlelight and red velvet, so maybe a VIP room at some nightclub?—but I remember asking my mom, "Why am I a 'poor girl'?" and she said,

"The shape of your love line indicates that you will fall in love —hard. And trust me. People who fall—get hurt."

I remember how her voice cracked with tears when she spoke.

How long was that before she left? A week? A year?

Tyler stands behind me, his breath warm on the back of my neck. He reaches around me and cups my open hand with his. "Now turn your wrist, just like this." The salt spills from my hand into the simmering pot. I watch white grains dissolve into gray clouds.

"See? That's it. You're cooking," Tyler says. His voice pulls me back to the moment, but my throat still tightens around the memory.

"I'm cooking," I repeat.

"I'll fix the sauce. You just stand there and tell me when it boils."

"Okay," I say, and I stand still, even though my body feels cold as soon as he walks away.

I can hear him chopping something on a wooden board. I resist the urge to run toward him. Instead, I close my eyes and lean over the pot, feeling the heat rising from the stove.

I try to pull myself back to that moment in time with my mom. My dad told me she left because she met someone new, fell in love.

Was that what she'd been referring to in that moment? Was she feeling sorry that she'd fallen in love with someone else? Did it make her sad to leave? Did she have a choice?

Can love make you do awful things — things like run away and leave your only daughter behind?

I don't mean for it to happen, but a tear slides down my cheek. It plops into the simmering pot, another drop of salt water.

CHAPTER 40

CHLOE

"I am proud of this spaghetti," I say, swirling the last bit of noodles onto my fork. "It's delicious."

"It only boiled over once," Mia says.

"Next time I'll watch it," I say, recalling the overflowing water hissing on the electric burner.

"It turned out just fine," Tyler says.

"Yeah. Even Mom ate some," Mia says.

"She never eats anything," Nevaeh adds.

I glance over at the tray the girls carried to Coralee's room: glass of milk, salad with ranch, small bowl of noodles with red sauce, slice of garlic bread.

Tyler whisked the tray out of his mom's room a few minutes after the girls put it in there. The scent of food, he told me, often makes his mom nauseous.

When Tyler notices me noticing his mom's barely-touched tray, I reach under the table and give his knee a squeeze. It's hard enough to lose a mom who doesn't really care about you. Imagine worrying about losing a mom who does.

After dinner, Tyler puts two battered laptops on the kitchen table. One is for me, he explains. The other is for Mia. He says he'll help Mia with her homework while I inspect the flash drive.

The time has come. I pop in the flash drive. Nothing happens.

Tyler looks up from Mia's laptop. "Give it a minute. It's a really old laptop. Word is the school district actually got them from Sweet Harbor High dumpsters." He taps the keys on Mia's laptop with one finger. "Okay, Mia, do you see that word?"

"It's hard," Mia says.

"No. You just got to break it down. What sound does a C plus an H make?"

I smile. Tyler is so patient to help Mia learn to read.

"Chuh," Mia says, sounding out the word.

The laptop I'm using chugs and groans like a hiker climbing Mt. Everest. Will it make it? The spaghetti dinner slithers around in my stomach as my anxiety mounts.

At last, the icon for the USB pops on the screen. I click it, and the computer grinds away before revealing the hidden treasures.

It's not bank account information.

It's documents.

Hundreds of pages of dense information. Emails, calendar entries, legal documents.

A headache starts brewing above my eyebrows. It will take some time to comb through all this.

The computer whines and moans. I half expect the ancient processor to start smoking as it works through all this data.

"Okay, what about these two letters? S and H? What sound do they make when you put them together?" Tyler asks Mia, patiently.

"Shhhhhh," Mia sounds out.

But Mia's not the only one putting things together. As I look through the documents, it's clear that Riding Industries, my family's corporation, was doing some seriously bad stuff.

I'm not somebody who pays a lot of attention to the news. But even I know you can't be going around dumping toxic chemicals everywhere. That's illegal.

And if what these documents say is true, the chemicals were making people sick, right here in Shady Cove. And Riding Industries knew about it and they didn't stop it.

In fact, they lied to everyone. They said they were following safety procedures. But it wasn't true.

"Let me type," Mia says. Her high, squeaky voice floats to me like something in a dream.

When I look up, things seem to move in slow motion: Tyler slides his laptop to Mia. Then he pulls his chair toward me, moving to look over my shoulder.

My hand snaps the laptop closed before my brain can catch up.

"What's on there?" he whispers, resting his hand on my leg.

Normally, his touch would fill me with butterflies; now it feels like an octopus tentacle clinging to my leg.

A new feeling—guilt, maybe?—oozes through me. I'm not sure what to do.

I stand up, brushing him away.

"Nothing," I say. "There's nothing on it. Where's your bathroom?"

Tyler's eyes grow wide with sympathy. "I'm sorry, Chloe," he says. It's obvious he thinks my dad led me on a wild goose chase.

"Don't be sorry," I snap. "Just—the bathroom?"

"Down the hall."

TYLER'S BATHROOM is immaculately clean. There's a row of bright yellow rubber ducks along the ledge of a gleaming white clawfoot tub.

I splash cold water on my face, trying to get it together.

Someone else might look at these documents and be confused.

But I'm not.

I know exactly what my dad wants me to do with them.

He wants me to blackmail my grandma.

TYLER KNOCKS on the bathroom door. Three quick knocks. "OK in there?" he asks.

I'm sitting on the bathmat, reeling. I've been here for a while, maybe half an hour. Most of that time, I've been freaking out.

At some point, I piled all the rubber duckies into my lap. Their tough, squeaky bodies aren't much comfort, but I hold on anyway.

"Yeah, just a minute," I say. But my voice sounds strained.

Great. Now my boyfriend thinks I'm pooping AND I have to blackmail Granny.

"Uh—okay, take your time. Only, Mia's computer crashed, so we're going to have to finish her homework on the laptop you were using." I hold my breath, not sure what to say.

I don't want Tyler to see those documents. But I also don't want it to look like I'm hiding anything. Because I'm not.

This is family business, right? Nothing to do with Tyler. I get to have my privacy. Right?

But I don't want Tyler to know I don't want him to see the documents. I can't explain why.

"Be right out," I say. Rubber ducks tumble to the floor as I stand up and turn on the faucet, pretending to wash my hands.

As I walk toward the kitchen, I can hear Mia sounding out words. "Ridd-ing. Ridding IN-Dus-tries?"

"Industries," Tyler corrects her, automatically. "Wait. Industries? Riding Industries?" Then he leans over and inspects the screen.

When I enter the room, he looks up from his laptop. For once, I can't read his eyes. Usually he's so expressive. Now it's like he's shut the door to his emotional vault, and I don't know how to pick the lock.

My mouth opens, but no words come out. A rush of cold sweeps through me, sharp and fast.

"Like I said, it's nothing. Just some old corporate paperwork. I don't know what my dad was talking about." The lie scratches at my throat as I say it.

"You don't know what your dad was talking about?" Tyler says, and his voice is low and harsh.

"I think I should go," I say. "I have to meet Micah. Go back to Granny's."

"Right," Tyler says, but he doesn't look up from the screen.

"Look, Tyler!" Mia says, pointing at the screen. "An X! You said we hardly ever see an X in the wild."

"That's right, Mia," Tyler says coldly. "That's an X. An X in Toxic."

My heart punches hard in my chest, and my body responds before my mind can catch up. I yank the flash drive from the laptop. My fingers coil around it, white-knuckled, making a fist I can't unclench.

"OK, Mia. You will have to work on your spelling by yourself. It's time I took Chloe home."

"Wait! You said Chloe was going to read us a bedtime story," Mia protests.

"The plan has changed," Tyler says, his voice gruff. He gives me an icy glare. "Let's go."

CHAPTER 41

TYLER

I'm a fair-minded guy. I can overlook a lot. It's not Chloe's fault that her family's company killed my dad and gave my mom cancer. It's clear she had nothing to do with Riding Industries or their dirty business practices.

Until now.

Now she's complicit.

Now she's hiding their dirty secrets for them.

Why would she keep what she saw on that flash drive a secret if she didn't want to protect her corrupt family?

I tear around the corner by Bleakers' Farm. I'm driving too fast, and I know it. The truck shakes and I hear a little gasp escape from Chloe. She clutches that big purse to her chest like it's a teddy bear, and I push away any soft feelings the tears in her eyes bring out in me. "Slow down," she whispers. "You're going too fast."

She's scared? Poor little Sweetie is scared? So what?

I've been scared for years.

Scared of losing my dad—and now my mom.

"Tyler," Chloe says, her voice faint. I ignore her. "Tyler!" she says again, forcefully. "Talk to me. What's wrong?"

"You know what's wrong," I say.

"I'm sorry I didn't tell you about those documents. I was just processing them, trying to figure out what they meant—honestly, I have never seen a lot of corporate materials before, I am kind of clueless—"

"Cut the bimbo act," I say. "You're smart. You knew exactly what they meant."

"It's not my fault my family did some bad stuff."

"But why would you lie to me about it?"

"I didn't lie, I—"

"You hid it!"

"Because it's none of your business!" Chloe shrieks.

"It's everyone's business," I say. "It's everyone's business if toxic chemicals are getting in the water. Because everyone drinks the water. That's the problem with you Sweeties. You only think about yourselves and how you're going to enjoy the next five minutes." My grip tightens on the steering wheel.

"That's not true, I—" Chloe tries to interject, but I'm on a roll, and I can't stop myself.

"You can fly your private jets, pump carbon into the atmosphere—so what? Climate change doesn't matter to you, because you've got flood insurance, a second house, and besides, who cares about the people left behind?"

"Tyler! Stop! You're not seeing me. You're seeing a picture that exists in your mind, like a cartoon, but it's not me—"

"Oh, I'm seeing you. I'm seeing you maybe for the first time." My heart slams against my ribs, the force of my blood roaring in my ears.

I should slow down, stop the truck—I know. It's not safe to drive when your anger is driving you. But I can't stop.

Chloe is crying now. "You don't understand. I was going to

tell you. I was just trying to figure it out on my own first. It's a lot to process. A lot of new information. I needed some time to—"

"To cover it up," I say. "I should have guessed. You may not have grown up here, but you're a Sweet Harbor girl, through and through. Sweet Harbor people will always protect each other—at all costs."

"I didn't think—"

"Of course you didn't," I say. "It's an instinct. Sweeties have an instinct for secrets and lies."

"That's not fair—"

"Face it, Chloe. You're a predator."

"I'm not a predator. I'm just trying to save my dad. Wouldn't you do the same?"

"Yeah? And who is your dad, Chloe? A nice little bunny rabbit? He's a liar and a thief—a predator, and so are you."

"Predator!" Chloe spits. "Says the guy who robbed a freakin' bank with me today? You're not better than me, Tyler. You just like to pretend to be. 'Oh, I braid my sisters' hair. I make spaghetti. I'm such a *good guy*, taking care of my mom who has cancer—'"

Chloe claps her hand over her mouth. She knows she's gone too far, bringing up my mom's sickness.

Something inside me jolts—sharp, electric—it's like a fuse, frying out. A darkness falls inside me, so deep I can barely see the road.

The best I can do is pull over and try to breathe.

I slow down, pull the car onto the shoulder of the highway, and flick on the emergency flashers.

"Are you kicking me out?" Chloe's voice sounds like she's far away, and it shakes with tears. "I'd understand if you want me to walk. If you never want to see me again."

I stare straight ahead, fingers still locked around the wheel. My jaw aches from clenching.

Chloe opens her door. "I'll show myself out."

I lean over her, forcing myself to keep my voice even, and pull her door shut again. When my arm brushes against her body, a tight, painful twist shoots through my chest. It won't be right for me to touch her ever again. But that doesn't mean I'd dump her on the side of the road.

"I can't let you out here. You're miles from anywhere. I'll bring you to meet Micah. That was the deal."

"You don't have to—"

I hold up one hand, silencing her, and pull back on to the road.

We drive in silence to the beach.

I park in a spot overlooking the water. The moon has been covered by clouds, though, so I can't see the ocean. All I can hear is the sound of the waves—a roaring void.

"We're early. Micah won't be here for an hour," I tell Chloe.

"You can just leave me here."

"No. I'll stay here until your ride gets here. Until you're safe."

"Please. Don't. It's better if I—I want to be alone," she says, and the jagged pain her voice makes me grit my teeth.

"Fine. Go and sit at that picnic table. I'll stay here in the truck until your friend comes," I say.

"Okay. Well. I guess this is goodbye?" Chloe says. But she doesn't make a move to leave.

"Guess so."

Her hand lingers on the door handle, and for a second I think she might stay—but then she pushes it open.

This time, when she goes to open the door, I don't stop her.

CHAPTER 42

CHLOE

J climb out of Tyler's truck for the last time. My body moves heavily, as if filled with lead.

I sit at the picnic table and listen to the soothing rush of surf. I try to remember that the ocean has known every kind of heartbreak: drowned lovers, shipwrecks at sea. It has swallowed worse pain than mine.

Water covers most of the world—so there's no reason for me to add more salt water to this earth. But there, alone on the picnic table, listening to the ocean in the dark, I let the tears come.

I stay like that, crying in the dark, for a long time. I don't hear Micah's Tesla pull up. So when I feel a hand on my shoulder, my heart jolts, flipping over like a coin tossed in the air.

Is it Tyler, making up with me?

No. It's just Micah, his handsome profile illuminated by the Tesla's headlights. I look past him to watch Tyler's taillights, glowing red in the darkness, as he turns the truck back on to the Shady Cove road.

When the truck disappears into the night, I scrub my teary, snotty face with the cuff of my shirt.

"Bad date?" Micah asks.

"The worst," I say.

"Me too," he sighs. "Come on. Let's go home and lie to our parents."

"You're so tense," Micah observes, as we drive back toward Harborview Drive. "Try to relax. Should I put the seat massagers on?"

He presses a button. I yelp. It feels like some very strong hands have reached up from below me and begun rubbing my butt. The sensation is so weird, I start to laugh. My giggles bubble up through my tears.

"Oh, is the shiatsu hitting a little low? Here. Let me set it to shoulders," Micah says, adjusting a setting on the touchscreen. "These seat massagers are an aftermarket customization. Only the best for my butt."

The steel shiatsu balls embedded in the leather seats slide up toward my neck and begin to knead. It does feel good. I lean back, let out a sigh.

"Better?" Micah asks.

"Do you have one of these for my heart? I need like... a feel-ings massage."

"How about this?" Micah presses another button, and Beethoven floods the vehicle.

The sound system is amazing; I feel like I'm inside a row of violins, each playing perfect, rippling chords. I close my eyes and feel the beautiful ache of the music.

"Classical is the best for breakups," Micah says. "Not that I would know. I've never been dumped before. Until now."

"You got dumped tonight, too?"

"Yup. Rajiv wanted to go public with our relationship, and I wasn't ready. He said he needs to date a, and I quote, an 'actual brave man.'"

"Oh, Micah," I say. "I'm sorry."

I hear the pain twisting through his words. "I tried to explain I *am* brave. Just strategic. Bravery isn't just about running into a fight you can't win. It's about assessing your options and defining a path to reach your target objective."

Target objective. Wasn't that what Riding Industries was doing? Being strategic—and secretive—in order to reach their target objective?

"But how do you know if it's worth it?" I ask. "Your target objective?"

"Hell if I know," Micah says.

He drives me back to Granny's. I can see her silhouette in the curtains. She's reading a paper newspaper, waiting up for me.

I unbuckle my seatbelt and start to say goodbye to Micah. I notice that his jaw is quivering a little. On instinct, I lean over and give him a hug. He hugs me back.

It feels nice, warm and comforting. His scent of Chanel soap, fizzy champagne and something earthy—like roots, growing in a riverbank—washes over me.

He strokes my hair, and I give in to the relief of shedding a few tears against his cashmere sweater. It feels good, like the massage for my feelings I was hoping for.

"Feeling better?" Micah asks, and I nod against his chest. "That's what they say," he says, brushing my hair out of my face, "laughter is the best medicine... if you're out of Valium."

I look up at him and smile. His dark eyes twinkle at me, and I feel a flicker of warmth—not romance, but human connection.

I like having a friend.

"We should at least pretend to make out," Micah says. "For your grandmother."

"For Granny," I repeat, and then I somehow manage to turn my head just in time, so his kiss merely grazes my cheek.

"Sorry," Micah says. "I thought maybe, since we're both single—"

"It's okay." I manage a shaky smile. "My brain's just… confused right now. I don't know—"

"No problem. Let's change the subject. Did I tell you about the haunted restaurant?"

"Oh! Right. With the ghosts. The ghosts who make people kiss. I forgot to ask." My heart's still racing, so I feel like my words come out fast and strange.

Did Micah really just try to kiss me? I don't have feelings for him —but there's something comforting about his presence.

Imagine a life where I could date Micah and be Granny's perfect little granddaughter. A life where I didn't have to black-mail anyone. Or run.

All I'd have to do is sit around and wait until I grew up and became another Granny: a perfect gray woman in a perfect gray house.

It would be like living as Sleeping Beauty. A princess in a castle, with servants at her beck and call, and everything she needs. But living life asleep.

Out of the corner of my eye, I watch the light in the living room flick on and off. I smile. That's Granny. She's signaling that it's time to come inside.

For some reason, that little flicker of light settles something in my chest. It's nice to know that someone is waiting up for me.

"Muddy boots," Granny says, approvingly, eyeing me up and down. "Looks like a good hike."

"It was," I lie.

I picture Nevaeh, tromping through mud puddles in these boots. Making my alibi with her tiny feet.

"What's wrong?" Granny says.

"Nothing. I'm just tired."

"I think I'll turn in too," Granny says. "I am far too old to be waiting up for a teenager."

But Granny isn't the only thing waiting for me. There's a letter. On my pillow.

The envelope is marked with an upside-down cross. All the letter says is: YOU HAVE ONE WEEK.

The window is open. Someone has been here. A Renegade.

My skin prickles. I can smell them—the scent of leather, gasoline, and B.O. lingers in the air. I run to the window, look out. The night is still, quiet. I close the window. Lock it. Lock my doors, too.

Not for the first time tonight, I wish Tyler were here.

CHAPTER 43

CHLOE

I've never blackmailed anyone before. I've seen it done. But never done it myself.

Plus, it's one thing to blackmail a stranger, like my dad does.

It's another thing to blackmail your own grandmother.

Maybe there's another solution, something other than blackmail? Maybe I could just ask Granny about these documents. Print them all out—she's practically allergic to screens—and who knows?

Maybe she'd volunteer to help Dad?

Fat chance.

I can picture her face, how the conversation would unfold. "What is this—blackmail lite?" she'd ask, her steely gray eyes piercing my soul. Then she'd throw her head back and laugh, daring me to go through with it.

I'm in a fog all day at school, my thoughts shuttling between my dad, the flash drive, and Tyler. My actual heart hurts. Like a physical pain. I keep checking my pulse in case I might die.

Under it all is this strange ache I can't shake — like I'm home-sick, but for a person. Tyler.

I'm in such a mood that I almost crash into The Sophies in the hall. They're standing in a row in the main hallway, fashion policing everyone's outfit as they file into school.

Sophie V. aims her phon camera on Addie. "I can see your bra strap," Sophie V. says.

Addie's green boat-necked top *has* slipped slightly off her shoulder. I can see a bit of her white bra strap peeking out.

"So?" Addie says, defiant.

"It doesn't match your top," Sophie E. says.

"Snip-snap!" Kyra barks, and Sophie C. zooms in with scis-sors. While Sophie V.'s films, Sophie C. snips Addie's bra straps, two quick snips.

Addie's mouth opens and closes. Her face turns deep red, a shade somewhere between Horrified Rose and Humiliated Ruby.

Addie needs a distraction. I've tripped waiters carrying full trays of pink daiquiris, pulled fire alarms, and set small fires in department-store dressing rooms.

I know how to orchestrate a distraction.

"Hey, Sophie!" I yell. I watch four honey-brown blowouts swivel on skinny pencil necks.

I shrug out of my tweed jacket and rip open my starched white button-down so hard the buttons pop off and fly in all directions.

"What?" I yell, sticking my chest out defiantly. "Y'all never see hand-knit lace bra before? La Perla?"

It feels like a hundred eyes and a thousand phones are watching me. My pulse is thundering, but under the panic, there's a flicker of satisfaction — like I can do more than just wait around for boys to break my heart or motorcycle gangs to kidnap me.

I can use the fact that I don't care about this stuck-up small town to actually *help* someone.

When I see Addie, making her escape around the corner, undetected by The Sophies, I smile and chalk this up as a win.

But fifteen minutes later, Addie and I are both sitting outside the principal's office. Someone texted the principal with a pic of my bra distraction stunt, and she pulled us both out of class—which wasn't fair.

"Sorry," I tell Addie. "I didn't mean to get you in trouble."

"It's okay," she says. "It was worth it, to see someone shock The Sophies into shutting up."

Behind us, Ms. Burberry, the school secretary, sniffles. She's Xeroxing flyers advertising her lost dog. It's a tiny terrier named Buster who wears a Burberry plaid sweater and a matching leash.

"He escaped on Thursday," Ms. Burberry says, when Addie asks. "He could be anywhere."

As Ms. Burberry blubbers into a Burberry plaid-patterned handkerchief, I remember something Granny said about the school secretary being a shirttail Burberry, a distant cousin of the famous fashion brand founder.

"Excuse me," Ms. Burberry sobs, and runs away, presumably to the bathroom, to cry.

With Ms. Burberry gone, Addie and I have an unobstructed view of the aquarium wall that divides the outer office from the principal's inner sanctum. Through the glass, we can see Principal Annan talking to a man with spiky blue hair.

An angelfish glides past.

"Who is that guy?" I ask. Parents and teachers at Sweet Harbor High all sport sleek, conservative hairdos.

"My dad," says a smooth, melodious voice. I glance over and see a tiny girl with long blue hair, the color of her eyes.

She pokes her head up from behind the far filing cabinet. I can't believe I didn't see her there. But looking at her now, I have the strangest feeling I've seen her before.

"What'd you do this time, Faye?" Addie asks.

Faye laughs. "Illegal wiretapping."

My jaw about hits the floor. Who is this girl?

She extends her hand to me, saying, "Ah, the dognapper. We meet at last." She smiles crookedly. There's something familiar about that grin, but I can't quite place her.

"Seriously, what did you do?" Addie asks, eyes sparkling with anticipation.

"Someone dyed the pool green," Faye says. "And the dye may have stained the swim team's hair, skin, and teeth."

"No way," Addie says.

"But they look like mermaids now!" Faye's eyes sparkle.

She reaches into her backpack and pulls out a brown paper lunch bag. Inside is a tuna fish sandwich.

As soon as the fish smell hits me, I remember where I've seen her before. The bus. She was on the bus to Sweet Harbor, the one that broke down. She stared at me in the oddest way.

The door opens. Principal Annan glares sternly at Faye. Faye grins, looks her in the eye, and takes a huge bite of her sandwich.

Her dad says, "Come with me, young lady," in an equally stern tone, and Faye waves us goodbye, still chewing.

"Chloe and Addie, I'll be with you in a moment," Principal Annan says. "Wait here."

"Faye's dad is kind of famous," Addie whispers as the blue-haired father and daughter leave. "He's very talented."

"Talented at what?"

"He's a fixer. A lawyer who finds unusual solutions for his clients. My mom told me all about him. Corporate espionage. Theft. Surveillance. Hostile takeovers. Blackmail."

My ears perk up. Maybe I'm not the only one facing moral gray zones today.

"He knows everything about everyone in Sweet Harbor," Addie says. "And so does Faye. In fact, she was asking me about you and Tyler."

"She was?"

Why would this random girl care about me and Tyler? Does she like him or something?

Addie shrugs. "She said she was following up some leads for her dad. Something about a lawsuit. Faye's harmless. But she can make a person feel a bit… watched."

"Strange," I say. "You'd think the Sophies would suck up to her if her dad has all kinds of strings he can pull."

"Faye's too weird for them," Addie says. "They can't stand it — she's like a walking defiance of their authority."

"I like that about her."

"Who doesn't?" Addie sighs. "I don't know how she does it, but Faye manages to seem like she doesn't care if she has friends or not."

"I've been a loner, like Faye, before," I say softly. "I never had friends till I came here. Trust me. It's better to have a friend."

I squeeze her hand, and she squeezes mine back. For the first time today, the pain above my sternum eases. Maybe I haven't lost everything.

I'M EXPECTING to get a big lecture in the principal's office. And I do.

What I'm not expecting is that the Sophies have filed Bullying Complaints against me—and Addie.

"What?" I say. "The Sophies *were* the bullies."

The principal's mouth is a hard line. "We take bullying very seriously at Sweet Harbor High. All bullying complaints are investigated by a student-faculty committee."

"Let me guess," I say. "The Sophies are all members of that committee?"

"Sophie Vuong, Sophie Edington, Sophie Cortez, and Kyra Cross are leaders at this school," Principal Annan says. "They're on many school committees. They do a lot of service work."

"Right. It's like how oil companies are always trying to infiltrate climate change organizations so they can take them over," Addie mumbles. I grin. She's sharp.

Principal Annan gives a stern look. "That's not a very Sweet attitude. Return to class. We will refer you for a disciplinary hearing."

"Sorry again," I tell Addie, as we head back to class. "I didn't mean to make life harder for you."

"It's okay," she says. "How's Tyler, anyway?"

"I think we broke up," I say. The words choke in my throat. Saying it out loud makes it real, like breaking a spell. My eyes sting, but I blink hard.

She gives me a hug. I'm not used to hugs. But I like them.

"I'm so sorry. Are you okay?"

"What does 'okay' mean?" I ask.

Addie laughs. "Do you need to talk?"

"I'm good," I say. If I actually open up to her, who knows what might come spilling out right now? Still, just knowing she's here… it's enough. For today.

"Okay. Well, if you change your mind, just let me know." She gives me one last hug.

So. That's what friends are for.

CHAPTER 44

TYLER

"Tyler? What are you doing?" My mom is standing in the kitchen doorway. She looks fragile in her night-gown and robe. Her bony toes stick out of the holes in her old bunny slippers.

"Tidying up," I say, putting away a plate.

"At three in the morning?"

"Couldn't sleep."

"What, have you got a case of Girl-Induced Insomnia?" she jokes, but her voice shreds into a cough, and she puts one hand on the doorframe, leaning on it for support. I wonder if she's too weak to stand.

"I'm fine, Tyler," she says, reaching into the pocket of her pink robe for a cough drop. Moms can always read your mind. "But clearly, you're not okay. What's going on with you? Did something happen with Chloe?"

"No," I lie. Part of me wants to explain everything to my mom.

But I don't want her to feel that burden. Or remember what Riding Industries did to our family.

Chloe. How could someone who made me feel so alive do something that feels so crushing? I wish we'd never met.

Chloe's choice to stay quiet about the documents throws all her other choices into relief. Everything makes sense now. It was easy for her to put me at risk breaking into that bank, for instance.

Clearly, the girl uses people and throws them away. She's just like all the other Ridings. All the other Sweeties. And I fell for it. I fell for her.

"Come on," my mom says. "Tell me."

"It's nothing," I say. "Just a case of the Sweetie Sickness."

Mom sighs. "Life isn't fair, I know it. But sometimes we have to let go of things that are beyond our control. Find some serenity."

"Serenity? That's what the Sweeties want. For us to be docile dupes. Sitting ducks."

"It doesn't do you any good to get upset—"

"Maybe I'd rather tell the truth than feel good," I say—or maybe I yell it, because my mom's face turns white. She steps backward, away from me, and staggers a little, grabbing the doorframe to steady herself.

I close my eyes, take a deep breath. Try counting to ten.

But with my eyes closed, all I can see is Chloe. Her long, soft hair. The dimple on her chin. The way her eyes glimmer when she lets down her guard, just an inch, and I can see the real her.

Chloe. She's colonized my mind, sent her Sweetie spores everywhere, multiplying until everything reminds me of her.

I have to get free of her.

"I'm sorry," I tell my mom. "I didn't mean to yell."

"Do you want a hug?"

"I'm fine."

"I'm your mom. Let me take care of you for once."

"But—"

"Please. For me."

She crosses the kitchen floor and wraps her arms around me. She gives the best hugs. Warm and caring. But I realize how fragile and thin she's gotten.

"Did you know I was friends with a Sweetie once, back when I was your age?" she asks.

"Friends?"

"More than friends. It was before I started dating your dad." Mom has never told me much about her life before she met my dad. I know her family was troubled.

"Is there a story?" I ask.

"Yes. There is. I got a job with a cleaning company. I was assigned with a four-person team to clean a mansion on Harborview Drive."

"Which one?" I ask, suddenly suspicious.

"Oh, I don't know. It looked like a castle, all gray stone and towers and turrets."

So not Chloe's grandma's house.

"Anyway, I used to sneak away and read books in the library. My boss, the head housekeeper, was easy to trick. She was always wearing headphones—she was one of those blue-haired folks, from the holler?"

My mom's side of the family all believes that there's this kin group of "hill people" living near the woods who can predict the future and things like that. I don't know about that, but I urge Mom to go on. She doesn't tell a lot of stories about her younger life.

"Anyway, you should have seen the library in this place. Big leather chairs, crackling fire, winter sunlight coming in through the lace curtains, and hundreds and hundreds of leather-bound volumes. They'd created this amazing oasis for reading. And I got to enjoy it. Sneakily. Then, one day, I was interrupted in the very middle of *Les Misérables*—"

"This is straight-up *Beauty and the Beast*," I tease.

Mom shrugs. "Maybe so. But to me, it all felt like a completely unique experience. I suppose young love always does feel that way."

"Love?"

"Or something like it."

"So, who was the guy?"

"Philippe Devereaux."

"A Devereaux? You dated a Devereaux?"

"For one summer," Mom says. "I got to see the world in a whole new way."

"A yacht way," I guess.

"That," she says. "But I also got to see *my* world in a whole new way. I saw what other possibilities are out there. And I saw what strengths we have here in Shady Cove, that they don't always have in Sweet Harbor. Things not even money can buy."

"Like what?"

"Loyal friendships, like the ones you've got. Creativity. A willingness to look the truths of life square in the face."

"So what happened with the guy? How come you didn't marry him?"

"Oh, his parents found out about us. They packed him off to military school, pronto. We wrote letters for a while. But then I started seeing your father."

For a second, I imagine her life if she'd married Philippe. Tennis at the country club. No health worries. Living in some stone castle by the sea.

What would that have been like? Would I have turned out to be the kind of guy Benny and Cy siphon gas from?

"Don't be so hard on Chloe, or on yourself," Mom says. "Young love is tough. But when you look back at your life, you'll realize—it's all really been a gift."

I hate when she says far-away-sounding things like that. It makes me feel like she thinks she's dying.

"Mom?"

"Mm-hm?"

"She's a Riding. Chloe. She's Chloe *Riding*," I say.

"Oh," Mom says. "That makes things complicated, doesn't it?" She smiles, ruffles my hair. "But I trust you. I know you'll figure it out. Have you talked to Benny? He always makes you feel better."

I MEET up with Benny in the shop. He brings a case of beers. He always has plenty. He lives above a bar and is buddies with the beer truck guy.

We drink in silence for a little while. Finally, I say, "Go ahead. Start in with the I told you so's. This is what happens when you get mixed up with a Sweetie, etc. etc."

"Nah," Benny says. He takes a swig of beer. "Do you love her?"

The word hits me like a slap. Love? Yeah. Yeah, I do. "Yep."

"So, what's the problem?"

"What do you mean, what's the problem? She's a Sweetie."

"Eh. Rules were made to be broken."

"You think?"

"Yeah."

"But she's more than just a Sweetie. She's a Riding. You know, Riding Industries, the ones who—"

"I know which ones. May their bodies become the marshmallows in the Devil's S'mores, toasting forever in the fires of hell."

"Yeah. Those ones. Therein lies the problem."

"She's just a kid, Tyler. Like you. She didn't make any of those decisions."

But she's making a decision now, I think. *She's keeping their ugly secrets.*

Still, I don't say anything to Benny. Not about this. It feels too real. I hedge a bit. "But in the future, you know how she'll turn out. Just like all the rest."

"You don't know that," Benny says. "Look at my cousin Addie. She started out as a Sweetie. Then her dad died. All the Sweeties turned on her like the status-seeking succubi they are. She got to see who they are, up close. Now she's awesome."

"Yeah," I say. "But it's a risk."

"Well," Benny says, finishing his beer. "Guess there's no law that says *everybody's* gotta live dangerously." He smirks and returns to his engine.

Okay. Maybe he's right.

Maybe I can live dangerously.

I TEXT CHLOE.

> Can we talk?

Yes. Please.

> Tomorrow night. Can you sneak out? I can pick you up.

My grandma goes to bed around 11. Is midnight ok?

> OK. Midnight.

CHAPTER 45

TYLER

I'm in the bathroom, fresh out of the shower, putting on aftershave and getting ready to meet up with Chloe when I hear it. *Thump.*

At first, I think it's nothing. The girls, playing.

I run a comb through my hair. I don't know what will happen with me and Chloe tonight, but I want to look and smell good.

But something about that *thump* makes me uneasy.

Maybe it's the fact that it's not followed by a succession of giggles, but by a grim silence.

I crack open the bathroom door, listening. Cold air rushes into the steamy room, giving me goosebumps. All is quiet. Not a whisper.

Something's wrong.

I reach for my robe. When I swing it over my shoulders, something bad happens. The robe flies out, knocking my phone from the sink into the toilet.

No. Not today.

Before I can fish it out, I hear something even worse than that thump.

It's my mom.

Calling for help. Her voice sounds weak and raspy.

SHE'S LYING on the floor of her bedroom, bleeding from a cut in her head. When I touch her forehead, her skin feels burning hot. "We've got to get you to the hospital," I say.

I pull the truck right up to the porch. Mia and Nevaeh and I help Mom down the steps. I drive slowly all the way to Sweet Harbor, careful to avoid all the familiar ruts and bumps in the gravel road.

The lights are so bright in the emergency room. The white tile floor shines like a mirror. My head hurts just being in here.

I get Mom and the girls settled in the waiting area. Then I make my way to the front desk. I wait for what feels like a century before a curly-haired woman finally looks up from her computer and says, "Next?"

I give my best My Mom Has Cancer smile and try to explain. The woman at the desk barely looks up.

"Insurance card?" she says.

I pull my mom's card out of my wallet. I carry a copy, and so does she. The woman scans the card through a machine.

It gives a horrible beep.

The kind of beep you hear on a game show before a trapdoor opens and swallows up the unlucky contestant.

"We don't take this insurance."

"Are you sure? All my mom's doctors are here."

"We just renewed our contracts. We don't take this anymore."

"What am I supposed to do? My mom has cancer. And she has a fever. The doctor said to come in right away if—"

"Take her to Shady General," the woman says.

I'm nearly denting this hospital counter with my fingertips, I'm gripping it so hard. "You don't understand," I say.

But the receptionist looks past me toward a goofy-looking blonde kid. He has blood on his face and his head is stuck in a lacrosse racquet. The kid's mom is staring into her phone, videoing herself applying lipstick.

She's making a TikTok.

"Next?" the receptionist calls, and Lip Gloss Mom almost knocks me over, lunging forward with her injured kid.

It's no use arguing. This is Sweet Harbor. The hospital staff will never listen to us.

I go out and get the truck. Pull it right up to the entrance.

"Hey! You can't park here! This is the ambulance zone," an EMT shouts.

"Just a sec," I say. I run into the hospital.

"Come on, we gotta go," I tell the girls. Mom is drowsing on Mia's shoulder.

"But Mom's sleeping," Mia protests.

"I'll carry her," I say.

Mom's body is light. She's grown way too thin this year. Her breath is hot against my neck, and panic claws at my chest, but I force my hands to stay steady. She doesn't wake up, not even when I settle her in the cab of the truck.

We drive to Shady General as fast as I can go.

CHAPTER 46

CHLOE

*W*hat do you wear to sneak out of the house to win back your secret ex-boyfriend? Gucci?

I flip through the clothes hanging in my closet. I've built up an impressive wardrobe in the short time I've been here, courtesy of Granny and Madame Defarge.

But nothing feels right. Nothing is what I want. Because the only thing I want is Tyler.

I tie bedsheets together to make a rope. Doing something with my hands helps me think.

Is there a way I can blackmail Granny without her knowing *I'm* the one doing it? I don't want her to feel betrayed.

But I *would* be betraying her, wouldn't I?

The whole thing just makes me feel so sad and scared and tired. And underneath it, a horrible whisper: maybe Tyler's right about me. Maybe I'm just another Riding, hurting everyone who tries to love me.

Even Addie. I don't even want to think about that disciplinary hearing tomorrow. Why did I have to drag her down with me?

I anchor my bedsheet rope to my bedframe. I toss the white sheet-rope out the window. It's a dark night, but the moon shines brightly.

I tug on the rope, testing it with my hands, and pray it takes my weight. Then I'm out the window, clinging to the rope, slithering to the ground.

I jog down the lane as fast as I can in my lucky Louboutins. My breath fogs in the cold air as I climb over the gate and stake out my spot on the edge of Harborview Drive.

Fast forward ten fingernails (chewed to the nubs), five unreturned texts (three to Tyler, and two to Jessa and Addie), and about twelve owl-induced jump scares, and I'm still here.

I've been waiting in the dark by the side of the road for an hour.

I've texted Tyler three times.

Crickets.

Is this his game? Is he punishing me, or was I just stupid to hope?

Headlights flare down the road. They're pitched about the same height as Tyler's truck.

My heart races as my throat fills with all the words I want to say to him: *how dare you! I hate you, I love you, please forgive me.*

As the headlights approach, I step out of their glare and shield my eyes. The vehicle slows. I realize it's not Tyler's pickup; it's a furnace repair van. It pulls to a stop near me and the passenger's side window slides down.

"Can I help you, miss?" the driver asks.

"No. I just thought you were someone else," I say, and foolish shame bubbles up, hot and itchy under my skin. The shame is tinged with fear, too. I know it's motorcycle guys who are after me. But the last time I was kidnapped, it was in an ordinary-looking utility vehicle like this one.

"Well, stay clear of the road. You're liable to get hit. You're wearing dark colors," the driver says, then peels off.

I text Tyler again. *Where are you? Are you just messing with my head? Text me back. Last chance.*

Suddenly, I'm cold all over. How did I end up here, freezing in the dark, waiting for a boy who doesn't even want me?

When I hear the sounds of motorcycles barreling down the road toward me, I creep back and hide in the trees, the way I did my first night in Sweet Harbor, and watch the motorcycles approach.

CHAPTER 47

TYLER

*T*he brightness at Sweet Harbor Hospital made my head hurt.

But the darkness at Shady General is much worse. The dull lights flicker in a crowded waiting room. Muddy footprints criss-cross the floor, along with dead leaves and splatters of blood. It's like no one bothers to sweep or mop.

We wait and wait in the emergency room. It feels like there are always at least three babies crying, four people with hacking coughs, and someone throwing up. The sour reek of vomit curls in the air, mixing with the sharp tang of antiseptic.

Mom sleeps against my shoulder. Nevaeh sits on my lap. She's sleeping, too.

I feel bad for Mia. She's old enough to know that this situation is not okay. That Mom needs help. That it might not come in time.

"You all right, Mia?" I ask.

"Can I use your phone?" she says. "I want to play a game."

I reach for it in my pocket. Then I remember where my phone is: soaking in the toilet at home. "Sorry, Mia. I forgot it."

For a second, her lips tremble. But she gives me a defiant smile. "That's okay. I will just imagine something. Like an imaginary friend."

Mia grits her teeth. I can tell how hard she's trying to pretend. When she opens her eyes again, she's standing on tiptoe. She tiptoes around the waiting room.

At one point, she gives an elaborate curtsy and I hear her mumble, "Thank you. My friend Chloe gave me these high heels."

Chloe. Oh no. A jolt of panic shoots through me, cutting through the exhaustion. CHLOE.

She's waiting for me right now. Out there alone in the dark.

I hope she's okay.

She's going to be mad at me—she has every right to be—but for now, my major worry is her safety.

I haven't seen the mafia guys she's worried about, but that doesn't mean she's wrong to be scared. Everyone acts like Sweet Harbor is in some circle of protection because it's posh. Like bad things can't happen to rich people.

But bad things DO happen. They just get covered up.

I don't like the idea of Chloe hanging out by the road at night. Even something simple—an inattentive driver, or a stupid prank by the Sophies—could hurt her.

And it would be my fault.

I need to get to a phone. Call Benny, someone. Send them to check on Chloe.

But my mom is sleeping on my shoulder. Nevaeh is sleeping in my lap. And Mia is curtsying to a bleeding man, a man with a knife sticking out of his hand.

The waiting room blurs for a second, my own anxiety making it all shimmer like asphalt on a hot day—how am I supposed to hold this all together?

"Coralee! You're up next." The nurse's voice is gruff, but I wake my mom up.

As we shuffle in to see the doctor, a heavy weight sinks in my stomach.

I've been here before, with my dad. I know what can happen. And I know what bad news might come next.

CHAPTER 48

CHLOE

*P*ine boughs tickle my face. I hold my breath until the motorcycle passes. I give a sigh of relief and take a deep breath of fresh, pine-scented air.

But then I see another lone headlight cresting the hill. I retreat deeper into the trees.

One by one, motorcycles roar past. Their headlights carve paths through the darkness. Their growling exhaust makes my ears ring.

When the last motorcycle passes, silence returns. My body sags with exhaustion, but inside, I'm tight as a wire. Then, in the darkness, I hear living things stirring—creaking pine boughs, a dog barking in the distance, the blood in my veins pounding in my ears.

WHERE'S TYLER?

I'm about to return to the house when I see a set of familiar-looking, almond-shaped headlights coming toward me. The lights grow brighter and brighter as the car glides silently over the road.

The black Tesla slows to a stop. The driver rolls the window down.

"Micah!" I say. "I'm so glad you're here."

"What are you doing hanging around with a bunch of trees?" he asks as I let myself into the car.

Luxury cars have such a safe, sturdy feel. When the door shuts, I feel protected from everything. For a second, I want to sink into that safety and never come back up.

That's what money does. It keeps you safe.

"I was waiting for Tyler," I confess. "But he didn't show. What are you doing here? I thought you were at a swim meet."

"I was," he says. "But I'm back now. I was driving by to see if you were still up. I'm having a French fry attack. Want to hit a drive-through?"

"Sure," I say, my voice small, shaky, disappointment still swirling in my chest.

"I'm sorry about Tyler," Micah says.

"Yeah. Let's just go."

"Do you want to talk about it?"

"No!"

Micah laughs. "Good. Because I have something for you."

"What is it?"

"Gossip," he purrs.

"Knowledge is power."

"And power is the greatest aphrodisiac. Okay. So, I was in the principal's office dropping off a donation from my grandmother, when I may have seen an email. From Kyra Cross's mom. To Principal Annan."

"Ooh, this *is* gossip. I like it."

"I can tell. You're drinking it up like a vampire drinks blood."

I punch him in the arm and he pretends to veer off the road.

"Apparently, Kyra has a big-time modeling audition. With Pardone," he announces.

"How did she get that? She's too short. Aren't Pardone People all over six feet?"

"Maybe she's getting leg injections."

I snort. "More like Pardone is getting a cash infusion from the Cross family."

Micah laughs, and instead of slapping his thigh, like people sometimes do when they laugh, he plants his hand, warm and firm, on my knee.

My stomach flips—not the good kind of flip. The kind of flip that feels like when you're drinking something fizzy, and it goes down the wrong pipe.

"What's up?" Micah says, stroking my knee and sensing my uncertainty.

"Nothing," I lie. "I'm just hungry. Are we almost there?"

CHAPTER 49

TYLER

*E*ven if the hospital is dingy, the doctor seems to know what she's doing. She moves fast, scolding the nurse for making Mom wait, getting her in bed, hooking up an IV of antibiotics.

"We're going to take good care of her," the doctor says. "I think the best thing now is for you kids to go home and get some rest."

"I'll be fine," Mom says. Her voice is weak. She smiles faintly. "Take the girls home."

I can't stand to watch the girls say goodbye to Mom. Instead, I stare out the third-floor window, looking down into the tops of some scraggy trees.

The moon shines on a concrete parking ramp. Far in the distance, I spot a faint pink-orange glow.

I wonder where it's coming from. The light over the sewage treatment plant? No, that's to the north.

I squint, focusing all my attention on figuring it out, concentrating hard so I don't hear Mia crying.

The Shady-Sweet Drive-In must be the source of the light. It's a big, lit-up fast-food joint. Dad used to take us there.

There's a Ferris wheel, waiters on roller skates, and the best french fries I've ever had in my life. It's so good even the Sweeties can't pretend they're above it.

Once, I saw a waiter skate out with a huge tray full of what must have been two dozen hamburgers, each in a white paper wrapper. The waiter tossed them, one by one, into the open sunroof of a limousine. It looked like the car itself was gobbling them up.

"Look," I said, "the limo's eating lunch." My dad threw his head back and laughed. Then he threw a handful of french fries into the limo's sunroof and we ran away, laughing and laughing —until his laughs turned to coughs. That was my dad.

Now it's my mom's turn to cough. The sound cuts right through me.

When the spasms stop, the doctor says, "All right, kids. Your mom's gonna be okay. Time to say goodnight. Go home and get some sleep."

The girls climb off Mom's bed. They're trying to be brave, choking back sobs. I give Mom a quick kiss, my chest tight. I don't say much. The words are sticking in my throat.

I hurry the girls out of the room. I want to rip the Band-Aid off. If I stay a second longer, I won't be able to keep it together.

I carry Nevaeh because she walks too slowly. But Mia keeps dawdling. "Come on," I say.

"I can't walk fast, I'm wearing heels," she says, pretending, walking on tiptoes down the hall.

I bite my lip — it's not her fault, none of this is — and keep my mouth shut.

"I'm hungry," Mia says when we get in the truck. "Can we go get some food?"

For one second, I almost say no. Almost tell her we have to just go home. But Mia's little voice cracks that wall right open.

So I rummage in the glove box. I try to keep some emergency funds tucked away in there. And if being hungry and sad isn't an emergency, what is?

"All right," I say. "Special treat. We're going to Shady Sweet Drive-In."

"Yeah!" Mia cheers. Nevaeh grins her gap-tooth grin. I put on a fake smile and get onto the highway.

As I drive, the pink-orange glow grows closer. For a moment, just a flicker, it almost feels like heading toward something good.

But under it all, Chloe's still there in my mind — waiting on that dark road, wondering why I didn't come. My chest tightens. I'll fix it, somehow. Not right now. But soon.

CHAPTER 50

CHLOE

*W*e drive along the coast road toward Shady Cove. It's a route I've only ever taken with Tyler. Tears sting my eyes. I wipe them away, pretending like I'm fixing my bangs.

"Where are we going?" I ask. I keep my voice light. Micah's hand is steady on my knee.

I don't know how I feel about that.

Well. I do. I wish it were Tyler's hand.

My heart is breaking, and I hate that I'm so desperate for human contact.

I hate this clawing, choking need rising up in me.

I was fine before I came to Sweet Harbor. Fine before I met Tyler. Fine.

And now I'm broken.

"We're going to the Shady Sweet Drive-In," Micah says, "it's a local institution."

"A drive-in," I say, trying to steady my voice, trying to make my words come out normal. "Do people on roller skates feed you in your car?"

"Exactly," Micah says. "Plus, it's great people-watching. It's like worlds colliding. Sweet Harbor meets Shady Cove at the drive-in."

A horrible thought occurs to me. What if Tyler's there right now — and not alone?

My mind flashes to girls — Shady High girls, girls with drugstore eyeliner and easy laughs. Girls whose worst secret is a hidden vape pen. Girls who wouldn't wreck everything they touch.

As we reach the crest of the ridge, I see the drive-in glowing like a neon carnival.

Is Tyler somewhere down there, in the glare?

As we descend the hill, I can barely breathe. It feels like there's something stuck in my throat. I don't know how I'm going to choke down hamburgers.

At the drive-in, LED signs flash:

THE ORIGINAL SWEETBURGER!

TRY OUR DREAMSICLE PICKLES!

SWEET & SHADY SHAKES—SERVED ON SKATES!

It's past midnight, but the Shady Sweet is bright as daylight and still hopping.

I've never seen anything like this place. For a moment, wonderment takes some of the sting out of my pain. Rusted-out Crown Victorias idle next to Lamborghinis; semi trucks park beside Mercedes SUVs.

Carhops bring trays loaded with fried fluffer-nutter sandwiches, milkshakes, and whoopie pies out to beat-up Hondas and gleaming BMWs.

Hands — some rough, some manicured — reach from windows to grab juicy burgers and crispy onion rings.

As I scan the scene, my eyes widen at the sight of a pack of motorcycles parked next to an Audi convertible.

Could it be the Renegades? My chest clamps tight — but I exhale when I see the riders: plump senior citizens in leather, licking giant ice cream cones.

Micah pulls the Tesla into a slot next to a muddy Ford pickup. "Ready?" he asks. He presses a button, and the sunroof slides open. He climbs up through it and sits on the roof.

I squirm up after him and perch on the roof. Despite myself, my mouth tips into a crooked smile. "This place is nuts," I say.

From on top of the car, I can see dozens of roller-skating carhops zipping back and forth in bright uniforms.

As I watch, a carhop leaps into the air with a tray stacked with banana splits, spins in mid-air — a double axel, maybe? — and lands without dropping a thing.

"Wow," I say.

"Welcome to the Deep-Fried Olympics," Micah says.

Soon, a carhop skates up with menus, and before long, we're munching the best sweet potato fries I've ever had — sweet, salty, crisp.

"This is exactly the right place to take me," I tell Micah. "There's so much to see. So much life."

"I thought it would distract you from your sadness," he says. "And me from mine."

"Rajiv still isn't talking to you?" I ask.

"No. But maybe that's okay. You know, you have really beautiful lips."

"Not as beautiful as Rajiv's," I tease, but my voice comes out like a squeak.

"Different from Rajiv's," he says. His gaze holds mine. "And beautiful too."

Micah leans in for a kiss, and this time I'm too slow to react. His lips meet mine.

My heart sinks. It's not relief, or comfort, or anything close to right. He tastes like French fries, and all I can think is: wrong, wrong, wrong.

I push him away.

"Chloe! Who are you kissing?"

A high, squeaky voice cuts through everything.

Mia, Tyler's sister, is standing in front of the Tesla, holding a wad of pink cotton candy the size of her head.

"Um, hi, Mia," I say. My mind spins. What is Mia doing here? Is Tyler here, too?

A carhop whizzes past on skates, carrying a trayful of burgers. Then, in the pink-orange glow, I see him.

Tyler, carrying Nevaeh in his arms.

Seeing him is like being struck by lightning. My skin hums, my throat tightens, my heart thunders.

For a second, I feel guilty, being here with Micah.

Then I'm furious.

Tyler ditched me tonight. He left me standing on the side of the road. I have every right to be here, with whomever I want.

But none of that comes out when I say, stiffly, "Hello, Tyler."

Beside me, Micah lets out a low whistle. Somehow the whistle says both "Oops — you're busted, Chloe" and "Wow. He's hot."

"Nevaeh had to go to the bathroom," Mia says. "We're parked over there. You should come with us! We're tailgating."

I study Tyler's face. Cold. Stoic. Unreadable.

But as I watch, his jaw tightens. His eyes flick to Micah, then away. There it is — the crack in the ice. And it slices me open.

"Who's your kissing friend?" Mia says.

"What?" Tyler and I speak at the same time.

"Your friend. Who you were kissing. What's his name?"

Micah waves at Mia and smiles. "I'm Micah."

My whole body aches watching Tyler's eyes narrow.

"Micah, why were you kissing Chloe? She's Tyler's girlfriend," Mia says.

"Let's go, Mia," Tyler says, voice rough.

"But I want to talk to Chloe—"

"Come on." Tyler puts a hand on her shoulder.

I watch them walk away. I wait for Tyler to look back. To give me anything. He doesn't.

"Well, look at it this way," Micah says. "At least we made him jealous."

"I need to go home," I say. My voice cracks on the last word. "Please take me home."

I slip down through the sunroof. The leather seat creaks beneath me as I settle in.

"Chloe," Micah calls through the sunroof. "Come back up. Don't you want a sundae? The night is young."

I talk to Micah's knees. "No. Take me home. Please."

I can't be here anymore.

I can't be out in the world like this.

I need to be under the covers, at home, hiding, safe, where I can't hurt anyone.

Because I ruin everything that means anything to me.

CHAPTER 51

CHLOE

At school, I sit down at our lunch table with Jessa and Micah, maybe for one of the last times. The disciplinary hearing is coming up soon.

What if I'm expelled? Will Granny kick me out?

I guess it won't matter if the Renegades get to me first. I've got to figure out what to do about this blackmail thing.

I keep dragging my feet because deep down, I don't want to do it. I like Granny.

Why do I have to hurt her to save myself? To save my dad?

Not to mention, this whole thing has already destroyed my relationship with Tyler. My eyes are burning from staying up all night, crying. I've used up about half a bottle of Visine already, just trying to look normal for school.

"So, Chloe and I kissed last night," Micah tells Jessa, who gasps.

"You guys would legit be cute together," she says.

"Well, we are both very cute apart," he says.

"Exactly," Jessa says.

"But Chloe likes someone else. And I do, too. That's the horrible thing about falling in love. You can't exchange people like they're, I don't know, cashmere sweaters," Micah sighs.

"That's the tragedy of the human condition," Jessa says.

"Yes. Alas. Our mortal coil."

"At least there's cashmere," Jessa jokes.

Hearing their voices, I feel underwater, drowning.

All I can think about is Tyler. What he might be thinking. What he might be feeling. And why he won't text me back.

Last night, I messaged him. I tried to explain that nothing had happened between me and Micah. Just a kiss that tasted like root vegetables and hot oil.

But he never replied.

"... don't you agree, Chloe?" Jessa asks.

"Huh?" I haven't been following anything she's saying. Then, across the cafeteria, I see a flash of blue hair.

It's that girl, Faye Frost, whose dad is the fixer. I wonder if he's kind of like my dad. What's the difference between a fixer and a con artist, anyway? If anyone in this cafeteria knows how to blackmail someone, it's her.

I jump out of my seat and hurry over. "Hey!" I say.

Faye's eyes twinkle at me above another tuna fish sandwich. She must really like them.

"Can I sit here?" I ask. She's all alone at the huge cafeteria table.

She nods, and I sit. "Okay," I say. "This is kind of sensitive. But... I heard your dad has experience with blackmail. Maybe you know someone I could hire to help? For a cut?"

Faye chews, swallows. "Okay," she says. "I can't help you. But I know someone who can." She pulls a pen from behind her ear and scribbles on her brown paper lunch bag.

It's an address: 4859 Shady Road, Room 311.

My heart skips a beat. 311. That was the safe deposit box

number, too. It feels like a sign. But it must be a coincidence. Right?

"What's this?" I say.

"Go there, and you'll find what you need."

"Who should I talk to?"

"Just go. Get up and go right now."

"Really?"

"Really. Trust me. There isn't a thing that goes on in Sweet Harbor or Shady Cove that my dad doesn't know about."

I narrow my eyes. "Why would you help me? You don't even know me."

Faye smiles, sharp and knowing. "Oh, but you're interesting, Chloe Riding. You and Tyler."

I bristle. "What do you know about him?"

Faye shrugs, like it's obvious. "I watch. People talk. The Sophies can't shut up about you. And my dad — well, he listens for a living. He's been watching your family a long time. Watching the fallout from Riding Industries."

"Fallout?"

"A lot of people have gotten hurt." Faye leans forward, as if she's about to ask me question.

Before she can speak, something smacks into my back. I turn —and find myself face to face with the hard edge of a Gucci satchel.

"Excuse me," Sophie V. says in a pinched little voice. Behind her, a line of Sophies and their sycophants snicker. It's obvious she hit me with her bag on purpose. As they laugh, I notice their lips are extra plump, like they just shot them up with the filler injections from the school restroom.

When the Sophies move on to torment girls at another table, I study the address Faye has scribbled on the brown paper lunch bag. "So, ah, thanks for this," I say.

Faye smirks. "The Sophies hate you. Which makes you easy to like."

"You and me. We think alike," I say.

"The enemy of my enemy," she sings, taking another bite of her sandwich.

"Okay. Well, thanks."

"Chloe?" she calls as I leave. "Just remember. You may be an heiress. But you're a different kind of heiress."

"What do you mean?"

"You'll figure it out," she says mysteriously. There's a bit of tuna fish on her chin.

SHADY ROAD IS A NARROW, potholed track. Once upon a time, it must have been shaded by trees.

Now all that's left are big, round stumps.

I accelerate past them, and despite everything, I can't help noticing the Tesla is fun to drive.

In fact, I'm so accelerator-happy, I streak past 4859 Shady and hit 5000: a sad-looking Walmart. I turn around, scoping for a driveway, an apartment complex, something.

But there's nothing. Just an old brick hospital and a concrete parking ramp.

Is this it? Why would Faye send me here? Is this where her dad works? I'd pictured a more discreet, luxurious office.

My hands tighten on the wheel. This is probably a mistake. Who trusts a weird blue-haired girl who eats fish on a bus?

But it's the only lead I've got.

I park in the ramp. Walking to the hospital, I breathe in that familiar, sketchy parking ramp smell — wet concrete, stale pee, and no-one-can-hear-you scream.

A light flickers at the main entrance. An ancient receptionist dozes behind a tiny desk.

"Excuse me?" I say.

"Yes?" she rasps, eyes fluttering open.

"I'm looking for room 311."

She raises a bony finger toward the elevator. "Third floor," she whispers, eyes already drooping shut.

The elevator shudders between floors. What kind of hospital is this?

Before I can panic, it lurches back to life with a groan, and takes me to the third floor.

Room 311. It must be an office, I think, passing the patients' rooms. 306, 307, 308, 309, 310, 311.

Here it is. Another patient's room. I can see a bed, the shape of feet under the blanket.

I hesitate. Maybe this is a setup. Maybe Faye's dad has been watching me for the Renegades. Maybe this was all a test — maybe there will be some motorcycle monster waiting for me in the hospital bed, the way the Big Bad Wolf climbed into Granny's bed and waited for her.

"Get out of the way!" An orderly pushing a cart of dirty laundry slams into me, sending me stumbling into the room.

And that's when I see who's lying in the hospital bed.

It's Tyler's mom.

CHAPTER 52

 hloe

TYLER'S MOM'S eyes are closed, and her blue headscarf has slipped on her head, so I can see the veins racing over her pale scalp. She looks different than the warm, lively woman I met in the kitchen. But it's her, definitely.

The heart monitor beeps. The sound pulls me back into the room where death looms.

Tyler's mom sleeps. I don't know what to do. I don't know how I can help her, or anyone.

I slip the medical chart from the holder at the foot of the bed. Quietly, I open the folder and skim through it. I can't understand all of the jargon, but I know what I'm seeing isn't good.

I read about Tyler's mom's long journey. Cancer. Surgery. Chemotherapy. Immune suppression. Infection.

She's been dealing with this for years. Since Tyler was in sixth grade. I picture him at twelve, trying to help baby Nevaeh, toddler Mia. Trying to hold up a house already caving in.

I keep reading, searching for reasons to hope.

And then I stumble across a sentence that hits me harder than anything ever has—harder than when Tyler said goodbye. Harder than when my dad left me in a hotel with a note.

Patient's disease is likely resulting from second-hand exposure to toxic industrial chemicals. Patient reports her husband died of same illness following repeated workplace exposure. Patient's insurance coverage provided via settlement with Riding Industries. Reduced benefits led to patient's transfer from Sweet Harbor Hospital to Shady General.

Riding Industries.

My family is responsible for Coralee's cancer. For Tyler's dad's death.

The house I live in. The tailored jacket I'm wearing. Helga's salary. Granny's pearl-gray manicure.

Tyler's dad paid for it—with his life.

I swallow, trying to think. Trying to understand and process all of this information. It suddenly makes sense why Faye Frost sent me here.

No doubt her dad is monitoring Tyler's moms case—*because he's compiling information on Riding Industries.*

Maybe he's already doing my blackmailing for me. Or building a case for a competitor to exploit.

There's a faint stir—like paper rustling—and I hear Tyler's mom whisper.

"Water," she murmurs.

I rub the tears from my eyes. There's a plastic mug with a straw on the bedside table. I bring the straw to her lips. She takes a sip and sinks back into the pillows.

My hands tremble. I have no right to be here. No right to stand in this room. Because my family has done its best to kill this woman.

I press the nurse call button and hurry, through a fog of tears, into the parking ramp.

The cold air slams into me. A crushing weight settles on my chest. I can't breathe. I only know I need to get away. To run far from the guilt, the pain, the suffering. From the love.

In the parking ramp, I step into the elevator. Footsteps echo behind me, just as the doors begin to close. A man slips in, and I barely glance up, too busy wiping my eyes.

But then I see it.

The upside-down cross gleaming on the front of his leather vest.

I force a shaky laugh. "This place has the worst elevators," I manage, smiling through clenched teeth. "This is the second time I've gotten stuck today."

The man smiles, dazzling white teeth against spiky white hair.

"Hi, I'm Bob," he says, holding out his hand.

Confused, I shake it.

His grip tightens, iron on my fingers. "Hello, Chloe. Orphan children are the easiest to catch. They're always hoping to belong to someone."

He spins me, pins my arms behind me, and cinches my wrists with plastic zip ties. I try to headbutt him, but he slams the control panel, and the elevator jolts upward. I crash to the floor.

When the doors open, all I can see are boots—black, shiny motorcycle boots. I count six—three pairs—before I'm hauled to my feet.

"Ow!" I yell.

"Pipe down," Bob snaps. He yanks me up by my ponytail. "Shut up, or I'll bash your face into the wall."

"She's got nice teeth," one of the men says, twirling a toothpick between his lips. "I'd hate to see them fall out on the ground."

"You're with the Renegades now, kid," says a third guy. There's a reddish stain on his white beard. I tell myself it's pizza. I pray it's pizza.

Pizza Stain pulls my flip phone from my pocket, snorts, and

snaps it in two. "You don't know how lucky you are. You're just an ordinary girl. And we're about to turn you into money."

"Ransom money," the heavyset one with the nose ring says.

"Walking debt," Bob says. "Human cash."

"Where are you taking me?"

"Motorcycle parking," Toothpick Guy smirks, spit flashing between his teeth.

I square my shoulders. *Think, Chloe. Think. Stall.* "You're kidnapping me on a motorcycle? How's that going to work?"

"We're not kidnapping you. You're coming with us willingly. Because if you don't, your dad gets it." Bob draws a finger across his throat.

"Okay," I say, swallowing hard. "Prove it. Show me you have him. I want to FaceTime."

"You're not really in a position to negotiate, little girl," Tooth-pick Guy says.

I scan the lot. Fire extinguisher? Car mirror? Anything to kick or grab—nothing. Empty concrete and painted lines.

I know the rule: never go to the second location.

But they drag me anyway.

We reach a dark corner of the lot. My heart thuds as I spot a blue-glitter sidecar bolted to a hulking Harley.

"A sidecar?" I blurt. "You're going to kidnap me in a sidecar?"

"Shut up," Nose Ring snarls. He slams a motorcycle helmet over my head, jams the visor down, and crams me into the sidecar.

The engine roars, the world jerks, and we're off.

Every bump and pothole rattles through my body. If I die—if they kill me—Riding Industries' secret might die with me.

And Tyler will never know I'm sorry.

Or that I loved him—despite always screwing everything up.

We tear down the highway. I think of Granny. Will she ask Helga where I am? Will she call the school, the police? Or will she assume I'm just like her sons—that I ran off, disappeared?

Well. If they kill me, at least I'll miss the disciplinary hearing with the Sophies. I laugh bitterly inside my helmet, and even that slight movement of my chest makes my ribs feel like they're splitting apart. My heart aches.

The bikes slow, crunching over gravel.

They flip up my visor, and I blink into the glare.

A cabin. Ramshackle, splintered, its roof sagging under tufts of grass. Behind it, a maple forest burns with autumn reds.

I think to scream.

But who would hear me?

Nose Ring shoves me toward the door.

Inside, light slants through a hole in the roof, illuminating a chair, a table, a glass of milk—and my dad.

CHAPTER 53

CHLOE

*M*y dad.

He's here.

He's here, and he's dunking Oreos in milk.

"Chloe!" he says, brushing crumbs off his hands. "You made it!" He stands up and bows. "My apologies. This place is hardly the Four Seasons Hotel."

"Dad? What's going on?" I ask. *I'm not sure whether to hug him, or cry into the collar of his crumpled suit, or attack one of the motorcycle guys to help us escape.*

"Oh, it's a simple matter of Yankee Swap," Dad says breezily. "Bob?"

Bob snaps open a switchblade. Even in the shadowy light, the knife has a lurid glare.

"No! Stop!" I yell as he approaches my dad.

The Renegades all laugh.

Because Bob isn't about to stab my dad. He's about to free him.

He slices through the zip-ties at Dad's ankle. Dad kicks his leg free and says, "Cheerio, chaps," in his poshest British accent.

He brushes off his gray bespoke suit and gives me a quick peck on the cheek. "See you soon, darling."

Then he walks out into the green field and leaves me to my fate.

Through the open doorway, I watch him vanish. His figure gets smaller and smaller until he reaches the road. Then he turns and disappears.

"Awww. Parting is such sweet sorrow," Toothpick Guy coos.

"Get her ankle," Nose Ring says.

Pizza Beard drags me to the chair where my dad was sitting.

Bits of Dad's Oreo cookie float in the milk, staining the liquid gray.

When Pizza Beard bends down to secure my ankle, I kick him in the head.

He yanks my hair, slamming my face onto the table. Blood trickles from my nose. That doesn't make me less cautious. It just makes me more angry.

"What are you idiots doing?" I shout. "You just had my dad. He's the one you want. He's the one who racked up debt. I can't do anything for you."

Toothpick laughs. "I thought your dad said you were a smart girl. You think your little old granny would've paid a ransom for your loser dad?"

Bob laughs. "Nah. Your Granny ain't shelling out for your pops. She knows he's a two-time con artist. But you. You're just a kid. Granny Moneybags will pay anything for you."

A sick, crawling feeling climbs up from my gut.

My dad traded me for his freedom.

"Aw, sugar," Nose Ring says, leaning in close. He smells like sardines. "It was business. Your dad cut a deal with us. If we let him go, he promised he'd lead us straight to you in Sweet Harbor, and we'd split the ransom money with him."

Pizza Beard sucks his teeth. "Seems like someone should've done that blackmail when she had the chance. But you, you took your time. You dilly-dallied. Now we gotta do things the hard way."

"I think it's 'shilly-shallied,' not 'dilly-dallied,'" Bob mutters.

"You wanna go, Bob?" Pizza Beard flicks open his switch-blade, lunging toward Bob.

"Settle down, fellas, we're gonna be millionaires," Nose Ring says. Reluctantly, Pizza Beard snaps his knife closed and spits on the floor.

Toothpick smirks at me. "Got milk?"

He shoves the gray milk toward me.

"Come on," Toothpick says. "Drink it."

"I can't," I say through gritted teeth. "My hands are tied behind my back. Untie me, and I will."

"Untie me, and I will," Pizza Beard mimics in a mocking tone.

Nose Ring crams the helmet back on my head. It muffles the sound of their voices. I guess that's something to be thankful for.

"Come on, boys. We've got our future ransom money secured. Let's go get drunk," Toothpick says, ducking outside.

Through the tinted visor, I watch them gather at a bonfire. They dance in their leather, passing jugs of whiskey.

The light fades. Cold seeps into my bones.

Micah will wonder where his car is. Granny—when will she notice? But Dad. My dad isn't worrying at all.

AT SOME POINT, I fall asleep.

I wake to the sound of footsteps.

It's so dark I can't see, especially not through the helmet's tinted visor. When I feel someone in the room with me, my whole body goes cold.

Someone slices the bindings at my ankles, and then a hand hooks under my elbow and hauls me up.

Instead of leading me out the door, whoever's with me shoves me through a small hole in the cabin's rear wall. The wood scrapes my helmet, splinters snapping against the plastic.

As soon as I'm free, I run, wrists still bound behind me. I can barely see, but I charge forward. I duck a branch just in time.

My feet skid through wet leaves. I trip over a stump, and no sooner have I landed on the ground than someone rips the helmet from my head.

Cool air floods my face. I gasp to breathe the fresh Oxygen. My lungs can't get enough of it.

And then I smell it—green lava soap, cedar, something clean and sharp that cuts through the dark.

Tyler.

He's here. He's the one who helped me out of the cabin. He's the one breaking me out of my wrist ties.

"Come on," he murmurs. "We have to hurry. We've got about as long as their favorite song before they notice."

My heart lurches. He came. He came even when I'd hurt him. Even when he should have turned his back. Even when no one else stayed. And maybe that's what matters most.

Through the creaking trees, I hear the Renegades belting out *Bad to the Bone.*

Tyler helps me up, and we run through the woods.

At the riverbank, the water rushes black and fast. Tyler parts the brush to reveal the little souped-up johnboat. Benny's boat.

He helps me climb in, shoving it into the current.

As the boat spins away, I reach for him—but he's gone. Just a brush of fingers, then air, as the river snatches me away.

"Wait!" I cry, searching for paddles. Nothing.

"Shh! I'll be fine," Tyler calls softly. The way he says it—steady, calm—makes my chest twist hard.

Because I can't escape two truths.

My dad ran. And Tyler came back for me.

I get a last look at Tyler before he disappears into the woods.

Now I'm alone on the river.

The boat bucks on the waves. Frantic, I tug the starter chain. The motor sputters, before finally roaring to life.

I grab the tiller. Ahead, the moon glints off a fallen log—and there's Tyler, standing on it.

I steer toward him, biting back panic. If I can just get there in time, I can pick him up.

But what if I overshoot? What if I crash into the log and knock Tyler into the water?

Shouts split the night, interrupting my anxiety.

The Renegades are on shore. They're drunk and mad and they've found Tyler.

"You think you could steal our ransom money, boy?" Nose Ring growls. He grabs the log. It spins.

Tyler dances to keep his balance, and as he does, his pants start slipping down his hips. Even now, his grin flashes toward me—and for a second, it's just us again, hanging out in Tyler's shop, joking about his pants always fall down. Rhyming *liar, liar, pants off Tyler*.

My throat tightens. I almost laugh. I almost cry. Even now, he's still him. And I still care.

At the last second, as the pants fall, Tyler yanks them up—and the gesture causing him to tumble into the water with a splash.

"Tyler!" I wrench the tiller, swerving wide to avoid hitting him.

From shore, I hear Tyler's voice, sharp, commanding, even as he's splashing in the water: "Hey! That girl stole my boat! Let's get her!"

Even now. Even here. He's protecting me.

I hold the tiller, eyes scanning the dark. The river, the rocks, the trees. When I look back, I can see the Renegades, fishing Tyler out of the water.

I've got to get help.

I can't rescue him alone.

I'm twist the throttle so the little boat rockets forward. I'm leaving—but I'm coming back for him.

CHAPTER 54

CHLOE

*W*hen I hear the roar of the highway, I beach the boat in the shallows and climb out. I wade through thigh-deep water and crawl up the low, slippery bank. Then I trudge, muddy as a swamp thing, to the road.

The sky is rosy with dawn light. Birds twitter in the fresh, pine-scented air. Then, an enormous dog bounds out of the woods and races down the road.

I jump back at the sight of her. She's huge, lion-like, like an escaped circus beast. Her coat is caked with mud, but beneath the layer of dirt, I can still detect the deep red color of her fur.

It's Sweetiepie!

So this is where she's been all this time—running around in these woods?

Then another dog bounds out of the woods, a tiny terrier in a tattered Burberry sweater, dragging a leash behind him like a parade streamer.

Could that be the school secretary's escaped terrier? He's gone wild now, romping and playing with Sweetiepie. As the two dash off together, I smile.

I'm freezing cold and wet, but the sight of this canine elopement makes me feel warm all over. It gives me the burst of energy I need to keep going.

When I see the sparkle of the harbor, I realize I'm only about half a mile from Granny Riding's.

I break into a run, mentally rehearsing my next steps.

I just need to get to Granny's, call the police, and lead them to Tyler. Also: give the flash drive to the media.

But when I get to Granny's, my to-do list evaporates. Because there's a police car in her driveway.

Instantly, I know I'm in trouble.

If I thought Granny Riding was mad when I pulled that stunt in the courtroom—that's going to be nothing compared to this.

Disappearing? Stealing Micah's car? From now on, Granny is going to think of me the way she thinks of my dad. To her, I'll be a former grandchild. Dead to her.

Focus, I tell myself as I hurry into the house. Tyler is what matters—keeping him safe is the goal. It's not about me or my need for Granny to like me. It's about getting people to that cabin to rescue Tyler.

When I open the front door, I smell fresh coffee and hear the crackle of a police walkie-talkie. I set one bare, muddy foot on the carpet runner, and then, from the foyer balcony, Helga shrieks.

She rushes toward me down the stairs and throws herself at me.

At first, I think she's angry I'm leaving footprints on the rug. Then, once her arms close around me, I realize she's capturing me—dragging me in to Granny like a prize animal—and it's only when I feel her tears on my neck that I understand.

Helga is hugging me.

She actually cares about me.

"Oh, your grandmother is sick to death worrying about you," Helga sobs. "Come on with me. I'll take you to her." She locks my hand in an iron grip and leads me upstairs.

Helga doesn't knock on Granny's door. She just shoves it open, shouting, "She's here! Chloe's here! She's home!"

Granny sits up in her gray silk peignoir. She rips her lace sleep mask off her face, and Helga shoves me into Granny's bony, silky hug.

"I thought we lost you, my darling," Granny says, and as her misty-scented perfume envelops me, I've never been more surprised in my life.

I allow myself to bask in the hug for one moment before pulling away. "The police," I say. "I have to go talk to them. Tyler —my boyfriend—my ex-boyfriend—is in danger." I break free from Granny's arms and run downstairs to—for the first time in my life—tell the police everything I know.

But the cops don't seem to find the situation nearly as urgent as I do.

"Ah, the old Frye sugar shack," Officer Tran says knowingly when I describe the place.

"Officer Frye's dad owns that property. I'll call over there and have him take a look. Meanwhile, dispatch'll send the Shady County sheriff out."

"Don't you think we should go over there? Right now? Tyler could be in danger!" I say.

"Almond croissant, officer?" Helga beams, proudly passing pastries on a silver tray.

As Officer Tran reaches for one, his sleeve rides up—and my heart sinks.

There, on his wrist, is the telltale tattoo: the Renegades' upside-down cross.

No wonder he's acting so meh about a biker gang holding someone hostage. He's one of them!

"Helga, doll? Did you put some kind of cream in this croissant? It's delicious," Officer Tran purrs, all innocence, shoving another puff pastry into his Renegade mouth.

"Almond paste," Helga beams, her whole face lighting up. It's the first time I've ever seen her smile.

"Is that the same as marzipan?"

"I just told you someone was in danger!" I say, but my voice is suddenly shaky. I'm exhausted, not thinking straight.

"It's out of our jurisdiction, Miss Riding," Officer Tran says. "The Shady sheriff will take it from here."

What are the chances the Shady sheriff is a Renegade, too? My guess is 100 percent.

They'll leave Tyler to the Renegades. And as soon as they figure out he has no money, he's in danger.

Tyler is tough and smart. But there are four of them. They're armed.

If Tyler's going to get rescued, I'm going to have to be the one to do it.

"Well, I trust you to do what's best," I say, in my demurest, most deceptively heiress-y voice. "Now. If you will excuse me. I have to go to school. Please don't hesitate to stop by should you need a contribution for the policemen's ball."

"The Ridings are always very generous, ma'am," Officer Tran says, reaching for a third croissant.

"Goodbye, Officer. Oh—and there's an almond stuck in your mustache." I glide upstairs, mind buzzing with plans. If I'm going to get Tyler, I'll need help. And I need to get the flash drive to the press, too. No matter the consequences, the truth needs to come out.

But escaping Granny's clutches today feels almost impossible.

She doesn't want to let me out of her sight. She doesn't even want me to go to school.

"I kept thinking of my son, Lewis," she whispers, voice tight with pain. "He disappeared. I couldn't live with myself if the same thing happened to you."

Normally, I'd empathize. I might even welcome the occasional hug—but come on. This is an emergency.

Finally, I pry her off me, saying, "Granny! I have to go to school." Never thought I'd beg for this. "Come on, let me go. I'm getting you all muddy. I have to take a shower."

"You are filthy," she agrees. It's a relief to see that familiar, steely glint of criticism in her eyes.

I turn on the shower but don't bother getting in. Rescuers don't have to be exfoliated.

I pat my pocket—yes, the flash drive's still there.

The sound of the shower will buy me an hour.

I slip out the window. It's easy. My sheet-rope is still dangling from it.

Then I run down the road toward town. After half a mile, a stitch in my side forces me into a walk.

I'm doubled over, gasping, when a black Rolls Royce SUV slows beside me.

The back window rolls down. Kyra slurps an iced latte.

"Oh, hey, we picked you up Starbucks," Kyra says. She flings the cup out the window.

It smacks me in the forehead, drenching me in icy, sweet milk.

Then Sophie C. guns the engine, and the Rolls roars away.

I keep going.

But when I glance over my shoulder, my gut tightens.

Another SUV slows down.

I dive into the ditch—until I hear a familiar voice.

"Chloe? Is that you?"

Jessa.

"Thank God," I say, climbing out.

Inside the car, I tell her everything.

Tyler, the Renegades, the cops, the flash drive. "That's why we have to find Benny," I say. "He'll know what to do." I can tell that Benny is the friend Tyler trusts most.

Jessa shakes her head. "If you're going on a life-or-death adventure with Benny, then I'm going, too."

I grin. So *this* is what it feels like to have friends.

"Here's the plan. We'll go to school. I'll hover in the drop-off line. You run in and grab Addie. We'll fill her in on the way. She can help us find Benny."

"Good idea."

"Great. And I know a shortcut that will get us to the front of the drop-off line."

When we near town, Jessa suddenly pulls the Lexus off the road. She veers through a set of bristly hedges, skids across a clay tennis court, rumbles over a patio, and shoots out an alley—cutting off the Sophies' Rolls Royce.

We beat The Sophies into the drop-off line, whooping and cheering.

Then I run inside to get Addie.

CHAPTER 55

CHLOE

*B*ut just my luck, Principal Annan is waiting for me just inside the school entrance. She sweeps her eyes over me, taking in my mud-caked hair and damp, dirty clothes.

"Chloe, think a minute. Is your outfit communicating respect for this judicial process?"

"Judicial process?" I try to peer around the principal, looking for Addie.

"Your disciplinary hearing is starting right now," the principal hisses.

I can't be trapped for hours in some mock court proceedings. I've got to get out of this.

I stick with the classic escape. "Can I go to the bathroom?"

The principal's eyes narrow. She's suspicious. "Why don't I escort you."

"Oh," I mumbl.e. "The royal treatment. Thanks."

As Principal Annan leads me to the bathroom, we pass the

football team. They're all crowding around the trophy case. I can't help noticing Kyra's boyfriend among them.

But it's not Kyra he's watching. Jackson's gaze is fixed on Addie, down the hall, tucking books into her locker.

I grin. Jackson's done my work for me. He's scouted Addie out.

I lift a hand and call out, "Addie! Hey!"

She turns, her ponytail swinging, and starts toward me—just as Principal Annan steers me into the bathroom. "Here we are. Go on in."

"You're just going to stand outside? Like a bouncer?"

She crosses her arms.

"Got it," I mutter, slipping inside.

Inside, Mimi, the restroom attendant, beams, her silver tray gleaming. "Good morning! Gloss? Lip filler? Eau de parfum?"

"Not today," I say, scanning for escape routes—ceiling vent? Air duct?

From outside comes Kyra's voice, all sugar and chainsaw: "But Principal Annan, I have to do a quick touch-up! It's for my modeling audition!"

Annan sighs. "Fine, Kyra. But just you—your friends can wait in the hall."

As the door swings open, Mimi's lips go thin as the needles on her tray. Clearly, she doesn't like Kyra, either.

Kyra clomps in on her gold platforms. "Good morning, Chloe. You look tired. What, haven't had your morning latte?"

Then, without even glancing at Mimi, she snaps, "Chanel No. 5. Now."

Mimi offers the iconic bottle. Kyra snatches it, uncaps it.

"You know, Chloe. You'd be a lot easier to deal with if you didn't smell." She lunges at me, aiming the perfume at my face, spritzing like it's a squirt gun.

She's fast, but I'm faster. I back into a stall, jumping onto the toilet.

"What's your problem, Kyra? You've hated me since day one. Are you that insecure?"é."

Kyra blocks the stall. "You Ridings think you're so special. You think you have everything, but—"

"You do have something I don't, though."

"What's that?"

I pause a minute, pretending to peer, from my elevated spot on the toilet, down at her head. "You have a bald spot."

Her hands fly to her head—and that's my opening to escape.

I leap past Kyra but she grabs my ankle, sending me crashing into Mimi.

The tray goes flying. Perfume, palettes, lipsticks scatter.

I scramble to my feet—expecting Kyra to chase me.

But she doesn't.

Kyra isn't coming for me.

She silent.

Dangerously silent, like a predator.

"Oh my goodness," Mimi murmurs. "How horrible!"

I turn. Kyra has a needle sticking out of her forehead. Her eyes cross as she stares at the syringe.

"Get it, get it out!" she squeaks.

I reach toward her to help. "Not you!" Kyra hisses.

She swats at me—and accidentally presses the plunger, injecting lip filler into her forehead.

A lump swells between her eyes, the size of a nectarine.

Poor thing. And on the day of her big modeling audition, too.

Seeing herself in the mirror, Kyra screams. Principal Annan bursts in, sees her, and screams too.

"Oh God, no, this looks like a lawsuit!" Principal Annan wails.

A screaming principal is the perfect cover.

No one notices me pocketing a few just-in-case syringes as I slip out the door.

That's one way to get out of a disciplinary hearing.

Now all I have to do is hunt down Addie, and we're off to Shady Cove.

CHAPTER 56

CHLOE

*a*ddie's wedged in the shadows next to the kombucha vending machine, crying, hands full of hot pink yarn— her half-unraveled sweater. I don't bother to ask what happened to it.

"I need you—come on." Before she can react, I grab her arm. There's no time to explain; Tyler's life is at stake.

Addie stumbles after me as I steer her toward the exit. Jessa is waiting in the pickup line, idling the Lexus.

"Are we skipping school?" Addie balks. "I can't. I have a quiz."

"Nope, just grabbing you a new sweater from Jessa's car," I lie. I open the back door and shove her inside, piling in after her.

Jessa floors it.

"What's going on?" Addie demands.

Suddenly, Jessa slams on the brakes, and we all go flying, along with school folders, a tennis racket, and a storm of Starbucks cups.

Micah has planted in front of the car, palms on the hood.

"Chloe Riding! I know you're in there! Where the hell is my Tesla?" he bellows.

"We're going to get it right now!" I say, heart racing. "Just—get in!"

Normally, stress kills your credibility, but for once, the universe cuts me a break and Micah softens.

"Fine. We're not doing anything in Econ today anyway. Take me to my Tesla."

He climbs, and as Jessa peels onto the highway, I fill everyone in on Tyler, the Renegades, the useless cops, and the danger confronting us.

Addie texts Benny. "He's in. The boys have already been thinking of an extraction plan for Tyler. But we have to meet him behind the school. Benny says they'll only join if it's on their terms."

"Of course," I mutter. How Ponyboy of him.

Jessa turns down a crumbling Shady Cove street and heads for a low, battered school building. .

"Drop me at my Tesla," Micah grumbles.

"Later," I say firmly. "Urgent situation, remember?"

"This is why we should call the authorities," Micah sighs. "But —oh my God. Who is THAT?"

Benny Kim struts through the school parking lot, all swagger and midnight eyes. Even though Cy, who's walking next to him, is a head taller, Benny is the one who attracts attention.

"My cousin," Addie says primly.

Jessa exhales. "He's so pretty it's unfair."

"Focus," I hiss, as Micah scrambles out of the Lexus to introduce himself. "Hey, man! I'm Micah. Heard your friend's in trouble. Let's go."

Benny doesn't shake Micah's hand. Instead, he turns to Addie.

"Little cousin. Who's the Sweetie crew?"

"They're here to help," Addie says.

Benny's eyes narrow. "Help? From Sweet Harbor? Please. Take your savior complex back to your sailboats."

I step forward, pulse drumming. "Enough with the Ponyboy attitude. Tyler's in danger. The cops won't help. If we're going to save him, we need to work together. Can you handle that—or should we leave you behind?"

Benny sizes me up, his grin slow, sharp. "Alright, Sweetheart. My boys are around back. We've got the box truck."

"Yeah, you remember the box truck, Chloe" Cy says, and I flash back to the night of the dognapping, and remember how it felt to be riding around the pitch black back of that truck with Tyler.

"Let's go," I say. Because every second we waste, Tyler's time runs out. But for the first time, I have real backup. I have a crew. And we're not stopping.

CHAPTER 57

TYLER

*I*t's a good thing I can fix motorcycles.

The Renegades are all show and no strategy, swaggering like they run the world. It wasn't hard convincing them to keep me alive—I promised I'd tune their hogs for more speed. They handed me a wrench instead of a gun.

While I work, my brain hums with everything I'm trying not to think about. Chloe—did she make it home? My mom, my sisters—are they okay, or panicking without me?

Benny, Zane, Cy—they know where I am. I left a trail, a note on Ash's windshield, after tracking the gang here. They'll come. I just hope they come fast.

Morning's breaking over the trees, soft gold on my back. Around me, the Renegades snore, spit, bark with laughter. One pees on the fire. Another nearly chokes on his bacon. Idiots.

For a flicker of a second, I wonder if this is what I'm headed for—a life wasted in someone else's gang, somebody else's dirty work.

I force the thought away, fingers tightening on the wrench. Stay useful. Stay quiet. Stay alive.

The motorcycle engine sputters, coughs—and then purrs.

I wipe my hands on my jeans and glance at the trees. Hang in there, Chloe. Hold tight, Mom, girls.

My boys are on their way. Right?

CHAPTER 58

CHLOE

*T*he boys' re-purposed U-Haul truck groans up the hill, the metal box rattling like a tin can. I can feel the folded loading ramp underfoot, heavy and cold where it's strapped against the floor. Cy fidgets by the roll-up door, ready to swing it open at the signal.

The plan's simple: Benny distracts the Rengades. Cy cracks the door. Tyler jumps into the back of the truck, and we're gone.

The truck lurches on two wheels around corners. Benny grinds the gears like the truck insulted his mother. I have to brace myself against the steel walls of the truck to keep from crashing into Cy, who's scarfing down a meatball sub.

Through the wall of the truck, I can hear giggles. Jessa somehow wormed her way up front, next to Benny.

I can't entirely blame her for using the opportunity to flirt with him, but she'd better focus when it's important. It will take everything we've got to free Tyler.

Zane, Micah, and Addie took Jessa's Lexus. They'll meet us at the rendezvous point. We figured having extra vehicles might help if the motorcycles give chase.

My HEART JOLTS when the truck turns off the main road. Gravel pings against the truck's undercarriage. Cy finishes his sandwich and burps.

"Satisfied?" I whisper.

Cy pats his stomach. "Indeed."

I don't know how he can eat a moment like this. We outnumber the Renegades—but they have guns. We don't.

The truck slows and reverses into position, just as we planned. Cy, surprisingly light on his feet, cracks open the back door. A slit of light. A burst of birdsong.

And then—the voice that ices my spine.

"Can I help you, fella?" Bob. The white-haired Renegade who zip-tied me in the elevator.

"Hope so." Benny's voice, casual. "You know how to get to 411 Whisper Lane? Got a delivery."

This was the plan.

Cy rolls up the door an inch further. I peer out—and there's Tyler. Alive.

My breath catches. He's crouched, working on a motorcycle, fingers tight on a wrench like it's a weapon.

Looking through the crack in the door, I can see Pizza Stain, Toothpick, and Nose Ring. Benny's distracting them. He's climbed out of the truck and is fumbling with a giant paper map.

Even motorcycle gang members *love* competing to give directions. Toothpick's telling Benny that he's got the map upside down, and Pizza Stain is arguing that Whisper Lane isn't even going to *be* on the map, because it's now called Tulip Way.

I watch Tyler watching the Renegades. His eyes are sharp, calculating. Predator eyes.

Wait, I tell him silently. *Let us help. Don't—*

Tyler moves like a switchblade. One second he's crouched by the motorcycles, the next he's stealing a set of keys from Pizza Stain's back pocket.

My heart jumps. He's a pickpocket too? Of course he is. Could Tyler be any hotter? But now I want him to go slow, keep his cool. Let us help.

I can hear an edge in Bob's voice now, as he negotiates with Benny. "I already told you! There's no Whisper Lane here. Now get out of here before there's trouble."

Cy slides the door open another inch.

And that's when Tyler sees me. His eyes change—soften. A flicker of summer cuts through the cold.

I hear Jessa, making a scene in the front seat. "Wait!" Jessa calls. This wasn't in the plan, but I'm learning you can count on her to bring the theatrical skills when needed.

"I have to pee! Do any of you fine gentlemen know if there's a ladies' room near by?" She's using a fake Southern accent, sounding full-on pageant queen. As she exclaims dramatically, Cy cranks up the door fully.

I motion to Tyler. *Come on. Get in the truck.*

But he shakes his head, indicating that we should lower the ramp for him, and swings a leg over the bike.

No. No no no no.

I make an X with my arms. No! Forget the bike! *Just jump in the truck!*

"Y'all really ain't got no powder room?" Jessa drawls.

Tyler grins at me like a dare.

It's now or never.

I leap from the truck, yank the steel loading ramp down, and scramble back inside, screaming "Benny! GO!"

The truck jerks forward—just as Tyler turns the key, revs the engine, and rockets up the ramp.

He's going so fast he nearly crashes into the back wall of the truck as we peel out, but he manages to brake just in time. He pops the kickstand and swings down, smooth as silk.

"What?" he grins. "Never seen me park a bike?"

Behind us, the Renegades charge. Bob lunges, fingers outstretched, for the ramp—but Benny floors it, and Bob face-plants in a puddle of motor oil.

Laughter bubbles up in my throat, until Tyler grabs me, kissing me breathless.

The ramp clatters against the road, spitting sparks. Inside, I feel like I'm made of sparks too.

"Tyler! Bro!" Cy yells over the engine roar. "Stop sucking Sweetieface and help me bust off this ramp! They're on our tail!"

CHAPTER 59

TYLER

*T*he Renegades are after us on their bikes. The white-haired Renegade's face is dripping with engine oil—it looks like war paint.

When he bares his teeth, Chloe moves closer to me, and I pull her tight. Thank God she's okay.

The ramp drags along the highway, scraping and squealing, shooting sparks. The front Renegade's tire is inches from the lip of the ramp. He's so close I can see the grease on his teeth, the whites of his wild eyes.

"Go in the back," I tell Chloe. I crouch down, balancing carefully near the ramp, stomach churning as the highway blurs beneath me.

Cy pounds the metal, fists ringing against steel. Then I spot it —the emergency ramp release.

One swift kick with the toe of my boot, and the ramp pops free, clattering onto the road.

The flying ramp nearly takes White Hair off his bike—but the old bastard veers just in time. I have to admit: he can ride.

Behind him, the Renegade in the sidecar shakes his fist at me, his dirty white beard whipping in the wind.

I burst out laughing—that deep, helpless kind of laugh that only hits when things have been so bad, all you can do is howl. The kind Cy and I have laughed through before: my dad's funeral, Cy's juvie stint—now this.

I sling an arm around Chloe, and she dips her hand into her sweatshirt pocket and pulls out three needle-tipped syringes.

"What the hell?" I say, as she takes an expert dart stance, squinting.

The needles fly. The first misses; the second sticks in White Hair's nose. He jerks, overcorrects—and wipes out hard on the pavement.

His crew blows past him without a glance. A minute later, he's up again, shaking his arms loose, the needle still wobbling from his nose.

Chloe dusts off her hands. "Botox," she says coolly. "FDA approved effective."

Damn. I love this girl.

But Nose Ring is closing in now, so close I can see spit flicking at his mouth's corners. His hand dips to his hip.

Gun.

"We're sitting ducks—Chloe, get behind the bike!" I shove her down, scrambling for cover, and as Nose Ring draws his gun, a Tesla slides silently onto the highway, cutting him off. Nose Ring swerves, the gun flying from his hand.

A Lexus roars up behind the Tesla, both cars weaving to block the lane.

"Sweeties to the rescue!" Cy whoops, hammering on the metal walls.

· · ·

WHEN THE TRUCK finally lurches to a stop, I hop out and gaze around, then help Chloe out of the truck. Lifting her down is the least I can do to the girl who Botoxed a biker game.

I've never been here before.

"Where am I?" I ask.

All three vehicles are parked in a circular driveway in front of a white-columned house. A maid in a crisp uniform pours fresh lemonade from a glass pitcher.

"My place." Micah—the guy who kissed Chloe—offers me his hand. I shake it. His palm's too warm, like a sun-warmed snake, but I shake it anyway.

"Thanks, man," I say. "You saved my ass."

"Nothing doing."

He hands me a glass of lemonade. I hadn't realized how thirsty I was. I tilt the glass and take a long drink, finishing it all, and when I set the glass down on the maid's tray I can't help but smile.

Jessa, Addie and Chloe are hugging and talking animatedly under a weeping willow tree. Micah and Benny are arm-wrestling on a fragile-looking glass patio table, while Cy and Zane egg them on.

Chloe slips away from the girls and tugs me under the shade of an old oak, her fingers still curled around a half-empty lemonade glass. "We have to talk," she murmurs, her voice low, eyes searching mine. "About Riding Industries. About... all of it."

I brush my thumb across the inside of her wrist, feeling the quick thrum of her pulse. "We will. But not now."

Her breath hitches—a soft, surprised sound—and she smiles, the kind that's a little shaky but sincere. Something swerves in my chest. Something good.

"You scared me," she whispers. "Out there."

"You scared me first," I murmur back, and it's only half a joke.

For a second, we just stand there, the hush of the trees wrapping around us, the late sun slanting gold through the leaves. Her hand finds my shirt, fingers twisting in the fabric like she's anchoring herself.

I tilt my head, brushing my mouth to hers, and it feels, like the first deep breath after surfacing from underwater.

When we pull back, I rest my forehead against hers. "We've got time," I say softly. "We've got us."

And for the first time in a long time, it feels like the truth.

CHAPTER 60

CHLOE

I have to get back to Granny's. It's been hours. She must have figured out I'm not *actually* in the shower by now. There's probably another set of squad cars in the driveway already. Maybe an Amber alert.

I pull back from Tyler, but he pursues me with urgent kisses. "Wait, wait, stop," I say. "Granny's going to be worried sick. I have to go home, I have to go back to—"

"Can't we just forget about reality a little while longer?" Tyler asks.

I shake my head. "That wouldn't be fair to Granny. But you know what would be? Stopping at the post office on the way."

"Huh?"

"To mail this to the New York Times." I reach down my shirt and fish the flash drive out of my bra. Tyler's eyes follow my every move.

"Granny doesn't deserve to worry about me. But that doesn't mean Riding Industries shouldn't pay for what it's done."

"Are you sure?" Tyler says. "I've thought about it. Maybe you're not to blame for what your family does. You're you. Just Chloe. And I don't want you to wreck your relationship with your family. I know you've never had a family. I just want to be with you. We can figure everything else out together."

His words bring the tears to my eyes.

Fortunately, Tyler's T-shirt is extremely absorbent.

He holds me close while I cry into his chest. As I cry, all the feelings I've pushed down for so long wash over me.

I've been like that dolphin Tyler and I rescued on the beach. Stuck. This emotional wave pushes me out to sea, out to freedom, to where I can move. Salt tears, salt water.

And all the while I'm crying, Tyler strokes my hair, and let me blubber out all my apologies. I'm sorry for making him break into the bank. For letting Micah kiss me at the drive-in.

"Shh," Tyler says. "Forget about it. We were broken up. Plus, I stood you up."

"Yeah, about that," I say, making my tone firm. "You can't disappear on me."

"I know. I had to take my mom to the hospital. I would have called. But I dropped my phone in the toilet." He winces, sheepish.

"Seriously?" I don't know whether to laugh or cry. "All of this happened because you dropped your phone in a toilet? I got kidnapped, and you got held prisoner, because of a phone fell in a toilet?"

I'm laughing through tears, the kind of laughter that feels like shaking off chains.

"Really, it's okay if you want to talk to your grandma before you go to the media with the flash drive," Tyler says.

I nod, holding his gaze. "All right. But I want you to meet Granny. I want her to know the truth about us. That we're together. No more lies. No more pretending."

I don't *quite* have the nerve to say *I want her to know the truth about what's happening to your mom.* But I'll get there.

We say goodbye to our friends and hop on the stolen motorcycle. I hold on to Tyler and lean against his strong, warm back as he drives us to see Granny Riding.

"There aren't any squad cars in the driveway. That's a good sign." I yell into Tyler's ear over the sound of the motor.

He parks the motorcycle between the two stone lions that guard the steps. "Maybe you better wait outside for a minute. I'll calm Granny down. Then you can come in," I suggest.

"Take your time."

Tyler leans back, gives me a wink, and pulls a paperback out of his back pocket.

Inside, the house is quiet, gray and calm.

I find Granny sitting in the living room, reading a magazine while her pedicurist kneels on the floor, painting her toenails a cloudy gray color.

Granny fixes me with a gray and puzzled look. "Chloe. You're filthy. Haven't you been taking a shower?"

"For two hours?"

"I thought you needed a little time to compose yourself," Granny says. "Apparently not. What happened?"

"Granny," I say. "That's a long story. But first, there's someone I'd like you to meet."

Granny's face turns to granite. She shoos her pedicurist away. Once the woman leaves, Granny's eyes turn flinty. "Is it your father?"

"What?"

"Is *that* who you've brought to see me?"

"No, I—"

"Because I am not interested. He came poking around here

yesterday, Chloe. I'm convinced he had something to do with your kidnapping."

"I know."

"Oh, Chloe," Granny sighs. "It's hard to learn such a bitter truth about your father. I always wanted to protect you from him. You should know that a security team has been monitoring you for many months. I was worried something like this would happen. But you're so good at giving them the slip—"

"A security team?"

"Big guys? Black Suburbans?" she says.

"You sent those guys? I thought they were the mafia."

"Well... they are. We just occasionally do business together. And I was *right* to engage them to protect you. Your dad's relationship with the Renegades is no joke. But I thought you'd be safe here, in Sweet Harbor." A tear escapes Granny's eye, and I go to hug her.

She only tolerates my hug for for a minute before settling back in her chair, wiping her eyes. "So, who have you brought to see me? Micah?"

"No. It's someone else." My voice cracks a little. "I haven't always been honest with you," I say.

Granny snorts. "Obviously."

"I've been seeing someone. And it's not Micah. It's someone else. His name is Tyler, and I'd like you to meet him."

Granny closes her gray eyes. "I trust there was a reason you concealed this from me?"

"Yes."

"I imagine the reason had to do with my snobbery."

"What?" I'm shocked, and Granny can tell.

"You credit me with very little self-awareness, Chloe. As you grow, you will learn these social rules are in place for your safety. It's not snobbery for the sake of snobbery. Life is war, Chloe."

"Okay."

"It's because I love you."

What???

"Yes, Chloe, you are, in fact, lovable. Though your clothing is doing very little to advertise that fact. Go upstairs and change, and I'll meet you and your visitor on the patio. I trust he's not—as you young people say—a Cove-Man?"

I refuse to hang my head. I look her straight in the eye. "He is."

Granny's whole body seems to spasm, but her gray mask descends quickly. Presumably, for my safety. "Very well. Don't look at me like that. I have a clean bill of health from my personal physician and am at very low risk of cardiac arrest from any such news. Go on and change, and I'll see you and your young man on the patio."

ON THE PATIO, I can see the silver sweep of the harbor reflected in the depths of Tyler's eyes.

"Never thought I'd have a rich girlfriend," he says, taking in the scene—the harbor, the rose bushes, the stone turret by the guesthouse.

Girlfriend. That word sounds even better than *heiress.*

Tyler takes my hand. He turns it over, tracing the lines in my palm with his fingertips. As his finger skates the arc of my love line, I'm reminded of the palm reading my mom gave me.

This time, I think, *lucky girl. You fell in love.*

"How did you find out my mom was in the hospital?" Tyler asks.

"Faye Frost told me. I have no idea how she knew to send me there... apparently her parents have some corporate espionage business. So maybe they were watching your mom for dirt on Riding Industries?"

"Huh. Well. All that matters is she helped bring us back together," Tyler says. He squeezes my hand. "Chloe... I heard some of the Renegades talking. They were saying some stuff about your dad."

"You were right about him," I say. My throat tightens, tears prickling behind my eyes. Tyler pulls me close, and when a tear escapes, he catches it with his thumb.

"I wish I hadn't been right about your dad," he says softly. "Or so rude about it."

"You were just trying to warn me," I say. "I'm so sorry my family is such a mess. Your mom is so lovely. And my family, we're monsters. I think Granny's gonna kick me out."

"If your grandma kicks you out, I got you. We'll figure it out. You don't mind a leaky roof, do you?" Tyler whispers.

"Not if I'm with you."

I hug him tight.

THE FRENCH DOORS OPEN. Granny steps onto the patio, carrying a platter loaded with Helga's pastries.

A platter? I've never seen her carry anything other than a purse. She usually has servants for that.

She sets the pastries on the table, smooths her skirt, and sits down. She smiles at Tyler as if he were any other guest—Micah, Kyra—and says,

"Read any good books lately?"

Fortunately, he has.

CHAPTER 61

CHLOE

ㅤa few months later ...

TYLER LOOKS HOT IN A TUX. I lean in to adjust his bow tie, and he distracts me with a kiss. Which is not good, because in a few minutes, I have to make a speech. And I need to concentra—

"Chloe?" Addie pokes her head into the green room. "Sorry to interrupt."

Tyler and I break away from each other reluctantly.

Addie smiles. "You guys are so cute together."

"You look great tonight," I tell her. Addie's wearing a simple black dress and a shiny nametag that says "Volunteer."

"You're on in three minutes," she says.

"I think you have lipstick on your cheek," Tyler says.

"Wait," I say. "How did I get lipstick on my cheek?"

"I think you kissed it onto me, and then I kissed it onto you," he says.

"Aww. It's like we're chewing the same gum," I coo.

He wipes the lipstick off my cheek with his thumb. Then he takes my hand. We walk to the ballroom and wait in the heavily curtained wings of the stage.

Granny Riding stands on the stage. She's dressed head-to-toe in silver sequins. Her hair is done up in a frosty silver swoop, and she clutches a gleaming platinum trophy.

Frankly, this is a familiar sight. Granny collects awards the way other old ladies collect thimbles or Beanie Babies.

But this time, Granny is not receiving an award.

She's giving an award away.

The recipient, Dr. Suarez, walks on stage. She's wearing a white lab coat over a rainbow sequin dress. When I see Dr. Suarez's familiar smile, my throat aches. I want to cry with happiness.

Because Dr. Suarez's experimental treatments worked.

Tyler's mom's cancer is in remission.

Dr. Suarez saved his mom's life.

When Dr. Suarez takes the stage and bows, the room shakes with applause.

"I have to follow Dr. S.?" I whisper.

"You'll do great," Tyler says, and plants a little kiss in my hair.

I inhale, square my shoulders, and step into the spotlight.

For someone who spent her life making things up, pretending to be someone I'm not, you'd think going on stage would feel easy. It doesn't.

Because what I was doing all those years traveling around running cons with my dad wasn't performing. It was hiding. Running and hiding.

Now I'm stepping out on stage to tell the truth about everything.

* * *

I TEST the mic with a soft hello.

Then I glance over at Tyler, waiting in the wings, his eyes glowing.

He is obviously proud of me. That gives me the courage to keep going.

"I never expected to find a home in Sweet Harbor," I tell the assembled crowd. "But you never know where things will lead you."

How could I have known, that day running away from the mob, that I'd meet Tyler on the side of the road? And that our meeting could lead to his mom's recovery? And my finding a home with Granny? And friends, actual friends?

Out in the audience, I can see Tyler's boys, Addie, and Jessa. And Tyler's mom, Coralee, too. She sits in the front row, beaming. Her sandy hair has grown back, and it's trimmed into a cute little pixie cut.

Mia sits on one side of Coralee. And, miraculously, Granny sits on the other. Sitting on Granny's lap is Neveah. She's playing with the sequins on Granny's silver dress.

Granny picked out both the girls' outfits. They're wearing little pearl-gray party dresses, pearl-gray patent-leather shoes, and white anklets.

I smile. "I thought life was about getting away with things, doing whatever it takes to survive. If getting what I needed meant stepping on people, or lying—well, I thought that's just how life was. Now I see life doesn't have to be that way. There's no getting ahead, not really, if you're pushing people down or leaving them behind. That's what tonight is about. The fact is, Riding Industries, my family's company, lied. Our lies hurt people. But we're working to make things right."

I swallow. "At first, it seemed like being accountable for what happened would be really hard." I pause, picturing Granny crying over the golf course in Virginia sold to fund the cancer foundation.

She and my grandpa used to vacation there every year as a family. The day Granny sold it, she made me sit next to her on the couch by the harp, looking through old photo albums.

She pointed out my dad and his brother Lewis, both wearing plaid golf pants and funny hats. No one has seen my dad since I was kidnapped. (He did email me once, about an "investment opportunity." But that's it.)

And as far as my uncle Lewis . . . Granny hasn't seen him in years. She doesn't even know if he's alive.

Dad and I used to think having enough money would solve all our problems. But now I know that even if you're as rich as Granny, life still finds ways to hurt you.

And even if you're hurt, you can still find ways to love and be loved. And love can make people surprise you. For example, Granny never once threatened to disinherit me for dating Tyler. She just hugged me and said she was so glad I was home safe.

True, she was annoyed I wanted to go public about Riding Industries' unsafe disposal of chemicals.

But then she said it would be a good lesson for me in public relations, personal branding, and crisis management. "It's a chance for you to host your first charity gala," she said. "It's a key skill in an heiress's repertoire."

So here I am, wearing Prada, giving a heartfelt speech, saying, "Thank you, good night," hearing applause, and—seeing my dad in the crowd.

Dad? That couldn't be him. Could it?

My heart crashes to the floor and I shade my eyes with my hand, squinting into the darkened hall to see more clearly.

* * *

"Uм—" I squeak. "Could I have the spotlight go just over—just over there?"

The lighting operator sends a beam onto the seafood buffet.

My dad's not wearing a tux—which is surprising, because he usually knows how to dress the part. Instead, he's wearing an ugly checkered sport coat. And his hair is uncharacteristically shaggy.

As the man turns around, squinting into the spotlight, caught with an enormous plateful of shrimp, my voice falters.

"Sorry," I say. "I thought—I thought I saw somebody I knew—"

From the wings, Tyler whispers, "It's Louie! Louie, from the bank! I swear it's him. He shaved and cut his hair."

Granny lets out an undignified squeal, leaping to her feet. "Lewis? Is that you?"

He freezes, a prawn sticking out of his mouth.

"Lewis! My son!" Granny runs up the aisle to him, taking quick, tiny steps in her form-fitting gown.

Could Louie, the guy sleeping in newspapers in the bank, really be my long-lost uncle? Murmurs roll through the well-dressed audience.

From somewhere I hear Kyra Cross's voice: "Count on the Ridings to bring the family drama."

Finally, Louie speaks. "Well, Mother," he says. "I told you I was waiting until you told the truth about our family to come home. And, you have. So now I'm home."

Micah, who's emceeing, snaps his fingers at the catering manager. The waiters start clearing plates, moving things aside to create a dance floor. I step off stage, knees shaking, grateful for Tyler's stabilizing embrace.

He leads me into the crowd to meet Louie (Uncle Louie?) and Granny.

"Ahh," Louie says, when we approach. "The bank robber and

her boyfriend." Fortunately, Granny doesn't hear him. She's talking to the caterer, demanding more shrimp for her son.

Louie and Tyler exchange fist bumps, and I shake Louie's hand. Now that a beard isn't covering his face, I can see how much he resembles my dad. It's uncanny.

Thinking of my dad, and how he betrayed me, hurts. Instinctively, Tyler rests a hand on the small of my back, comforting me.

It's okay. This guy, Louie, might look like my dad. But he's someone completely different.

"Open your purse," Louie tells me.

"Huh?"

"Just do it."

I open my bag—the big Birkin, the one I got from my mom—and Uncle Louie starts loading it with free shrimp.

Well. Maybe he's not *completely* different from my dad.

"Go on and dance, you two," Louie says. "I'll watch your purse." Even as I hand it to him, I know he'll probably spirit it away to wherever he's sleeping—the bank, maybe. But I don't care. I have a feeling I'll be seeing him around.

The dance floor flashes with warm pink lights.

Even before the bass drops, everyone is dancing; the whole crowd of stuffy Sweet Harborites gets up out of their chairs and boogies awkwardly, jerking and flailing around on the dance floor.

"It's a bunch of klutzes in four-thousand-dollar gowns," Tyler marvels.

Even the Sophies are dancing, clinging tight to members of the Sweet Harbor High football team.

"Weird. I can't believe they're all dancing," I murmur.

"I picked a good DJ, didn't I?" Jessa remarks. She gives me a congratulatory hug.

"Yeah, who knew this crowd liked EDM?" Tyler says.

"They don't," Jessa says.

I look at her quizzically. "How come they're all dancing, then?"

"Don't you know who the DJ is? It's Governor Devereaux's daughter. Everyone in this place is desperate to impress the governor. So they'll dance to whatever tune the DJ plays," Jessa says.

I study the woman in the DJ booth. Pink lights flash over her. She shares her cousin Jackson's warm brown skin tone. A tower of lavender braids is piled up on her head.

She's one of the most powerful people in the room. She can say "jump" and this crowd will literally say "how high."

* * *

I SCAN the crowd for Jackson, which is easy because he's surrounded by Sophies, as usual.

Kyra and the Sophies are all wearing fringed white cocktail dresses. They glow brightly on the dance floor.

Kyra's body covers Jackson the way kudzu climbs a tree. But as they move around the dance floor, he keeps his brilliant dark eyes focused on one spot: the donation table.

Addie is sitting there, in her simple black dress, sipping punch and accepting envelopes stuffed with cash.

Does Jackson like Addie? Or is he simply scheming up more ways to help the Sophies torment her? He's Kyra's boyfriend... the odds of him being as nice as he seems are basically zero. Too good to be true generally is.

As my eyes move from Jackson to Addie and back, I catch Faye Frost watching me. She's wearing a navy cocktail dress. It's the exact shade of her hair.

Her eyes dart between Jackson and Addie, and she gives a little nod and a sphinx-like smile. Does she think Jackson likes Addie, too? Or maybe she knows some Devereaux-related corporate secrets?

I grin. If Jackson *does* like Addie, that would throw a monkey wrench into the entire social order of Sweet Harbor High. And honestly? That would be a good thing.

Tyler dips me so low my hair brushes the parquet floor, and I melt into a perfect combination of love and laughter.

LATER, after Uncle Louie has taken off with my purse, after Helga has driven Granny home, after the governor and her daughter have returned to the capital, after the waiters have collected all the shrimp and all the chairs, Tyler and I are still dancing in the dark in the empty ballroom.

He's loosened his tie; I've taken off my heels. My bare feet slide easily on the smooth, cool floor.

We're alone, dancing to the buzz of the vacuum cleaner in the hallway and the rhythm of our own hearts. It's a song that will go on, no matter what.

The big hotel falls silent all around us.

Tyler's pants fall down—just a little. (Some things never change.)

I reach back and hitch them up for him.

We keep dancing.

THANK YOU FOR VISITING SWEET HARBOR!

It means so much to share this fun, over-the-top world with you.

If you're not quite ready to leave Sweet Harbor, grab your free bonus short story, A Golden Bachelor for Granny—set on a cruise to Greece!

Chloe and Tyler team up to find the perfect boyfriend for Granny… who turns out to be someone you just might recognize from this book.

There's meddling. There's matchmaking. There's the Mediterranean.

Thanks so much for hanging out with me in Sweet Harbor!

Love,

Poppy

P.S. I have a favor to ask. Would you consider leaving a review (or a star rating) on Amazon?

Reviews help Amazon decide whether—or not—to recommend a book to readers. Even a five-second, super-quick star rating makes a huge difference. xoxo.

www.ingramcontent.com/pod-product-compliance
Lightning Source LLC
Chambersburg PA
CBHW052022240626
47153CB00006B/1914